BOOKS BY GAIL PASS

Surviving Sisters   1981

Zoe's Book   1976

SURVIVING SISTERS

SURVIVING SISTERS

GAIL PASS

New York

ATHENEUM

1981

Library of Congress Cataloging in Publication Data

Pass, Gail.
  Surviving sisters.

  I. Title.
PS3566.M773S9 1981   813'.54   80-69373
ISBN 0-689-11134-7

Published simultaneously in Canada by McClelland and Stewart Ltd.
Composition by American–Stratford Graphic Services, Inc.
Brattleboro, Vermont
Manufactured by R.R. Donnelley & Sons Co., Crawfordsville, Indiana
Designed by Kathleen Carey
First Edition

For my parents, Helen and Arthur Pass,

and for my sister Adrienne,

with love

OIDIPUS: I've watched my own soul—strange drives forcing
me higher and higher
to goals I can barely discern, and one of them
is beauty of mind,
true majesty; and one of them is death. I
am, I've found
a rhythm, merely: a summer and
winter of creation and guilt.
I'm the phoenix; the world. Thanatos and Eros
in all-out war,
the chariot drawn by sphinxes, one of
them black, one white:
one pulls toward joy, the other toward
total eclipse of pain.
With all that, too, I've made my peace.
I've fallen out of Time . . .

JOHN GARDNER, *Jason and Medeia*

ISMENE: What further service can I do you now?
ANTIGONE: To save yourself. I shall not envy you.
ISMENE: Alas for me. Am I outside your fate?
ANTIGONE: Yes. For you chose to live when I chose death.
ISMENE: At least I was not silent. You were warned.
ANTIGONE: Some will have thought you wiser. Some will not.

SOPHOCLES, *Antigone*
trans. Elizabeth Wyckoff

SURVIVING SISTERS

I

S WEATING BY THE DOORWAY, Irena's uncle grasps the hand of everyone who enters. Across the room, a dark-suited cluster of men solemnly waits for the priest to arrive. Sitting surrounded by women, Irena's aunt bites her handkerchief; no wail of lamentation will arise from there. In the past her quiet group would have been moving and moaning in ever-mounting rhythms, pulling at their hair and scratching their cheeks as agony pushed their song higher, and pain prodded them into dance. But such displays are unseemly now.

Alone, Irena does not look up. If she risks raising her eyes, she will see her brother's powdered face, and crisp military uniform. It is not the one he died in. Nor does that body bear any resemblance to the brother who has died. The fallen warrior. She cannot garland his head with laurel and celery, strew herbs and evergreens on the bier, throw nuts and fruit into the coffin. Ancient rituals would be absurd, performed to tunes of funeral parlor Muzak.

Reverend Kourides comes in and the wake begins. Circumspect. Formal. Afterwards, released from constraint, the mourners gossip in Greek while filing out. There is scandal rising, threatening to swell, should Philip and Alexandra also miss Eugene's funeral.

Far away, Phil must desperately want to come—his brother is lying in that coffin. But Irena knows Phil will not be there. Unlike him, Alex can choose her moves. Surely her sister will arrive by tomorrow.

"Rena, I'm with Gene, can you get over here?"

"Alex?" She gripped the phone. "But when did you get in, what are you doing? Everyone's expecting you here, at the house."

"Fuck everyone. Just come over." The phone clicked; it buzzed its dead sound. Her sister never wasted time on niceties.

Irena dreaded going to the funeral home on her own; she had to force herself to enter the building. Head down, avoiding views of caskets, she went into the room holding their brother. Cross-legged on the lowest step leading up to him and still in her Army surplus jacket and blue jeans, Alex followed her progress to the front row of chairs. Her expression was unreadable; she made no greeting. Without taking her eyes from Irena's face, she reached for a recorder on the carpet near her knee, and brought it to her mouth.

Long, mournful notes overrode the Muzak.

Irena looked around nervously. Some saccharine-voiced functionary was bound to tell them this was most irregular, couldn't be allowed. On and on, with Alex watching her while she piped. Eerie sounds. She was shivering.

At some arbitrary point, they stopped. Alex pulled her

4

knapsack close and began packing away the recorder. "It's not an *aulos*, but the next best thing. The best I could come up with." She stood, her hands resting on her hips too casually, making Irena wary. "Is that the best you could come up with? Shaking in your shoes?"

"What do you mean? What was I supposed to be doing?"

She leaned forward. "You were supposed to be getting into it, Rena. Sending our brother's soul off before old foul-breath Kourides comes here and hustles us all through some formulaic little prayers. Before Uncle Constantine defiles this room with that shiny American flag in his buttonhole, and dear, dreary Aunt Eunice starts to snuffle. This is our brother!" pointing to the coffin as if Irena didn't know. "And he's dead! Don't you think we owe him something? Something personal that comes from inside us and has some meaning?"

"Alex, you are really upset. I know Gene's—I mean, for God's sake. I'm sorry I didn't do whatever it was you expected. But I'm mourning him. Can't I do it my own way?" She walked nearer, hoping it was over, but Alex wouldn't reconcile, she turned away from her, going up the few stairs to the coffin's head. Irena couldn't follow her there. She could barely watch as her sister's hand hovered over the face, descended, then actually touched it.

"Gene." The normal tone seemed inappropriately loud. "Hey. Big brother. I'm sorry we had to argue, that last time." Her other hand jostled the dead shoulder. "Listen. I forgive you for losing my baseball mitt. I forgave you twelve years ago, but I never told you."

She couldn't control her discomfort. "Alex, people are going to be arriving any minute."

Her sister went on, belittling the danger and her. "You were a pretty neat brother, Gene. Phil and I were closer on some things, but I used to look up to you. Before. College changes a person, you know. I had to tell you what an asshole you were about the war. You see it now, don't you?" She ap-

5

peared to be listening to an answer. Her hands left the body. "You don't. You haven't changed—you're still just like *him*. Aren't you. *Aren't* you." Suddenly her face was within inches of the powdered one. "Hey, Mister Patriot. Was it worth it?"

"Alex!" She edged closer to the doorway. "Come on, let's go."

Alex waved a dismissing hand at her. "Was it, Gene?" She stepped back. Gesturing the length of the casket, she persisted. "Here you are, all decked out in your military splendor. All decked out, Gene. Dead." She gripped the coffin's rim with both hands. "What good are you to your country now? What good are you to us, to the people who loved you? Damn you Gene," knuckles showing white on the solid walnut, "what *good* are you?"

"Alex, please!"

Rigid except for a muscle moving in her jaw, she glared at their brother; then her shoulders drooped, her hands dropped from the rim. "I'm sorry." She patted the uniform. "I'm sorry, Gene." Her lips curved down, she bent over—Irena couldn't watch—she was kissing the mouth. "Goodby." She smoothed the carefully combed hair. "Goodby, Gene. Goodby, my big . . ." Her face contorted.

She came running down the steps, seeking Irena, clutching her. It felt strange, protecting her older sister. Alex shook inside her arms.

Their uncle walked in on them clinging to each other; over Alex's shoulder, she could tell that all he saw were Army fatigues and blue jeans. "How dare you show such disrespect!" The words were hissed at Alex's back. Spying the knapsack, he grabbed it and shoved it into their bodies. "Irena, find a bathroom, get her into decent clothes before the others arrive."

Alex hadn't been so defiant as to come without a dress. They slid into their seats just as Reverend Kourides started intoning.

A short prayer, sending mourners and coffin off to the

church. There, a censer swings, voices are raised. The cantor is new and sings with power. The priest owes his post to Constantine Lampros and somehow sounds sincere. They leave the church. Trail to the grave, where Jesus Christ conquers, and Alex steals flowers to throw on the lid.

At the memorial dinner, held in the church hall because of the crowd, the *kollyva* is passed, sweetened with cinnamon, almonds like flesh. Each person partakes of the ritual wheat.

"And now, we must raise our glasses." Their uncle had already raised his too many times, but he managed to stand as he spoke. His face was very flushed. "To Eugene, who was like a son to me. A good boy, always. A boy who showed respect. A boy," he stopped to look around the room, "who became a man of *philotimo*." Irena watched the old men near him nodding their heads in assent, thinking, no doubt, that personal honor was something most of today's youth couldn't even translate. "Let us drink to a brave Greek-American who gave his life for his country. I am proud to call him *son*." Tears rolled down his face as he guzzled a full glass of wine.

"That pig," Alex muttered. "That shit." Her face, too, was flushed, but dangerously.

She touched her sister's wrist. "Don't, Alex. Let him carry on. The last few days have really been hard on him."

"I bet." Alex moved her arm away. Grasping a bread knife, she held it straight above the table, then lowered it and began pressing harmless circles into the cloth.

Their uncle's voice again rose above the clatter of people eating and talking. "Theo! Stand up, my friend." It was embarrassing, the gigantic sweep of his arm. "Stand up and tell us about Eugene's—"

"What about your other son?" Alex was on her feet. "There's another *man* in the family," yelling right next to her, "what about him?"

The room was quiet as he tried to get her into focus. "I have no other son. There is no such person."

7

"You deny Philip Lampros?" her voice climbing into shrill-ness. "In front of these people who know him, you deny that he exists?"

"Yes!" His fist slammed the table. "I tell this room, I tell the world! I have no other son!" Beside him, Aunt Eunice stared at her plate.

Heads twisted from uncle to niece, eager for the next volley. Irena followed the stem of her wineglass twirling between her fingers. How could Alex possibly think it would do any good? Their trying to outface each other and glaring across tables would just be a standoff of futile pride.

The crowd lost interest, started talking and clinking silver-ware again; Aunt Eunice smiled weakly at no one in particular. Even *they* seemed to know it was over. Uncle Constantine fell heavily onto his chair as Alex, wheeling, strode past the tables toward an exit. She poured the rest of Alex's wine into her glass. Their uncle was in no condition to drive; she would have to stay where she was, then take what was left of the family home.

Her dented VW sits parked in their street. Alex has not raced back to school, or crashed at a friend's. Feeling relieved, Irena helps groggy Uncle Constantine get to his bed; accepts haggard Aunt Eunice's kiss on the cheek.

"Thank you for staying behind tonight." Her aunt was too tired to smile. "I'm sorry that had to happen. You'll see if she's all right, won't you? I'm sure Alexandra would rather have you checking on her than me."

"You shouldn't feel that way—really. Alex is just—"

"Don't bother, dear." She managed a sad little one. "I know I'd only make things worse." Turning away, "Good night. Tell her not to worry about tomorrow; your uncle will sleep it off."

"Good night."

She walked down the hall, to the bedroom she and Alex had shared during childhood. Her knock pushed the door

8

open. Alex was sitting on the floor, hunched over, her long, dark hair falling forward and hiding her face. "You okay?" Alex nodded, but despite the light from the bedside lamp, she wasn't certain. "Want company?"

"Sure."

Closing the door, going to sit across from her on the twin bed, she spied the open plastic bag and small pack of cigaret paper balanced on Alex's thigh; her sister *would* be calmly rolling a joint.

"You don't mind, do you?" Mock concern.

"Give it a rest, Alex, please?"

"Sorry." She licked the paper. "You've been a real handy punching bag. I apologize." Lighting up, she took a deep drag, and held out an acrid peace offering. "The tyrant in bed?"

"Mmhm." Knowing Alex never lost a chance to evaluate her, she was inhaling the smoke with as much air as she could and keeping it for as long as possible, so that when she finally exhaled only a faint trace was visible. She was pleased by the surprised way Alex cocked her eyebrow. "Aunt Eunice said not to worry, he'll sleep it off."

Her sister reached for the joint. "I'm sure he will."

"Maybe you will, too."

"I don't want to. I'll be there at breakfast reminding him."

"Why, Alex? Another argument's not going to change things." The weed was scratching her throat, but she kept on taking her turn.

"You know he has to be shown he can't get away with it, Rena. Why do you and Aunt Eunice let him go on pretending Phil doesn't exist? It's such a sick fantasy. It's a monumental act of aggression, much worse than the other one."

Triggered, the vision hits before she can turn away. Outside the rim of light, her brother's face approaches. There are tears mixing with the blood coming from his nose. A plaid jacket whirls through the air and whips against his open mouth. A suitcase strikes Phil's leg; he falls on the muddy lawn. A door slams. Screams die in the house.

9

". . . were actually killing Phil, I mean physically," Alex nudged her to take the joint, "would we stand by? Just be passive witnesses and not do anything to stop him?"

"But what, Alex? You know how impossible he is—if he's not charging around the house like some mad bull, he's giving us the silent treatment. You don't live here every day anymore. It's easy to come back for a few hours, and say 'Do something!' "

"Reenah," her most exasperated tone, "the prick needs a conscience! Don't you see that? 'There is no such person,' " she mimicked gruffly, " 'I forbid you to speak his name.' What a load of crap, and you let him dump it!"

She sighed, waving away the minuscule butt. Things were always easier for Alex. She watched her carefully split a match and insert the bit of cigaret; holding the flimsy holder in both hands, Alex sucked on the joint, then passed it forward. She tried to smoke it exactly the way Alex had, and succeeded in burning her lip. "Looks like I can't do this right, either," returning it.

Alex gave her one of her more significant stares. "I didn't mean to put you down, Rena."

Then why did you? She was even taking another deep drag.

"You know me, I always come on too strong."

Yes, and some day Alex would patronize her and she wouldn't feel that she deserved it. The three years separating them were a chasm, with her sister self-confidently on the other side.

Another unbidden image. The gaping cleft between them needs to be examined. Dark. Dizzying—Irena fears she will lose her balance.

"Where are you?" Alex, smiling at her.

"Here." She blinked rapidly. "I'm here. I was just . . . I don't think I'll ever have what you do. Your toughness."

"Maybe you shouldn't." She started expertly rolling another joint. "I used to envy Phil sometimes and wish I had his trusting nature. But look where it got him." When both ends were twisted, she couldn't decide which one to light. "If you're going to make it as an idealist, you can't be naive about humanity. Phil's problem was . . ." she lit the smaller and the match flared brilliantly, "he thought people would actually do right once the circumstances were explained. So he just sat down with Uncle Constantine, and calmly presented his reasons for refusing to fight in the war. Because our dear uncle would understand. Of course he would! Well, sure!" She leaned her head back against the bed. "Dumb. That was dumb, Phil, the one thing you hate is violence."

He truly was the gentlest of them all. Sometimes she thought Phil was her real sister, and Alex was another brother, hiding in a female body. "I wish Canada wasn't so far away. Do you think he's all right?"

"Don't worry about it. There are lots of groups helping guys get out of the country now. He's with one."

"How do you know that?"

She wasted her drag on a smoke ring. "I haff my vays."

"Come on, Alex. How do you know? Phil wasn't going to communicate with any of us because they might trace it."

Alex looked at her from under heavy lids; she was being appraised again. "There's a network, Rena. It's big." Her sister sat up straighter. "A lot's going on. I hardly go to classes anymore."

"But what about grad school?"

"Poly sci's a joke. I'm not going to study power under some asshole who wrote a book when the real thing's in the streets, with the people."

"What if Uncle Constantine finds out? He won't foot the bill for that—he didn't want you to go there in the first place."

"Don't remind me." She pulled over the ashtray and started shredding burnt remains. "I had to beg that bastard. And he loved it. He likes nothing better than seeing some female grovel so he can play the big man. Well, two can play —I've learned the game, Rena. As long as I know what I'm doing, he can't touch me. Every month when I get that check," she paused to let her see the extent of her sneer, "I *laugh*."

Irena lay back full length on the bed. She couldn't even hate as strongly as Alex did. Was she afraid to? Her uncle and aunt, the house—they were all she had. She was the only orphan left now, everyone else . . . Maybe it had weakened her for life, she would always be left. "Alex . . . do you ever think about our parents?"

"Jesus. Not very often. I mean, how old were we? Two and five?"

"Things would have been different, wouldn't they?"

"If our parents hadn't been hit from behind by some drunk? Sure. I don't know about better, but different, definitely."

She remembered a fur coat. That was all, just the feel, the softness against her face when her mother . . . New Year's Eve, she had thought it meant her mother, a funny sound, then Eve. Her mother . . .

"Rena? Are you going on a bummer?" A hand entered her hair. "Hey." It felt good. "You've got *me*."

Her sister's touch is soft, reassuring. Pretty hair. The voice floats near her ear, so pretty. Strands fall slowly down a hand, like copper, like bronze, they ripple across a palm. Pretty Rena feels lulled, and pleasantly lost. She is soothed by the sister closeness.

It lingered after Alex moved away. "Greg Roussas says, the only area where we look like sisters is around the chin. I guess he ought to know." She was poked. "Here. The last of the grass, alas."

Her fingers accepted the joint.

"If you're still interested in him, Rena, now's the time to say so. Because if you are, just tell me and I'll . . ."

"What're you talking about? Never was in Greg Roussas."

"Really? But he was in you, wasn't he? In. You."

"Not in me, ever."

"Rena. You never balled Greg Roussas?"

"No. Is that what we're talking about?"

"Well, shit. That creep." The joint left. "So. Who have you done it with?"

Hairy body, on the wrestling team. Never love, just . . . did it to do it. Was okay. Got a little better. Something wrong with her, though. Liked it best when he brought her with his hand.

"Come on. You have to have done it, you're my sister."

"It wasn't very good." But that time, the hand time . . .

"More than one guy?" She shook her head no. "But more than once." She shook her head yes. "Nothing to worry about—it can take a while. Unless of course the guy's a bum lay. God this stuff is making me thirsty." Getting up sounds. "Don't go away." Cautious, cautious, opening the door. The hallway creaked near the top of the stairs.

Guess that told her. She wasn't the prissy twit Alex thought she was. Alex didn't know her. Nobody did. She didn't either, but she wasn't a sissy twit. Prissy twat. She wasn't . . .

Alex came back, carrying wine. She had to be told. It was so clear, what Irena had to say. "Listen, Alex . . ." She swung her legs over the side of the bed in order to share the clarity, make her see it. "I am not . . ." She grasped the neck of the bottle Alex was holding out. "A sissy twat."

A spray of wine burst from her sister's mouth. "Wha-a-t?"

She tried to draw herself up very straight. "I . . ." Alex was interrupting this important, dignified moment with hysterical cackles; she was rolling from side to side with her arms wrapped around herself and being ridiculous. Irena was offended; she threw back her head and swigged from the bottle.

"That's the funnie—" Alex couldn't finish, she was still laughing. Suddenly she wanted to laugh, too. She did, and it was glorious! The laughing was all around her, she was the center, they were whirling together, she and the laughter, and they were going to go on forever.

Foul wretchedness coats her mouth. Despised light pricks her eyes unmercifully. Demented drums boom within her head. She is awake, and it is morning.

She dares to look in a mirror. Reflected, a mouth in sensual repose despite what lies inside. Her long-lashed eyes do not show a thousand scratches but instead are miraculously clear. There is no pulsing beneath her unblemished forehead. Her straight nose innocently hides a residue of grass. However, the bronze hair of yesterday is merely brown today, and gentle waves have lost their contour overnight.

Greg Roussas was right, she decided. Alex was animated, dark; she was amorphous, brown. Taller, but Alex had never needed to be tall. She hadn't spent her childhood willing herself to grow to five feet six so she could be above average in something. Height had seemed such a good idea then. When she was marking inches on the wall and continually staring into mirrors, wondering what she would look like fully grown. Even now, the face in front of her didn't seem quite her own. And she'd failed by an inch. So much for growing.

Yanking her hair into a knot, she slipped a rubberband around it and turned her back on herself. A somber turtleneck jersey, her denim skirt; she left the room without image-checking again.

The aroma of sausages and coffee met her on the stairs. Nothing would ever stop Aunt Eunice from providing the comfort of food. She was standing by the stove whipping pancake batter as Irena walked into the kitchen and went over to kiss the top of her head. "Anything I can do?"

"Thank you, dear, you can pour the juice. Did you sleep well?"

"Like a log." A stoned one. "How come the table's only set for three?"

14

"Your uncle's gone to work. He shouldn't, with the funeral only yesterday, but I didn't try to stop him. I think he wanted to avoid unpleasantness."

"Did he say that?"

"Of course not, your uncle has his pride. He mentioned going over the books before the accountants come on Friday." The batter sizzled; masterfully she controlled two frying pans full of bubbling buttermilk circles. "He'll be giving Delos Street something to talk about when he opens up the store. But I suppose that's better than some terrible argument with Alexandra at breakfast. They're just alike, those two—she's every bit as stubborn as he is. I wish your sister would realize what a disagreeable trait that is."

"What about your husband? Don't you think he ought to, too?"

"Your uncle is almost sixty, Irena. He's not about to change."

Great, go back to Day One and start arguing from there. She heard Alex clumping down the stairs; wearing hiking boots in the house again. Aunt Eunice was too busy stacking pancakes to notice.

"Good morning, ladies!"

She winced. Either Alex had fantastic recuperative powers or she was inured to midnight marijuana.

"God, Aunt Eunice, that smells dee-vine!" A parody of ecstasy, a simulated swoon. Hugging the cook, "I'm famished!" she twisted around, winking, "Aren't you, Rena?"

"Ravenous." It was true, her stomach roiled with hunger.

"I'm glad you girls have found your appetites. You didn't eat a thing at the memorial dinner."

Every occasion had its food. Every brother had his day, and Eugene's was over. They never even mentioned him last night. Not once. She hadn't even thought of Gene. Till now. Too busy worrying about herself, grieving for herself. And Phil. She had given some attention to him at least; she hadn't been totally self-centered. The living must go on—what a

15

lame excuse for selfishness, when the dead were hardly buried.

"What's the matter?" Alex plunked down a plateful of crisp sausages and pulled out a chair across from her.

"It's strange. Here we are, about to eat a normal breakfast when . . ."

"A good Christian nourishes her body, Irena." Aunt Eunice took her seat. "If Reverend Kourides were with us, he would say eat, and your prayers will be even stronger. Alexandra, pass your sister the pancakes."

She expected Alex to make some crack about the good reverend, not simply pass the plate. But her mouth was busy; by the time Irena had dotted each of her pancakes with butter and poured maple syrup over them all, her sister had eaten halfway through a stack.

"Aunt Eunice . . ."Alex spoke between mouthfuls, "you're the best cook in the Western world."

"Not the entire universe anymore?"

"Kid's hyperbole. This is a realistic, adult appraisal." She pierced another sausage.

"Well, it's nice to have you both around the table again. Just the three of us, like it used to be." Irena caught the puzzled look Alex threw at her. "It was always my favorite time of day, when the boys were out, and your uncle had gone to work. You girls would practice on some recipe, and then we'd all sit down for a tasting party. Just us *women*; it was fun, wasn't it?"

"But there were four of us," Alex reminded, reaching for the pancake platter.

Aunt Eunice couldn't quite bring herself to smile. "Of course. But your grandmother Agnes always placed her chair by the stove, where she could oversee everything."

"Baking the Saint Basil's cake—I remember that," Irena offered. "And . . . dyeing Easter eggs! Remember, Alex? Grandmother Agnes's Easter eggs were always redder than anyone else's. You were so sure she was using real blood, you purposely cut your finger and tried to dye an egg with it."

16

"That's what you thought. Phil and Gene didn't have to stick around—I just wanted to get my polka-dot apron off and go outside. Pass the syrup, please."

"You were a very determined little tomboy, Alexandra. You'll be grateful for those lessons someday when you have your own kitchen to take care of."

Both sisters rolled their eyes. Usually it was husband or family, now it was kitchen; the new wrinkle on the old sentiment made it weirder, almost inhuman.

"I think Grandmother Agnes was neat." Alex must have decided not to let Aunt Eunice get to her this morning. "Really tough—smart, too. Just because she couldn't speak English very well, I didn't appreciate her enough."

"Your grandmother may have been intelligent, but she was not an easy mother-in-law to have around."

"I thought you liked her." Alex poured more coffee into each of their cups.

"I respected her. Only a strong woman could have survived those times in the old country. Did you know she was the first person your uncle sent for when he had made enough money?" She lowered her cup, oblivious to the fact they were nodding their heads yes, they knew. "Other men were buying passage for their sweethearts; he brought over his mother. They laughed at him in the coffeehouses, but he didn't care. He venerated her." She sat back, her hand still on the cup, her eyes narrowing. "The bond between them . . ." She shook her head.

The thought stays inside, impossible to share. She knows about futility. Feelings no one has ever questioned; depths no one has bothered to explore. So what if once she was a young wife, newly married and struggling to break in? Her nieces will not see that, they never look beyond. Just an everyday aunt, to them she is nothing more.

Lines of bitterness marked her mouth. "He was the first-born male, the fulfillment of her marriage. She spoiled him, always. That's why he is the way he is."

17

"A wife should have more—"

"But they were always arguing." Alex had to be stopped. "It used to scare me, the way they screamed at each other in Greek."

"Pah. Greeks discuss everything at the top of the lungs. No," Aunt Eunice clinked down her cup, "they spoiled each other. Shamefully."

"So he took good care of her in her old age. What's wrong with that?" Alex, unperturbed, met their glances.

"I'm surprised to hear you standing up for him, Alexandra. It's too bad your uncle isn't here to enjoy it."

"Yeah, too bad."

"You haven't asked where he is this morning."

She had to bring it up.

"I didn't think I needed to."

"You know where he's gone, of course."

"To the store, where else?"

"And of course you know why."

"Sure. Gotta keep those drachmas rolling, folks. Can't shut down forever because of a little funeral in the family."

"I don't think you have ever even tried to understand him."

Irena closed her eyes; Aunt Eunice really was a masochist.

"I have spent . . . my entire life! understanding that man. God *damn* it. It's a stupid one-way street and I'm sick of it! I'm sick of getting nothing in return."

She didn't have to see her sister trembling; maybe Aunt Eunice would fall back now and not push her any further.

"Some of the money your uncle makes today will pay for another textbook. Have you thought of that?"

"Yes! I've thought of it! Uncle Constantine likes having women leech off him! But at least *I'm* not making it my life's work!"

No rejoinder. She opened an eye. Alex was shakily ripping the cellophane off a pack of cigarets. Aunt Eunice had picked up her fork and was very carefully pushing bits of sausage to the side of her plate. One of her shoulders sagged, as if there had been a physical blow and this her silent claim of injury. "There will be services at the grave Thursday. Will you be staying?"

Alex jerked a cigaret out of the pack. "Can't. Midterms."

"I'm sorry to hear that. I hope," she said to the plate, "you're enjoying your classes."

"They're fabulous."

"Political science seems such a strange course of study for a girl."

Even Alex couldn't believe Aunt Eunice would set herself up again so soon. "You think so?"

"Well, I don't know much about it, but isn't it really a man's field?"

"Guess not, since I'm in it." A mild reproof; she was probably cursing herself for having lost control before. "Incidentally, Aunt Eunice," she flicked an ash in the direction of the ashtray, "I'm a woman, not a girl. And I'll study anything I please."

"*There*, you see?" Triumphant, Aunt Eunice lifted the salt and pepper shakers and set them squarely in the middle of the table. Alex and Irena looked at each other wide-eyed; was she crazy or were they? "You can do whatever you please. But I never had that freedom—any girl without a husband was a burden on her brothers. That's what I was taught. Here or in the old country, it didn't matter, you married a Greek and raised children. That was our job." Her body swayed toward Alex although she addressed the wall. "And no one paid us to be good wives and mothers. We just worked hard at it. Everything we had to learn, we did. *Without*," she faced her then, shoulders straight, hands clasped before her on the tablecloth, "the benefit of textbooks."

"You won't hear any argument from me. What people sell their souls for is their business."

"My soul belongs to the Lord, Alexandra. Not your uncle."

"Excuse me. I thought they were one and the same in this house."

"Well, you're the only person who does. He's a man like any other. You used to call him The King behind his back; now you say he's God, but it's you who keep elevating him. I wish you would see that; it isn't healthy."

"But Aunt Eunice, didn't he expel Phil from this paradise of domesticity?" When Alex faked innocence, watch out. "Of course the *good wife* let him do it. The *good mother* must have been looking the other way."

"Alex . . ."

"That isn't fair." Her eyes watered from the wound. "You know you've always been my blessing, the four of you. You know we couldn't have children—I lived for years with your uncle and grandmother blaming me for that. Heirs, sons—I just wanted a baby. When your parents . . . I know it was selfish of me, but when the Lord took their lives, I felt He was giving me the chance to complete my own."

"Four little bundles literally from heaven, huh, Aunt Eunice?"

"I don't care if you think it's something to be sarcastic about. It's the way I felt. And your uncle—he never once complained about the responsibility. If he paid a little more attention to Eugene, it wasn't because he didn't love all of you. Eugene was the oldest son, that's all; when he went away, of course your uncle expected Philip to—"

"Hunt and fish," Alex interrupted, "and kill and maim and drink retsina with the boys. Except that wasn't Phil's way. So lo, the great God grew offended by his *unmanly* son, and banished him forever."

"It was his running away from the draft; you know that. Your uncle loves his country."

"More than his family? I guess Uncle Constantine would have been happier if there'd been two coffins yesterday. That really would've been something to be proud of."

"You're a harsher judge than he ever was."

"Bulloney! And so what? My judgments don't mean a thing around here, they don't affect anybody's life. 'Fight like a man and die like one!' he thunders. 'Okay,' says Gene, and he strides out the door. 'Uh-uh,' says Phil, and he would have been thrown right through it if the *good mother* hadn't opened it first."

"What could I have done? Tell me!" She was grasping Alex's wrist. "I want to know what I could have done."

Alex looked down at the fingers on her arm with such distaste, they shrank away. "*You* couldn't have done anything. You've always let him get away with murder; that iron hand of his has hit out lots of times, and you've never done a thing to stop it. All you do is cry and cater to his excesses and blame Grandmother Agnes for what he is. And oh yes, you pray. It helps a whole bunch, having a holy mother in the house."

"No! I won't listen," actually covering her ears and closing her eyes, "I won't. The Lord is my judge, not you, the Lord, He's the one—"

"There's no one up there, Aunt Eunice!" Alex shouted. "You don't have to answer to anyone!"

Aunt Eunice squeezed her eyes shut even tighter. Her head shook from side to side. "I can't hear you! I'm not listening."

"For Chrissake, Alex, let up."

To her surprise, Alex leaned back in her chair. She grinned without warmth, and lit another cigaret. There was silence, if not peace. Aunt Eunice cautiously opened her eyes; in stages she lowered her arms. The only sound came from Alex, steadily inhaling and exhaling through that strange, cold grin.

"Goodness it's late." Aunt Eunice stood and gathered the sticky plates together. "We'd better get started on these."

Irena got up too. She stacked the cups; piled the silver. Alex simply teetered on her chair, watching them. "C'mon, Alex, since when are you excused?"

Her grin grew wider. "Just us *women*. It was fun, wasn't it?"

They both stopped to stare at her. "But I meant that, Alexandra." Her voice was soft with surprise.

Alex brought the chair legs thumping to the floor. "Well, just count me out of your kind of womanhood, Aunt Eunice. Because if being a woman means being like you . . . I'd rather slit . . . my . . . throat."

Irena was aghast, could find no words.

Her aunt is slumping onto a chair, her sister callously leaving the room. What is there to do? Deny the thing Alex said? Show pity, pat Aunt Eunice on the head and tell her . . . What? Feebly her aunt motions her away. Irena hesitates. Helpless, she obeys. Leaving Aunt Eunice alone in her kitchen, to heal herself if she can.

Needing succor like a child needs the breast. From whose bosom can she gain strength? For her, arms that offer shelter and a moment's pure, uncritical love belong to the Virgin Mary. The Holiest of Mothers. In a bedroom above, Her body glows in an icon's rendering of grace. But to pray is to acknowledge, and that, Aunt Eunice cannot do.

No, over this she is better left, among frying pans and silverware, soap suds, scouring pads, an oven to clean, floors to wax. Let her attack her pain with elbow grease. If the wounds are deep, the needs severe, no one will know. No one will hear. Her aunt will survive—she has all these years.

She leaned against the doorjamb. "Did you have to do that?"

"Yes." Alex angrily stuffed a shirt into her knapsack.

"Because he wasn't here, and you just had to take it out on someone?"

Her sister yanked at a flap. Her jaw was tight, she wouldn't answer.

"She's down there crying, you know."

"Shit!" throwing the bag against the wallpaper. She turned to her with clenched teeth and wild arms. "You were there! You saw what she did! Why does she always . . . why must she . . ." Her hands tried to express it; they gave up. "Fuck it." She righted the overturned knapsack.

"Alex, you knew that would happen. I don't know why she does it. But you're smarter than she is; you're stronger. Can't you shut yourself off from it somehow?"

"Didn't I try? Damn it, you saw me trying! I'm not a saint!"

"If you go back to school without apologizing, you'll—"

Lunging, she stabbed a finger toward her face. "Don't tell me what to do, Rena! Just stay out of it. Stay . . . out."

Irena bit her lip. Alex, menacing, backed away; walked to the bureau, started rummaging in a drawer. She watched silently, trying to judge from the anger in her sister's body when she could speak again. Carrying a handful of underwear to the bed, Alex jammed it inside the bag, and went back to the bureau.

"Can I just say something?"

Hands on the open drawer, she sighed, slowly looking around. "Go ahead."

"Do you realize . . . you've been home less than one day, and you've already told off everybody in the family?"

"So?"

"So, how did you get a monopoly on self-righteousness?"

Her mouth twisted. "Little sister's growing up."

"Don't patronize me, Alex. I am really tired of it."

Alex stared, testing the depth of what she had heard. Then she casually moved to the nightstand, where her cigarets were.

"All I'm trying to do," she wanted to keep her voice level, devoid of any pleading, "is get you to see what an ego trip you're on. None of us measures up to your expectations; no one does things the way *you* think they should; we're all inferior to Alex."

23

She eyed her over the match flame. "I can't help it if my sister sees superiority in everyone but her."

"Not after this."

A raised eyebrow was her only reply.

"That was bloodshed down there; I didn't respect it."

"But you respect Aunt Eunice."

"That's not the point—she does the best she can."

"Don't I know it. There's all sorts of refined hostility behind her little games—which both of you refuse to recognize. She resents me like hell, Rena. It's true!" Nodding against her disbelief, she mouthed *true*. "Aunt Eunice doesn't have the guts to take on Uncle Constantine, so she dumps on me. But that's only part of it. The other is, she can't stand seeing me accomplish things that she never did, and couldn't. Because she made her decision a long time ago to be a mild-mannered house prostitute, and it's too late to change."

"That's unreal, Alex—they don't even do it anymore."

"Right! Her kicks are all in the ass; they always have been. But she's got a roof over her head, groceries in the cupboard, and nice, middle-class respectability. So what if her husband walks all over her and treats her like shit. Just ask her, she'll tell you it's worth it. Maybe she tells her blessed Virgin Mary something else, but not you. You're the one she wants to convince, Rena. Then maybe you'll be just like her, grow up in her image—I'm out of reach, but you can still prove her life hasn't been one big waste."

"You don't honestly believe that."

"You bet I do. And if I see you going that way, don't expect me to applaud."

"What should I do instead, Alex? Be just like you? At least Aunt Eunice doesn't hurt anyone; she isn't out for blood. So she's meek, that doesn't give you the right to take advantage of it like *he* does, you're just as rotten to her as—"

"Stop it!" Her anger had flooded back, warping her face. "Don't *do* that! I've had it with that line, I am *not* like him! You've picked that up from her, she's the one who's made me

24

a stand-in for him and now you're doing it!" She jerked the knapsack toward her. "Jesus." The buckles jingled as she pulled each one tight. "I don't see where you've been so fucking sensitive about her feelings. She's been a doormat for you just as much as the rest of us."

Dizzy from standing, she crossed to the bed she had spent hours on, just last night, when they had been close.

"Phil's the only one who ever treated her decently." Alex shoved the bag to the foot of the bed. "Out of principle and simple, basic kindness." She sat where the bag had been, tucking a leg under. "Look how she paid him back."

She had no response, no desire to defend anymore. Her tiredness was that awful heavy kind depression brings. Alex would be going soon, and they hadn't even started talking about things that were really on her mind. How could they now, with this stupid argument between them? "When are you leaving?"

"In a minute." She was prodding at a cuticle, obviously ready to go but not making a move to. "I'd have to now anyway. There's a big strategy session tonight; I promised I'd be there. We're really gonna bring 'em down, Rena."

"Oh." She nodded, pretending to know what that meant.

Alex tossed back a long strand of hair; it fell forward as she bent over her nails again. "Listen, I'm sorry. We didn't need that."

Needing to show her she could shrug it off, she mumbled, " 'S'all right."

"I wish you'd accept the fact we're different. I'm not asking you to be like me. Or saying you're exactly like her. Just be yourself, be your own person."

Fine, she wanted nothing more, but who was that?

"I know it's hard. I remember. You're sure it'll never happen, but it does. One day you simply wake up, and you know. You don't even think about it anymore, you stop hassling yourself about who you are, and you just start doing . . . being."

Sure. Except it wouldn't happen that way for her; she was bound to have more of a struggle than Alex. "Did you really not know? I mean, for a long time? You never showed it."

"Of course, dummy." She bounced off the bed. "I'm real good at bluffing, you know that."

Alex is kissing her hair. To cling to her, just for a second—rest her head against that denim waist. But she is afraid of looking weak.

"C'mon, I gotta go. Walk me to the car." Alex swung the knapsack off the bed and hoisted it onto her back.

She stood but didn't move from between the beds. "Alex . . . ?"

Her sister turned at the doorway.

"I . . . can I call you sometime? Would it be okay?"

"You don't have to ask." She motioned for her to follow and disappeared.

Her eyes were stinging. Alex? Why couldn't she say it? "Alex? I love you."

Outside, the sun was glaring, making the VW's blue paint oily bronze. The motor started with a sewing-machine whine. Alex squinted up at her. "You ought to think about getting away from here, Rena. Transferring to State or something. It'd help." The gears ground into first. "See you." The car spluttered as if it were dying, jerked forward, then gained power; halfway down the block, a khaki-clad arm waved from the window. She hadn't apologized to Aunt Eunice, only called out goodby. Irena loved her, but sometimes her sister was very hard to like.

II

THREE SIT SILENTLY in the room. Having prayed and returned, they stay without words, bound by remembrance. It has been forty days since Eugene's body was sent beneath the earth. "O Lord, give rest . . . and of Thy goodness and mercy remit . . . the sins of Eugene Lampros." Commemorate, lest the family forget. Mention his name; exhume the dead. Dig him up for the sake of his soul, and remember. Commiserate. Regret.

Uncle Constantine is uncommonly quiet, puffing on his pipe. Stomach too big, collar too tight, he normally would have changed from his Sunday clothes. Aunt Eunice, rocking her chair with a muted creak, rests her head, eyelids lowered. Is she dreaming? thinking? seeing Eugene in his prime? or is there merely light behind?

Lord knows. So many real pictures fill this place. A shrine to Eugene now; images are all around. No one can escape

Gene in the Little League, batting on the mantel. In cap and gown, he graduates on top of the piano. Under the lamp, he kneels with a troop of scouts. Always in uniform of one sort or another; they mark the stages, the passages, the rites. The last: ending basic training near his uncle's favorite chair. Like a little girl who masquerades in mother's grown-up wear, he stares out at them; a boy dressed to kill for his country. Posing, serious and impressed; falling for the fantasy, the manly make-believe.

Dear Gene. Did he know? Irena swallowed. Before it happened, did he know it would go the other way?

Irena sees herself and Alex in a miniature double frame. Gap-toothed and pinafored: two innocents in braids. How quickly that would change, yet not a shadow, not an inkling, crosses those silly grinning faces. The only ones to sully the shrine, as if Phil had never been. Someone went through this room removing every trace of him.

She realized how little Phil would have minded.

He always was the unseen one, the child content with a private corner. Yet Phil was well liked, and something more, he was respected. He never knew a bratty phase, or teased gratuitously—tormenting squirrels and fireflies to see how their insides worked, then walking away indifferently from bodies that writhed, still half-alive—let others play boygod and bore themselves with pain. Phil was unique.

But not queer, she thought. That was Uncle Constantine's mistake. Shy, yes—but not withdrawn, as Aunt Eunice used to think.

Growing up, Phil never worried about what they said, or felt he was developing too late. Unlike Gene, who would lewdly boast of conquests the next morning, Phil had no need to broadcast success. To shore up his manhood by making whores of his dates.

Her sister said he was too idealistic. Surely that was a minor flaw, small, like the others.

Such as caring for everyone without discrimination and refusing to argue despite provocation, so that no one was special and he accepted too much. You would not want Phil in a political campaign, or choose him as advocate should you wind up in court, or expect him to love you above anyone else. Gene was for that. He was impassioned and loyal; too sure of the issues, of right and wrong, but quick to defend or offer support.

God. She smiled, recalling the brat he had been.

Gene was the terror, the terrible kid who blustered and broke things and left lots of bruises. He knew about torture. And he teased with true pleasure—waved boxes of Kotex just out of reach; tied brand new brassieres to the branches of trees; bragged to his buddies about seeing your tits. He was awful, they thought he would never mature. Then suddenly, he did . . .

Her eyes were burning. What she would give, to have him here. Gene.

Why now and not then? Why have the memories, the mourning, the hopeless nostalgia come swirling today and not at his grave or during the funeral? "Give the last kiss to him who hath died." Alex had done it, in her private goodby. And when the cantor had called out, others obeyed. But she, recoiling from lips that belonged to a corpse, had walked past the casket without looking in.

Does remorse make her see him come into the room? Run joyfully toward the mirage of his face? Drench it with kisses— bathe him with love! Watch how he laughs now! See how . . . he fades.

She hadn't done it enough when he really was there. And now was too late. Gene and the others—they'd all flown away.

She leans back, hoping to trap the tears. No brothers, no sister share the nest. Like the two who sit with her, she is alone, in a chair.

* * *

Before she approached *them* about it, she wanted to be absolutely sure. That's why she'd called Alex, to test it out—she'd done enough silent thinking in the past few weeks.

"He's not going to like it, Rena. You better be ready to crawl." Voices were arguing in the background; Irena kept expecting her to yell at them to pipe down.

"Should I call back later, after the meeting?"

"No, they're still getting their rocks off arguing policy—last time I mentioned tactics they treated me like I was some dumb broad who can't follow a conversation. I should've learned by now that I gotta get one of the guys aside and work on him, then when he brings it up, they'll all say 'Yeah, right, tactics!' "

Alex had said it was okay to phone her anytime. Even so, "This must seem pretty insignificant in comparison. I shouldn't be keeping you."

"Will you stop it? When His Greekness finds out you're thinking of dropping out of school to take a job, he is going to shit! What will people think, he can't support his own? You belong to the Great Provider, lady. You're supposed to get educated so the grocer won't rook you and you can be an asset to your husband."

"But it wouldn't be forever; I'd go back." After she had experienced a few things; given herself time. "I just don't seem to be making any progress there right now. I mean, what good's another A going to do me?"

"There's more to college than a classroom, Rena. If you came here you might—hold on." Close male voice, the word "coffee"; Alex yelped as if she'd been pinched. "Bastards, let someone else make it for once."

"I've thought about transferring, but . . ." If she followed in her sister's footsteps, she risked getting absorbed by the bigger shadow. "I'm not as committed as you are, I haven't sorted out enough yet—I'd only be a cipher marching in the streets, Alex."

"Listen, I don't want to pressure you, okay? You've got to

make your own decision." She thought she had; her resolve had seemed so firm before she called. "If you don't want to memorize a zillion more art-history slides, it's fine with me. But suppose you do get him to agree, and then you can't find a job that'll pay you enough to live on?"

She hadn't considered moving out of the house right away —Alex was pushing her in deeper than she had intended. "I thought I'd . . . the job I'd really like to try for is only temporary. And it won't open up till next semester, which is perfect."

"What would you be doing?"

"Working as a research assistant for some archaeologist at the museum."

"Gee, Rena, that might mean sorting potsherds all day in a musty room."

"Oh." She thought the job had sounded nice. "Well," attempting her breeziest, "I probably wouldn't get it anyway."

"What am I going to do with you? If that's what you want, then go after it. You gotta fight for *something*. Change your —wait a sec." More muffled voices near the receiver. "Vote's coming, I have to hang up. Let me know what happens."

"Alex?" Wait, everything was confused now. "Are you coming home for vacation?" They could talk about it then; there would still be time.

"Uhm, I'm not sure, I might . . ." her voice had dropped, ". . . north." Irena could barely hear. ". . . wild geese . . ."

"What? You mean visit—"

"Right!" Loud, cutting her off. "Thanks for calling, Rena, bye." The connection was broken before she could say more.

She had stretched out on her bed during the call. She stayed there, the phone resting on her stomach. If only she could reach Phil, too; talk to him for a while. She would have loved to go to Canada, but she hadn't been asked; even if she had, there was no way she could get past her uncle without money and an alibi. But just to call him; hear his voice. "If it's what you really want, Rena," his baritone still cracked oc-

31

casionally, "then it's good. Don't worry about school. When it's right for you to go on, you will." She could see him smiling, lips surrounded by a curly beard; blue eyes shining with acceptance, and love. No conflicting signals from Phil; her brother would have given her the confirmation she needed.

It used to be comforting, knowing what to do and automatically doing it. She had liked having routine in her life, but lately she'd been losing patience. Reading the message by the phone—Dear, gone to church meeting. Please preheat oven to 350, put roast in (uncovered!) at 3:30. xoxo, Aunt Eunice—she groaned. Ex oh ex oh Aunt Eunice; love and kisses as if she were four years old. Uncover the roast—she had only done it a thousand times. She crumpled the note.

Her aunt had left the mail by the phone as always; she flipped through it with rising irritation. The bottom envelope was addressed to her, in Alex's handwriting; but Alex was in Canada and would never have dared write her from there. She peered at the postmark; mailed yesterday, from school.

"Damn you, Alex." Changing plots again, after telling the family she had to stay at school to do a paper, then swearing Irena to secrecy over the fact she was going away. Because Aunt Eunice's name-day celebration fell in the middle of vacation and Alex wasn't coming home for it, Uncle Constantine had thrown a fit. "Upstairs she has a desk!" he had stormed; "Her own room!" he had ranted; "But our *scholar* needs a library! Our *scholar* cannot take time out from her busy, important schedule to honor a woman who has been a mother to her all her life. Our Miss Smartypants is so smart she has forgotten what a family is!" Neither she nor Aunt Eunice had had the temerity to tell him he was hardly the person to preach family togetherness. "I pay through the nose for her to go to school, and this is what she learns!" If Alex had come, they probably would have argued the entire vacation and ruined Aunt Eunice's day anyway. But that wouldn't have mattered to Uncle Constantine so long as the ritual had been observed.

She ripped open the envelope; the letter was dated several days before the postmark.

Dear Rena,

Big trouble! I am where I said I'd be and can't take a chance on calling. A friend will take this back and see that you get it.

The Gentle Idealist is in really bad shape from some stuff he took. Got him to a hospital yesterday and it doesn't look too good. Won't know for a while yet so I'm staying on. Problem—money! You've got to get <u>as much as possible</u> out of The Bastard any way you can. Don't, for godsakes, tell him what it's for. Someone will call you Tuesday evening—he can pick it up and get it to me quickest.

Love,

A.

P.S. This isn't bullshit, so don't waste time wondering if it is, just <u>get money.</u>

But how? Damn it, Alex, how? What could she say, Dear Uncle Constantine, I need an abortion? Listen Uncle Constantine, I have to buy a dozen textbooks and they're fifty dollars each? But Uncle Constantine, all the other girls are wearing . . . Jesus! It wasn't possible, she couldn't do it! How was she supposed to do it! What right did she—how was . . .

She leaned on the hall stand for support, tears of frustration taking over. Loud, desperate. She was splashing Alex's letter. Trying to brush it clear, smearing the ink. Making it run, like blue diluted blood, onto her hands. Her hands, shaking, upraised, blood on them—Phil's blood, staining her hands with his—No! It was *ink*. Bobbing her head, *ink* coming out of her mouth, assuring her. She could hear ink, see ink as she nodded.

Responding, her tears start receding. Her fingers stop quivering.

She shuddered. Becoming quiet, she wiped her eyes and face with the back of her hand. Picking up the blurred letter, she reread. What was the "stuff" Phil had taken? What was wrong with him—why a hospital? How could Alex keep that to herself, not tell her any details, as if Alex were the only one who cared?

It feels good, goading anger, driving before it the last of the horror.

Alex was so secretive and manipulative. Caution was one thing, but this was more than that, it was Alex in control. Alex the judge, deciding who should hear what without giving anyone a chance. Well, she was just as entitled to the truth as Alex was. She didn't have to earn her precious confidence like some kid whose mother thought she wasn't mature enough to hear what the grownups were saying. All that cloak and daggering—"Someone will call you Tuesday." Nobody knew the master plan except Alex; her sister always had to surround everything with intrigue and stand in the center.

Which was where Phil belonged.

She begins shaking again; her face threatens to cave in.

How selfish could she be? To feel resentful when Phil . . . Someone had to be with him, see that he got the proper care. No one could top Alex at taking charge. She should be thanking God her sister was up there, handling everything and asking for whatever help she could get. The thing she had to get was perspective. She had to. Money, she had to get—

The front door opened. She whirled as if caught in a theft. Her aunt's smile faltered.

"Irena? What's the matter?" Peering at her face, she walked closer and Irena took a step back, shoving the letter inside a pocket. "What's happened?"

"Nothing! I . . . What time is it?"

"Ten after four."

"The oven! I forgot to preheat the oven!" She raced into the kitchen; turned on the stove; hurried to the refrigerator and was taking out the roast as her aunt came in.

"Did you just get home? I thought certainly you would be home in time to preheat the oven. How could you forget when I left you a note?"

"I just forgot, that's all." She put the roast on the counter.

"But you know your uncle likes to eat promptly at six. I don't understand how—here, I'll do it," brushing her aside. She took off the tinfoil and began prodding at the roast, checking for neglect. "It won't be done until at least six forty-five now. I don't know what excuse I'll give him, he hates—"

"For heaven's sake! So he has to wait an hour for the first time in twenty years. You act as if it were the most important thing in the world that Uncle Constantine get his dinner on time."

Grim-lipped, her aunt shook paprika onto the meat.

"Look, it was my fault. I'll confess, all right? We can make some hors d'oeuvre or something."

"Your uncle doesn't like hors d'oeuvre."

"Then we'll . . . fix him an extra drink."

"He drinks too much as it is."

"Okay! Then we'll just do nothing and wait for the house to fall!"

Her aunt put down the garlic salt and turned around. "Irena. Something *is* the matter. I'm not accustomed to your behaving in this fashion and I want to know what's wrong."

No, she couldn't—then why hadn't she acted smarter, cooler? She touched the note in her pocket. Alex had only said not to tell their uncle. But it wasn't right to worry Aunt Eunice; not now, with everything still to be done.

"Does this have something to do with the letter your sister wrote you? Is she in some sort of trouble?"

Yes and no; she could feel her face reflecting each response.

35

"I've always let you girls have your little secrets, Irena. You've kept things from me all your lives. That's natural, and that's your privilege. But if this is important . . . just once, it would be nice if you could bring yourselves to trust me."

Her head was aching. "The oven light went off." She watched her aunt put in the roast; resigned to denial, having asked for the same thing Irena wanted from Alex. All these years, she had lived without it; they had done that to her. Lined, graying, she closed the oven door. "Aunt Eunice . . . ?"

She has forgotten what her aunt's body feels like, pressed in an embrace. Staying, she kisses a papery cheek. Under her lips, there are smile creases; then rivulets, the seams merge, wet.

They separated without looking at each other. "Well." Aunt Eunice fumbled for a Kleenex.

Grasping the letter, she still didn't take it out. "If I tell you . . ." She searched her aunt's face for a sign she was doing the right thing. "It has to be confidential. I mean, if you tell Uncle Constantine—if you think you might—I can't go into it."

"There is a long list of things your uncle has never heard from me, Irena. And I assure you, if something were on my mind, he wouldn't notice. So please, tell me."

She took a deep, shaky breath. "All right, Alex isn't really at school—she's somewhere in Canada, visiting Phil."

To her surprise, Aunt Eunice chuckled. "I thought Alexandra knew. She's nobody's fool, whatever happens, she always . . ." Her hand went to her chest. "Philip—something's happened to my Philip!"

She chewed her lip to stop it from trembling. "He's uhm, sick—Alex didn't say what it was, just that he's in the hospital and they won't know for a while but she's staying up there until they do so don't worry, they're taking care of him and Alex is there."

36

"Sick!" She felt for the rim of the sink. "How sick? Why don't they know? Alexandra must have told you!"

"She didn't! She didn't go into any details at all, except . . ." Maybe her aunt would see it differently. "If he's in the hospital, it sort of has to be serious, doesn't it?"

"Serious! I should be there with him, I have to go up there."

"But you can't—Uncle Constantine wouldn't let you even if you could. Alex is doing everything that's necessary, she's running out of money, that's all, that's why she wrote, to ask me to get as much as I could out of him without telling him what it was for. But, I don't see how I can do it."

Her aunt wasn't listening, her eyes were too faraway. "Your uncle would have to know . . ." They came back, hard.

"Aunt Eunice, you said you wouldn't—you can't tell him!" How could she stop her? "You promised, I trusted you, you asked me to and I—"

"*Irena.*" The sudden severity jarred her into silence. "You didn't let me finish. Your uncle isn't going to part with any money without a very good reason, and there is no excuse you can come up with that will work. The truth ought to get it out of him—now wait a moment." Palm up, she halted another outburst. "If he were half the man he thinks he is, it would. But it won't; that wretched stubbornness of his won't let him lift a finger."

"Then what are you saying? That we can't help? That's not possible—we have to."

"I'm saying we can't go to your uncle. *I'll* get the money . . . somewhere else."

"You?" It had never occurred to her; or to Alex either. "But how? Where will you get it?" Incredible; her aunt wouldn't be up to this, she was constitutionally incapable.

"I have a little of my own—but don't you dare let him know it. If he thought I was managing to save any from the household expenses, he'd cut my allowance. Your uncle

37

George isn't so tightfisted; I'm sure Leona has a healthy emergency fund salted away. I'll go to her."

"But you and Aunt Leona haven't talked to each other in years!"

"That has nothing to do with it. Leona is my sister and this is family; she'd be offended if I didn't give her the opportunity to help."

Her aunt walked to where her apron was hanging on the kitchen door; Irena had never seen her look so determined, slipping it on and tying the sash like a surgeon suiting up to operate, calm even though a life depended on his skill. "We have to have it by Tuesday, Aunt Eunice." She couldn't help it if this image of her was so new it couldn't overcome every doubt. "Alex said someone would call for it then."

"We'll have it." She marched to the refrigerator. Briskly things were moved about on the shelves. "Here," she thrust a bunch of lettuce in Irena's direction, "clean this, I'll take care of the beans."

She shook her head in amazement; Alex would never have believed it.

Unless he is alone at home, Uncle Constantine never answers the phone. Tonight, that privilege of his makes waiting a little easier. Aunt Eunice is at church once more, praying for souls and the strength to endure the advantage she has given her sister. So Irena is free to pass the time in whatever room she pleases; even if she has to run dripping from the tub, no one else will pick up the receiver.

"Irena? Greg Roussas. Can you talk?"

She hadn't expected it to be him. "Yes."

"Did you get it?"

"Yes." Alex must have changed her mind about Greg, unless she had taken to trusting "creeps."

"How much?"

"Five hundred." All of which had better reach Canada.

"Not bad! Should I come over or would you rather meet me somewhere?"

She heard her uncle climbing the stairs. "Fine! I'd love to!" In case he could hear anything through the bedroom door.

"Let's make it the pizza place on First, about eight, okay?"

"Sure, I'll meet you out front. Thanks for calling!"

"Thank *you.*" He laughed, as if Irena had been eager for a real date. She hung up, wishing she hadn't overdone the enthusiasm.

It had been over two years since she'd seen Greg, and the change in him was striking. Neat and lean; that was the Greg she had dated a few times before realizing what lay beneath his polite, Greek school manners. This broad-shouldered and bearded man in denims was like him only in height, and the size of the hand he had placed around her shoulder when they went into the restaurant. She remembered his hands all too well; his long legs, sprawled under the table, were already grazing hers.

"So, how'd you manage it?" He nonchalantly stuffed the envelope into his shirt pocket.

"I didn't; my aunt got it."

"You're kidding. What'd she have to do for it?"

How she could ever have found him attractive . . . "Just tell Alex, Aunt Eunice got the money from her sister. Do you know how Phil is? Has she been in touch with you?"

"Alex and I are always in touch." He grinned salaciously. "In all ways, in touch."

"Look, Greg, I'm not interested in any details that don't have to do with my brother. Will you tell me how he is, please?"

Lifting his beer glass, he eyed her in an unpleasant, calculating way, even while he swallowed and slowly wiped the foam from his mouth. "What would you say if I said Phil's fine?"

39

"He is! Why didn't she let me know? Is he out of the hospital?"

"What if I said, he never was in it?"

She couldn't speak.

"Hey, would you rather he was dying? Would it be okay then? getting the five hundred? Does he have to be dying for the cause to be good enough?"

"What kind of insane game are you playing? We've been worried to death about Phil! Are you saying he's never been sick, that all this was some grotesque way of getting money for a cause? Alex wouldn't do that to us. She wouldn't."

"So, it is true you'd rather your own brother was dying than know you'd been duped."

"That's not what I'm saying at all."

"Sure it is. But don't get so upset, Irena, I was just testing. Now I know."

"Know what? Testing what? Is he or isn't he sick? For God's sake, Greg, do you have to be this sadistic?"

He shot forward, "Don't talk to me about sadism, little lady," jabbing the air between them. "Not when you're sitting comfortably on your ass in your comfy, middle-class home wondering 'Oh, should I take History 302 or work in an art gallery for a while.' There are thousands of guys getting their fucking heads blown off out there, haven't you heard? Cute little bombs are burning the flesh off kids, or haven't you seen them trying to run away from their own backs on the evening news? Yeah? Then what're you doing about it? You're not doing shit, that's what, so don't talk to *me* about sadism."

"You . . . are . . . crazy. I want to know about my brother. Will you please . . . tell me . . . if he's all right. I don't care about anybody else right now, just him."

"Typical. I bet you've never had a worry in your life that wasn't personal. Well, here's a big one to add to your earth-shaking list. Phil isn't fine. He's freaked out on dope. Okay? You satisfied now?"

40

"Dope! What kind—you don't mean heroin?"

"Christ, a lot you know. If it was heroin, he'd be nodding in a corner somewhere. But he's rattling the bars, man, he's shaking his cage in the psycho ward. He's dropped so much acid and speed and psilocybin he's a fucking atomic mushroom."

"I don't believe you. That's not my brother."

"Oh, yes it is. He's slipped it in sixty-year-olds for uppers and taken their bucks for tabs and that is a— Shit!" His chair fell back as he got up spluttering, drenched in the beer she had thrown, without thinking or knowing ahead of time, simply lashing out, throwing it in his face. "No you don't!" Her arm was caught, she couldn't get past him. Keeping his grip on her, he flung some money on the table and propelled her out of the restaurant. The moment they were outside she tried to wrench free.

"Let go of me, Greg!"

He started walking rapidly down the street, pulling her along beside him. Frightened of what he might do, she twisted violently. "Stop struggling, damn it! I'm not going to hurt you."

"You're hurting me now!" Stumbling, forced to keep pace, she tried again to yank her arm away. "Will you stop? Stop!"

He wouldn't even look at her. Intent on some private mission, he treated her attempts to wrestle free as mere annoyances. After two blocks she was exhausted and his huge hand on her arm showed no sign of weakening. She had no choice but to try to reason with him. "Greg. I can walk on my own. If you'd just let go of me . . . let go, Greg, so I can walk without tripping all the time."

"If I do, will you promise not to run?" He didn't stop; his fingers were still digging into her.

"I promise."

"I don't believe you."

"Greg! I promise!"

He stopped then, and the pressure eased. "Okay."

Pulling her arm from his loose grasp, she expected to see a large red welt on it even through her sweater. She rubbed the soreness and looked at him in bewilderment.

"I'm sorry. I didn't mean to hurt you."

"Then why did you?"

A pleading expression. "I apologize. For all of it, what I said back in the restaurant; this." His hand—before he could touch her arm, she turned and walked away.

"Irena. Wait." He caught up easily. "Let me try and explain." Eyes fixed straight ahead, she kept on walking. "Look," he held out his hands, "I'll even keep them in my pockets the whole time if you'll just let me talk to you." He actually did shove them into his jeans, but she didn't trust the sudden transition; all she wanted was the safety of home. "Irena, please. I need someone to talk to, someone outside of it who'll listen."

"How do you expect me to after that?"

"I'm not expecting, I'm begging—you have to listen when someone's begging you to, don't you?"

"Not unless they're prepared to tell the truth."

"I am, I want to. But I need help, I can't seem to get down to it on my own anymore."

Her pace didn't slow; she owed him nothing.

"Irena, I'm fucked—it's this goddamn war."

"Oh sure. Nifty explanation, Greg."

"You're not a man, you don't know. I'm not saying it's the same for all of us—some guys don't have any conflict about it, they're against the war and in the movement and that's that, even though their lives are totally disrupted if they don't have a deferment. Or a trick knee." She remembered him in language class, pushing his knee joint in and out whenever he had an audience. "You're smart. Don't you think being Greek, the warrior tradition and all, could have something to do with people like Phil and me getting kind of schizy? Because we are—you saw a prime example of it."

42

"That wasn't true, what you said about him, was it? None of that can be true. Phil isn't like that."

"People change. At least sometimes I think they do, other times I think we're so programmed we haven't got a chance. I know Phil and I seem real different to you, but maybe underneath we're not. Because if he's got it too, the guilt, then it's guilt and craziness for both of us. Old Ajax slaughtering the cows. We're not fighting—we're trying to end the war and save lives, but we've got to pay for that."

"Why? Just because you happen to've been born male? If you were a Japanese with samurai ancestors, you'd be telling me the same thing."

"Maybe. Probably I would."

"Then you're making yourself pay. And if Phil is too, I want to know in what way."

He stopped walking. "Irena, I don't know how to cushion it. He *is* in the psychiatric ward."

"But he'll come out of it, won't he?"

"It can take a long time sometimes. There can be after-effects, like shock waves."

"And the other? What you said about his . . . about what he did, to get pills?"

He looked at the sidewalk. "That's not important; don't let it be."

"Is it true?"

"I shouldn't have brought it up. I was pissed. Forget it."

"So okay then, it's true." She pivoted and jounced across the street. Every step jolted her head but Greg came loping alongside. "Why didn't you tell me straight out from the beginning instead of putting me through all that? Why did you have to be so vicious?"

"That's what I'm talking about—Phil's gone his route, I've gone mine, and I don't know which of us is worse off. Irena, I'm not bulling you. You've got to understand that for us the *Iliad* was yesterday. We—"

43

"Get off it, Greg. What're you going to do, bring in every war in history to justify yourself?"

"Not every war, Irena. Just the ones I can't seem to escape. They're a part of me—my heritage. Phil's too. Remember Papagapolous, 'the geek who taught us Greek'? I can't shake that guy out of me. When the last war came along, the Yalu River could've been outside Troy, the way he went on about the valor of our brave older brothers; every time we'd translate a passage, he'd stop us to draw parallels and inflame our little Greek hearts. Then there were those speeches we had to make at the school pageants, all dressed up in our best suits, reciting patriotic paragraphs about the Greek War of Independence. We'd go home and our grandfathers would be talking about how they rushed to volunteer in the First World War so they could prove they were worthy citizens in the making. Then in the Second, when it was their hometowns, their relatives, their land, our fathers, their good American sons, fell all over themselves to defend the sacred soil of Greece—the home of democracy. Christ, even Socrates was a soldier. It's been drilled into us and drilled into us. An M-sixteen and Achilles' spear—they're one and the same, the way we were brought up."

"Everyone says this war is different."

"Yeah, on the surface. But what happens in war, that doesn't change."

"Well, Achilles wouldn't have fought in this one; there isn't any honor to it."

"Those old guys sending us off think there is. Honor and death—they don't see it's a fucked relationship, to them it's sanctified, some kind of holy truism. *Still*. It's the biggest crock of propaganda disguised as principle the world's ever had."

"So what's the message, Greg? All this talk of wars and heritage doesn't relieve you of responsibility—it doesn't excuse or even explain what you did tonight."

"You mean you really don't see it?" He hooked her sweater

44

to make her stop. "After everything I've said, you don't understand the pressures?"

"Is my personal perspective at fault again, Greg? Or is what you've said just too complicated for a little lady to grasp?"

He squinted around at the trees, the houses, the street; acting perplexed, giving himself time. Then he sighed, weightily. "Okay." He faced her. "When I saw you coming toward the restaurant . . . you looked so fine. So pretty and untouched by it all, I couldn't help it, this wave of fury started rolling through me. You had a choice, you could stay outside it if you wanted to—all girls can—and it looked to me like you'd made your choice without even thinking about it. On the one hand I was really glad for you, but on the other . . . It's like I had to protect you and beat you over the head with it at the same time."

"You've got a very weird view of protecting someone."

"Look, if Phil were really dying, that would be the worst, right? So in comparison, what he's going through isn't that bad. But it's bad. The whole thing kept flip-flopping, and it came out wrong. I know that. What I don't know is, how much are we responsible for, and how much is kind of inevitable? If it's all our fault, then there's hope Phil and I can sort ourselves out. But for me that means the crazyrages, as Alex calls them, are controllable—through willpower—which they're not. Why? If it's beyond willpower, then I could go on like this forever. And, Irena, I don't want to, it scares me. I can deal with that, but it doesn't stop the rages from getting in the way. Take tonight. I was so angry—with you, Phil, me —even though two of those people, I happen to like. A lot." Her shoulder was gently squeezed and quickly left alone.

Still the wily adaptable Greg, always adept at turnabouts whenever they suited his purpose.

She recalls back-seat car endearments; not falling for his tactics; being made to feel inferior. Attention no longer deserved or bestowed as he drives her home in silence, breaking into a derisive laugh when she tries to defend her behavior.

So she never admits she wants it, too, but not with her skirt bunched up to her waist while he struggles to fit a condom on before she can change her mind or some car or person arrives on the scene just as he gets it in. She fought him off, having heard from her friends the pleasure would only be his, that a girl needs time in order to climb to the ecstasy daydreams envision. She also required words more inspired than "Honey let me do it," and "I love you I love you" as he groped for her pants—sounds aimed at sex, when she longed for romance.

But not now. Certainly not with him. The strategist; still trying to maneuver her. Let him use Alex; let them manipulate each other. They were equals, a pair. Unless Alex had fallen for him, gone blind like the typical lover. No. In bed or out, she would never be submissive; either they tossed for the dominant position, or Greg had to fight for the top when he came up against her sister.

"Hasn't what I've said made any sense? Maybe it's not the greatest apology in the world, but in the long run, explanations are more important."

"I'll have to think about it, Greg. What does Alex say? You must have talked it over with her."

"I said I needed someone outside it, Irena. When two people are as involved as we are, you can't be sure their perspectives are all that objective."

How gallant, *their* perspectives. "I see." So he hadn't opened up to her, given Alex that edge—she would've taken advantage, gained the upper hand permanently.

"I'm in love with her, you know."

"No, I didn't." Why was she being so harsh on them and judgmental? Something was making her—currents of resentment were still shooting through her. She couldn't locate their source; the area surrounding Phil didn't seem to be the right one.

"She has me coming and going sometimes, and I'm not

46

talking about trips over the border. I really admire her." His beard hid any blushing. "Alex is one gutsy lady. Of course she doesn't have the same pressures. Like I said, it's easier for a girl—excuse me, *woman*." He laughed. "Your sister would've made a great Amazon. Lucky for me she's short and two-breasted."

"Is Alex in love with you?"

"We don't talk about it much. Anyway, that's not the scene. You bed down with whoever happens to be around. I've got to admit, the first time she did that, it threw me for a few days. Big rage; scared me more than it did her. But that's cool now; Alex can still set me off, but only when she does something dumb—dangerous, you know?"

She stopped. "What are you two involved in?" She tugged him back from the curb. "Not bombs and things like that—you're not in that part of the movement, are you?"

Rather than meet her eyes, he watched his boot kick the sidewalk. "If we were, I wouldn't tell you." He looked up, his mouth twitching. "Don't worry, Irena. We want to stop the body count, not add to it." It was an insider's grin, wavering but smug.

"Look, I don't think it's right, not knowing how to reach her up there. Security is one thing, but keeping me in the dark like this is really paranoid. What does my sister think I'll do, go to the F.B.I.?"

"They might come to you, ever think of that? If you don't know anything, you can't tell them anything, even inadvertently."

"Well, you tell Alex for me I think it's lousy. I've got as much right to know how my brother is as she does. I don't care what your secrets are, if she has to send it by carrier pigeon, I want news about Phil, *when* it happens and not just when she needs money!"

He put up his hands in mock defense. "Okay! I'll tell her. What's got into you?"

"Nothing." But she knew what it was, now. "It's late—I have to go. Alex better find some way of letting us know she got the five hundred or Aunt Eunice'll be worried."

"Just Aunt Eunice, huh? Don't you trust me?"

"About as much as you trust me, Greg. Good night." She turned her back on his amusement and walked. History 302 or an art gallery; damn them to hell.

"Private Lampros, reporting as requested."

"Very funny, Alex. Where are you calling from?"

"A pay phone, and it's a hassle, so don't expect me to do it too often. Thanks for the bills, Rena. You did good."

"You ought to be thanking Aunt Eunice, she deserves the credit."

"Spare me. How much does she know?"

"Everything I do. Except for certain vicious details about Phil that have nothing to do with his condition right now. How is he?"

"Calmer, I may be able to get him released next week. Listen Rena, that other stuff about Phil. It's no big deal—Greg can be an ass sometimes. How's she taking the rest of it?"

"Better than you'd think. She said no matter how painful the truth is, it's better than not knowing, and imagining even worse. She's right, Alex. You didn't have to do that to us."

"Gee, I'm really sorry, you know? I mean, my brother's freaking out all over the place and I'm running around trying to fix a hospital card so I can get him in somewhere with no money in a strange city in a foreign country, but I can see I should have stopped to consider the fine points of your and Aunt Eunice's feelings. Forgive me for not putting you at the top of my priority list."

"Look, Alex, everyone appreciates—"

"Sure they do. I just hope you never have to be responsible for deciding what's best in a life-and-death situation."

"Aren't you overdramatizing just a bit?"

48

"Right. I forgot. You didn't see Phil after God called to tell him to fly on up for a visit. Yeah, I forgot you weren't here when Greg caught him flapping his arms ready to take off, three storeys down."

"Oh God, Alex, no. Oh my God."

"You want to tell all that to Aunt Eunice? Go ahead, but I don't recommend it."

"What's happened to him? I don't understand any of it."

"Greg said he tried to explain, but you weren't terrifically receptive."

"Alex, how could I be? Just because you've taken to trusting that 'creep' doesn't mean I do. I never was receptive to Greg Roussas. I don't like him any more than Aunt Eunice does."

"Who's asking either one of you to like him? Whatever's between us is between us."

"That's what you think. It was all over town when I was dating him, but we stopped seeing each other before Aunt Eunice had to say anything."

"About what? Christ, what's she been filling your head with now?"

"Oh, something a *well-meaning* friend told her. Made a special point of recalling the old days, the padrone system, just so she could let it drop that when Greg's grandfather was a boy, the man who brought him into the country wasn't his real father, who happened to be a Lampros, but a pseudo father named Roussas. Which makes Greg a cousin of ours to the fourth or fifth degree—the *friend* hadn't quite worked it out."

"So?"

"So, incest, Alex. Aunt Eunice is afraid you're committing incest."

"Jesus! Of all the stupid—fourth or fifth? that's ridiculous! She better not be wasting any prayers on that one. Phil needs them all, and if it weren't for Greg, he wouldn't be here—tell her to put *that* in her little incense pot and burn it."

49

"Without telling her the rest? That fits. First she has to stay in the dark and scramble up money, then—"

"Shit! You try coming here and doing the right thing! You handle it, and I'll criticize *you* from the comforts of home. Grow up, Rena."

"I'm trying to. And I would appreciate it if you wouldn't ridicule me behind my back."

"What're you talking about?"

"Just keep me out of future conversations with your friend Greg, and don't hand me any more lines about how much you understand. All that secrecy and games-playing must have gone to your head, Alex, because you've really gotten two-faced. You're about as sincere as the United States government."

She waited for another outburst. There was none.

"This is serious business," her sister said mutedly, "not games. Everyone's under a lot of tension here. I don't know what Greg said to you, but you're my sister and I love you. Maybe I don't show it enough to suit you, but it's true. I know that; I'm sorry you don't."

She wasn't prepared, it rocked her more than an explosion would have.

"I'm running out of change. Tell Aunt Eunice I'm grateful, I'll be in touch, she's not to worry. And try telling yourself that if I come on as a hardhearted bitch, I have to right now. I could use a little understanding from you, Rena, it's time you got on a two-way street, too." More depressed than angry, Alex hung up without saying goodby.

She replaced the receiver. Not since Gene's funeral had she heard that sadness in her sister's voice. Unsettled, unhappy, she lay on her bed before going downstairs.

To seek out her aunt, relay what news she can. But Aunt Eunice is not in the house. With the children grown her absence from home has increased in the past few years. Using the church and the women's auxiliary, she has fashioned a small life outside. An afternoon here, an evening there—her

50

husband does not like it. However, he cannot complain, his wife's activities are respectable; they add to his good name. He thinks they stem from faith and the rewards of community service; only she is aware that an evening spent alone with him has no enriching ingredients.

He sits downstairs, after-dinner cigar and Greek newspaper in his hands. Having been well fed before she left, he must sustain himself till she returns. What then? Nothing. Just the sense of her there, completing the place; responding to whatever he might think of, more coffee perhaps, or a remark on his day. Chances are he will choose to ignore her. Still, it nags him that his life is not quite in order; something is missing. The house is not right. Some thing is missing; his wife.

Standing unseen, Irena peeks in. How long has it been since she looked at him? How gray he's become—even his mustache has started to turn. There is gray in the hairs on his arms. The head of hair is still thick and abundant, but gray mars the glory of boot-polish black. Unnoticed, she watches him read; follows the smoke as it leaves his mouth; listens to breathing, labored and old.

Her uncle, father-figuring since she was two. Overbearing; inflicting his rule. But not a bad man, really; he has always provided, always been there. Like a rock, he is solid, stable; obtuse. He cannot be budged once his position is taken. Yet, he can play on occasion, when his dignity allows. And he laughs, he enjoys a good joke. But men know this best. The men he works with who understand; the men he drinks with who have had the same life of hardship, hard work, setbacks, success. They like him, they ask his advice and have awarded him honors to show their respect. Constantine Lampros, a prince among men. But to his family, the despot. Irena cannot talk to him; seeing, she does not go in.

She climbs the stairs wondering how Alex could make the comparison. After the funeral, at the breakfast table, she had said she was tired of one-way streets; angry, fed-up with zero returns. And now the same charge, thrown at Irena. But it is Alex who blocks herself off and will not let Irena come near her. Alex who treats her the way he treats Alex, refusing to see or acknowledge. Her sister may hate being told, but the resemblance is unmistakable. And yet . . . if they really are so similar, her feelings for both should be . . . Awful—she shudders at the thought of loving him, or wanting his recognition.

The only thing she cares for in him is his predictable behavior. Unlike Alex, and the rest of the family, her uncle does not vary. She is no longer sure what the others will do—or who will show up to do it. A person needs security. Back in the confines of her room, she makes a resolution: when she finds her own private core, she too will be consistent. At least Uncle Constantine knows who he is; how comforting, to rely on that, regardless of what happens.

School, then home, the usual vague anxiety edging around her as she walked, too aware of space; the pressure "to be" in it. Turning the corner, she slowed. What was his car doing in front of the house in the middle of the afternoon? Almost always the street was empty when she came back from the library. Cars were taking up half the block, and the Lincoln in their driveway—it had to belong to Aunt Leona. She ran.

Took the porch stairs two at a time. Reached the landing just as "Uncle" Theodore came out, closed the door behind him, and stood before it. Family friend, business partner, he held out his arms.

She moved back, sure he had been posted there to meet her and tell her something horrible had happened inside the house.

"No hug for your old Theo?"

Wild-eyed, she shook her head no.

"Then come, we'll take a little walk." A heavy arm drew her to his side and down the steps. "A little walk to the garden, where it's nice and there will be just the two of us." She was guided along the stone path bordering the drive. "Why don't you visit me at the store anymore? You shouldn't hide such a pretty face from an old man who has so few pleasures left. I tell Constantine it isn't fair to keep you to himself when we share everything else, but your uncle is a hard man sometimes." The gate sagged on its hinges as he pushed it open. "We will sit on the bench in the arbor, all right?" Dried things rattled underfoot.

"Ahh," she had been pulled down next to him and could feel his bulk expanding. "Eunice has a way with flowers. Yes." Her hand was being held prisoner. "How many years have I known the family now, forty? As well as my own. Do you know what *kaladelfia* means? The good brother relationship. So, I have been elected, Irena, and you must listen to your old uncle who loves you." Squeezed even closer, she was kissed on the top of her head.

"It is your brother. Philip. An accident I am sure. When children play with matches—but I made promises to myself not to moralize today. So. His head was not right lately, that is no secret anymore. Good. He cannot be held responsible; the church will forgive him, the law can do nothing. The doctors said they did not think he would do damage to himself or others—maybe they needed his bed, maybe doctors are not so smart as they used to be—who knows? They released him from the hospital this morning. Your sister Alexandra took him home, to a house there, and left Philip upstairs to go to a meeting in the basement. Beware of people who meet in basements, Irena—you will forgive a little lapse now and then from an old man trying to share a bit of wisdom?" Her body was crushed now beyond breath. "Your sister says no one heard Philip leave; what they heard was the sound of the explosion. Outside. Believe your old uncle, Irena. When

53

things blow up, pain comes to the living; pain is for survivors. Your brother knew no pain. Do you understand?"

She was not hysterical; ice cannot cry. The words flowed around her at a distance.

"Alexandra will not tell us what they were keeping in the garage—it does not matter, the police will find out soon enough. There have been many phone calls back and forth; I am glad you missed them. Your sister is not thinking clearly. For Philip to have done such a thing on purpose would deprive him of God's blessing and make a burden too heavy for your aunt to bear. She must be allowed to find comfort. It is one thing to claim that only Philip knew what was in the garage; that way they save themselves, the real crazies, they emerge unharmed. All right, no one wants more children hurt, and expediency saves misguided necks. But it must stop there. Whatever your sister thinks, it is time she learned the value of kindness and a closed mouth."

In front of her, a man's handkerchief appeared. It made hesitant advances toward her face. She didn't think she needed it, but the white cloth blinded her, dabbing again and again around her eyes.

"You are a good girl, Irena. When the shock wears off, that is when you will have to be very strong. You will feel then, and it will be more than grief. People have a way of adding to misfortune, as if God on His own did not provide enough."

The handkerchief became a bulge in his suit pocket. "You know your uncle is a man of principle; many times have I been grateful for that in our business dealings over the years. But, old as I am, in this instance I could kick his ass, you will forgive me, up and down Delos Street. It would do no good—you cannot kick sense into a pig and that is what he is being, pigheaded. I can say this because there is no man on earth I love more than your uncle; no man, up to now, for whom I had more respect. I understand him maybe too well; it is not difficult for me to forgive him. Those are things you must try to do, Irena. Understand, and forgive him for not allowing Alexandra to bring Philip back for burial. Understand, a memorial service is also forbidden. There is to be nothing here, and no money sent there—the ban continues even unto death. He cannot retract it. Your uncle has trapped himself like a stupid, he has gone too far on this course to get himself out.

"So, I have taken it upon myself to send a check to your sister for Philip to receive a proper funeral. On company funds; Constantine will find out. His rage I am prepared to suffer because underneath, I know he will be relieved. He will even invent a pretext for paying me back my share. I know him; the man of principle must first of all delude himself."

Alex won't let him get away with it.

"Now, we will go in, all right?"

He hadn't heard so she repeated it, though the words had broken through the first time.

"We will go inside and you will be a help to your aunt." Wheezing from the effort, he got them up; she was guided past the gate, down the drive, to the front of the house.

Within, the curtains are drawn, the rooms lit by lamps. Mourners stay away from shadowed corners.

In the hallway, old men come and go talking not of sacrifice and war, but of damn fool kids who think they know it all. Where is pride? Where love of country? Sigh for fallen traditions. Remember the good old days. Blame the times one lives in. Pontificate and drink.

In the kitchen, well-trussed women willingly make food. Others take to solacing by standing over Aunt Eunice. Gripping her shoulders, touching her dress; puncturing their condolences with piercing cries of grief. As Irena appears, her name is wept; her sleeve is grasped; she is burdened with overwet kisses. But a path is cleared and suddenly Aunt Eunice sees her.

"Aaiireena!"

It is all in one, as if chorusing some black-shrouded ancestor who had, far back, kneeled on the sun-seared soil of Greece and opened her throat in rage and lamentation, victim of the gods.

"Ah, Irena! The first son was not enough?"

Arms spreading wide beckon her to fall on breasts that never knew milk. Stumbling, Irena is clutched to this barren chest. Pressed hard against funereal silk, her face starts to crumble. Ice disappears. The hot gush of tears, the pain gashing through—too much to bear! Hysterically she claws at the dress, and begs for relief.

"What can I do, Irena?" Aunt Eunice meticulously tucked a clean sheet under the mattress. "Not speak to him? He would regard that as a blessing. Refuse to cook his meals or launder his clothes? No." Despising her husband more than she ever had before, she would not relinquish her role—it was probably welded to her so strongly, she couldn't stand on her own without it. Irena knew it wasn't strength that had stiffened her aunt in the last week. Since hearing about Phil, she had been going through the house like an automaton; mechanically functioning, lifeless inside. "Pray for the soul of my son, that is what I can do." She centered the throw pillows in front of the bolster.

"But how do we know Alex even got the check, Aunt Eunice?" She followed her into the next bedroom. "What if she did but she's too upset to handle things? Or the authorities are giving her a rough time? We haven't heard from her, she doesn't answer the number up there—I think something is wrong or she would have called!"

Methodically her aunt stripped the bed. "Theo has sent money and Philip has been buried, period." She slapped a pillow into its case. "Did you change your bathroom towels?"

"No, I left them all wet and scrunched up in a corner to get moldy."

She came over to her side and pulled at the spread, correcting what Irena had just done. "When we're through here, please bring down the hamper."

"Don't you care anymore?"

"About towels I know you did no such thing to?" Her aunt briefly surveyed the room. On her way out, she straightened the lamp shade on her husband's dresser.

Hopeless; she might as well have been covering her ears again and saying I won't listen, I don't want to hear. Irena shoved the hamper out of the bathroom. They had to do *something*; something. A few weeks ago they had been allies. Where was the superwoman who had managed to get money? Gone, beaten. And what about herself? what was she doing? Docilely lugging a heavy clothes basket downstairs; drudging through domestic routines, just like her aunt. Waiting for what, Alex to come home and organize them into revolt? She had no business looking to Aunt Eunice when she couldn't take the lead herself.

She deposited the hamper in the laundry room off the kitchen. Going back upstairs, she heard the washing machine start up. It sounded strange, as if there were loose parts in the mechanism. The clanking got louder. She walked down a few steps; her uncle came out of the living room; her aunt appeared in the kitchen doorway.

"It's outside," she said.

Getting nearer, coming very close. On their way to the windows, they looked at one another frowning and shrugging, wondering what could possibly make that kind of racket.

They would never have guessed. The large black van slowing in front of their home is a bizarre creation. Cypress boughs garland its sides, from which hang bells and chimes and strips of twirling metal. The clattering, ringing noise they make is augmented by a gong strung from the passenger window, an arm swathed in saffron-colored cloth swinging back and forth, the hand incessantly beating.

To the amazement of those inside, the thing reverses into

their drive. At the wheel is a familiar figure. Alex climbs out, looks toward the house, and makes her fist a greeting. Power to the mastermind! It is she who transformed this second-hand van into an exotic funeral hearse. For coffined within, on a velvet-draped bier, lies the body of their brother. In triumph Alex has stalked to the rear, thrown open the doors, and revealed him.

"Constantine, the neighbors!" They were coming from all directions.

"Go home!" he bellowed, wildly waving from behind the windows. "Go home!" He hurried to the front door, flung it wide, and charged down the steps. "Go home!" Some retreated.

Grabbing Alex by the arm, he slammed the van doors shut and pulled her toward the house. Greg Roussas came running after, tripped on his saffron robe, righted himself, and got to the door just as it closed on him. He started pounding, making it shake in its frame.

"Go home!" Uncle Constantine roared, pushing Alex into the living room as Aunt Eunice seized Irena's hand. Alex grinned at them weakly and rubbed her sore arm. Greg still pounded on the door. Their uncle yanked it open. "Get off my property and take that thing with you!" "Alex! are you okay?" He was trying to get past but Uncle Constantine shoved him back once, "Out! Or I call the police!" twice, and he fell off the porch. Getting up, scrabbling at the dirt on his robe, he pointed a shaking finger. "Don't you hurt her, goddamn it! You better not lay a hand on Alex or I'll call the cops for you!" Uncle Constantine kicked the door shut; Greg limped to the van. He climbed in but didn't start the engine.

As calmly as she could, Alex was lighting a cigaret. Their uncle strode forward, ripped the cigaret from her mouth, the match and pack from her hand, and threw them on the carpet.

"How . . . dare . . . you!" His voice whispered rage; his

hand was up and ready to strike.

"Constantine, no." A feeble plea from Aunt Eunice in her chair.

The hand trembled; slowly it backed down. Smirking, Alex sauntered to the sofa and sat, legs splayed, arms stretched along the top. He stayed where he was, staring at the spot where she had been.

"I've brought your son home to be buried."

"I have no son!"

"You owe my brother a funeral."

"I owe him nothing!"

"You owe him honor."

He whirled. "Honor!" A spitting noise. "There! That is the honor I give him."

"You owe him," she said levelly. "He is as dead as the brother whose tombstone cost you thousands. You owe his body the decency you never showed the man."

"Man? Your brother was not a man, he was a coward! A weakling! A frightened woman! That was your brother. Let Canada bury him! Take him back to that country of panty-waist draft dodgers and let *them* put him in the ground. His body would pollute American soil."

"Phil died for what he believed in just as much as Gene did. He deserves a proper funeral, here, so the family can mourn him and the community can pay their respects. He's entitled, and so are we."

"*I* decide who is entitled in this house," thumb jerking toward his chest. "And it is I, Constantine, the community respects. Who are you? You're nothing! A schoolgirl with dirt under your fingernails and too much hair always in your face. You don't tell me what to do; you don't decide for me who is owed what." Straddle-legged, he towered over her. "You take your little games, your *high ideals*, put them in that playpen of yours out on the drive," his arm hit the air, "and go back where you came from!"

Not even Alex's eyes moved. "I'm not leaving until you give my brother his due. If I have to, I'll park that 'playpen' outside your store on Delos Street every day, and outside this house every night. Whatever I have to do, I'll do. And you can be sure the neighbors won't miss a bit of it. We'll see how long your name is respected then."

"What do I care about your threats? You think there aren't laws against parking dead bodies on the streets? You think I won't get the police to haul you away? You are stupid. My niece, the college graduate, comes up with plans that are so stupid a man who never saw the fifth grade can put a stop to them, easy!"

"So the police haul me away; so the law's on your side; so what? I'll go to court with a clear conscience—I'll pay a fine, but what're you going to do, buy off God?"

"Oh, now she's bringing in God!" He turned to see if they had heard this. "God is on her side!" Facing Alex. "Since when? You think He acts to suit you? You know what that is called? *Hubris!* This from a girl who gave Him up when she was sixteen. A girl who drove her aunt to tears proclaiming there was no God. I have served on the church board for over thirty years! We'll see whose side God is on."

Alex allowed herself a small, sardonic grin. "Talk about *hubris.* All you've got is a priest in your pocket."

"What do you know? There is nothing in the world you think you don't know! I pity the man who marries you! the poor husband who has you on his hands!" He raised his arms, imploring the ceiling. "Lord, where is he? I pray You, send the miserable soul who will take this treasure from my house. I give it to him willingly."

Alex jerked forward. "I'm not a fucking sack of potatoes you can give or keep as you want!" His instincts had finally found the way.

"Shut your filthy mouth. You don't use that language here."

"Words are free! They're not your exclusive possession and

60

neither am I! You don't . . . own me!" She was shaking, all composure shot.

Watching her struggle, he smiled maliciously. "A man owns what he pays for. And from your colic to your college, I have paid. I would have done better purchasing a cow. A cow knows her place; a cow does not talk back; a cow . . ." he leaned over the sofa, "is *worth* something after you have spent years feeding her stupid face!" Straightening, he hitched up his pants, swaggering victory.

Too soon. The red was fading from Alex's cheeks; she eased back against the cushions. "Then you owned Phil, too. He's yours. You're responsible for his body out there."

"Let it rot! Cart it to the city dump for all I care!"

"Constantine!" Aunt Eunice's eyes were horrified.

"Stay out of this!" He had whipped around to glower at her. "If you lift one finger, if you dare to borrow money from that sister of yours again—you think I don't know?—I'll put you out of this house without a nickel!" Returning to Alex, "As for you, not another cent! You get out of here and you don't come back! Never!"

If it was fear working on Alex's face, she stayed steady despite it. "You can kick me out but you can't get rid of me. People are going to hear about this. I promise you; I'll see to it. Your shame will be so great you won't be able to step foot outside this precious house of yours."

"Ooh, I am very frightened. Very worried." He shuddered mincingly. "This little girl simply terrifies me." Laughing, showing how preposterous the idea was, he lurched into the hallway; there he casually turned around. "I'll be home for dinner," he said to them. "See that she gets her nappies packed and is gone." He put on his jacket; opened the front door. "And make sure she takes her fairy friend in the yellow robe with her!" The door closed on another exaggerated laugh.

Irena extricated herself from her aunt's clutches, she couldn't wait to embrace her sister.

61

"Thanks for all your help, Rena."

The tone stopped her midway. "I didn't think . . . you were doing so—Alex, you were terrific!"

"Well, look at my appreciative audience." She gestured expansively. "Aren't I lucky. Look at all the support they gave me while the bastard pounded me into the ground and laughed in my face. Oh, but Alex is strong, Alex can take it! Sur-er." Her voice and face gave in at the same time; she would never have let him see these tears.

Aunt Eunice's pathetic chorus rose behind her as she got to the sofa and sat down. Alex hunched her body out of reach, "Go comfort Phil."

Lunging into the living room, Greg glanced around and rushed to kneel at Alex's feet. His large hands gripped her shoulders. "Baby, are you—"

"Don't call me that!"

His features contracted. "What'd he do to her?"

"Words." Irena wrapped her arms around herself. "Just . . ."

Alex was sobbing; Greg touched her hair. "Alex? Don't let him do it to you. Don't let him break you."

"Let her cry, Greg. She needs to."

He glared up at her. "You cry! You and your aunt both— Alex isn't like that!" He tried to lift her chin. "Hey. Amazon. You went into this knowing you could get hurt. You've still got big moves to make."

Nodding, Alex took Greg's hand in both of hers.

Irena sees their hands, fingers twining; envies their reinforced strength.

Alex's nods grew more vigorous; she was bringing the tears down to sniffles. When a tremulous smile appeared, Greg grinned and sat back on his haunches.

"Would . . . anyone like some coffee?" On the other side of the room, Aunt Eunice had risen.

The two of them looked at each other, then at Irena and burst out laughing; invited, she joined their relief.

"Yeah," Alex said, "that'd be great." Their fingers were sliding around, playful now. "And some sandwiches!" she called after her. She rumpled Greg's hair. "We haven't eaten since morning."

They leaned forward, kissing deeply. Severed—to them she was just an onlooker. They didn't know she'd been thinking, and had to share it. Offering her place on the sofa to Greg, she pulled an armchair closer. "Alex?" She sat with her knees almost touching her sister's. "Couldn't we take up a collection? Hit places like the church and the coffeehouse and all the businesses on Delos Street? It'd really embarrass him, and we could get enough money to take care of Phil." Hands locked together on the couch, they stared at her impassively. "I mean, he couldn't stop us, and it would accomplish both things, wouldn't it?" She didn't understand why they weren't reacting; making her feel foolish, a little desperate. "What's wrong with the idea? I don't see why it wouldn't work if the three of us went out and got people . . ."

"There are only two people in this who matter, Rena, and one of them is dead. If it were just a question of burying him, we could have done it with Uncle Theo's money. Don't you realize it has to be *his* money or the whole thing's pointless? He has to *claim* Phil. I told you before, the prick needs a conscience. I didn't go through all that crap over Phil's body just to come down here and do a number. I didn't decorate that van just for show. Despite what you seem to think, I didn't get it and my brother all the way here just for the sake of embarrassment." Her look was so contemptuous, Irena wanted to disappear. "I meant everything I said. This is the last stand, Rena. He is morally in the wrong, and he is not going to get away with it."

Aunt Eunice entered carrying a tray laden with sandwiches and hot coffee. Eyes stinging, Irena helped her set it down.

Alex turned to Greg. "Guess I'd better eat." Her voice was soft now. "We both sort of knew we'd have to go with the second plan."

63

Whatever that was, it made Greg solemn. Pulling back the sleeve of his saffron robe, he tore off a bit of bread, and gravely brought it to her mouth. Her sister took it on her tongue as if it were the sacrament.

III

IF ANNIHILATION darkens her dreams, Alex does not say so. She says her intention is to sway. Irena, in her new role as confidante, is too pleased to question further. Why should she—she appreciates history. She is also aware her sister will do this anyway. At least the weapon is fitting and common to heart-felt causes. Although in ancient times it was often used for taking one's own life, still, centuries have shown the same device turned truly against the world. And only decades ago, when women battling for rights were being forcibly fed, it publicized their fight. She readily admits the heritage is rich, the strategy classic—to protest, to change, the hunger strike is perfect. It may be a double-edged sword, but with Greg alongside for moral support, any risk in the handling will be borne by two until the tyrant retracts his decision.

* * *

"Not eating? But she'll starve if she doesn't eat! Irena, her body is God's creation, she has an obligation to Him to keep it healthy. She mustn't—it's heresy!"

"You've really put your finger on the essential issue, Aunt Eunice."

"Is that Gregory Roussas behind this?"

"No, it's Alex's idea and I think it's fantastic."

"Oh, yes, fantastic—who would believe it? Alexandra loves to eat. She won't be able to stay away from food for more than twenty-four hours. Does she think she can change the world in a day?"

"She's already into the second. And everybody on Delos Street knows it, Greg's seen to that."

"Yes, he has seen that the phone does not stop ringing. Rumor, gossip—haven't people anything better to do?"

"What they're doing is just what Alex wants. The pressure's on and she's not going to let up until he gives in."

"No matter who else suffers. What have they done with my Philip? Where is he?"

"I'm not sure, but he's ready—I mean, everything was taken care of in Canada—as soon as Uncle Constantine says yes, we can have the service."

"So, when hell freezes over, my son can go into the ground. Aii, such madness."

"It isn't mad, Aunt Eunice, it's brilliant! You wait and see, it's going to work."

"And if it doesn't? What will I see then? Two coffins? The church will not look at her—it's suicide! What is the matter with your sister that she turns her back on life?"

"That's not what she's doing! She is fighting for a principle."

"Principle. What *principle* is more important than life? Can you tell me?"

"Aunt Eunice, people fight for principle all the time. Fine people."

66

"And when they die for it, then they have won, I suppose. To a fool that must make sense."

"Alex isn't going to die and she isn't a fool! *He* is! She won't live on her knees, that's all. She's standing up to him, and I'm not the only one who respects her for it."

"I can just imagine the kind of respect Gregory Roussas has for her. Living in sin with that boy—I knew no good would come from it. Wrong breeds wrong."

"I suppose your husband's in the right. I ought to have known you'd take his side no matter what."

"Did I say any such thing? Your uncle has no respect for death, your sister has none for life—those are not sides to choose between."

"Then stay on your fence, Aunt Eunice. Go on letting other people fight your battles." She got up. "There's no question in my mind about who to support. If there's anything I can do to help Alex win this, I will."

"Win, lose . . ." Aunt Eunice's hands fluttered about her head. "I don't care which of them does what. Alexandra must eat. There must be no more bodies. That is all I care about— no more bodies! Where is she?"

"I don't know."

"Please don't lie to me, Irena."

"I'm not." Her aunt could sit in that armchair forever, for all she cared. Without telling her where she was going, or when to expect her back, Irena left the house.

Three times a day Greg appeared on Delos Street to give out bulletins. She easily tracked him to Markopolous's drugstore; hands cupped by the sides of his face, he was peering through the plate-glass window and mouthing something to the manager inside. Turning away, not noticing her, he withdrew a candy bar from his jacket.

"Greg!"

"Well, look who's here."

"He'll think that's for Alex."

"Not when he sees me eating it." He ripped off the paper; half the bar disappeared into his mouth.

"Do you think you should be doing that in public?"

"Where do you suggest I eat, in front of Alex? That'd be pretty sadistic, wouldn't it."

"But everyone knows now—if they see you eating, maybe they'll think she is, too."

"You've got a suspicion problem, Irena. I grew up in this neighborhood; these people take my word." He loped away, shooting the crumpled wrapper into a bin.

She was ignored, coming alongside. "I'm sorry." They would never be on the right footing with each other. "How is she?"

"Good. Hungry as hell but full of willpower." He pulled out a small drugstore bag and shook it. "Got her these, just in case."

"What are they?"

"Diet pills. Curb her appetite and give her some zing. Today she's got plenty of both; can't tell about later."

"I really want to see her. Will you take me?"

"Sure, she's been waiting for you to show up. Where've you been?"

"Dealing with our aunt, the calls . . ." It sounded inadequate even to her. "The phone's been ringing its head off," she ended lamely, feeling that failed to justify her absence, or acknowledge how well he was spreading the news.

As they crossed the street people appeared in doorways and looked toward Greg expectantly. All he needed to do was call out the number of hours Alex had gone without food. "Thirty-eight!" he said, approaching the shoe-shine parlor; Mr. Vlastos nodded grimly, raised his arm halfway in greeting as they passed, then went back inside. "Thirty-eight, Mrs. Pappas!" The wife of the delicatessen owner rocked her head against her hand. "Tell them thirty-eight, Stefan!" The moon-faced boy unhooked his legs from a wrought-iron grille and scurried into the dark hall of an apartment building.

"How many?" a woman called down to them from her fourth-floor window on the next block. "Thirty-eight!" She lifted her hand and shouted, "Anna! Did you hear? Thirty-eight!" Across the alley a woman's head and shoulders appeared. "Tell her a little fruit juice wouldn't be illegal!" Both neighbors waved; Greg smiled up at them, waving back.

"You sure have been busy."

"Rule number one. Word of mouth is worth a hundred flyers. In this neighborhood it's a cinch, the good old Greek gossip mill'll be the last thing to go around here. Everybody's talking. Alex is gonna be some kind of hero by the time this is over."

"When will that be, do you think?"

"Can't say yet. But there won't be any tears on Delos Street when that bastard has to give in. He's been playing cock of the walk too long, even his good buddy Theo's got a glint in his eye." He tugged her sleeve. "Up here."

They entered a narrow side street. "How did you find this place?"

"Friend of a friend. It's only a room with a hot plate." He gave her a quick scout's honor sign. "Just used for coffee and tea."

After climbing two more uphill blocks, Greg stopped in front of a red brick building with a peeling door. The tarnished brass knob had to be jiggled several times before he could let them into a dismal hallway, its decayed elegance a sad testimony to the past. Traces of gilt still lingered on the ornately carved bannister, so wobbly now she feared it would give way at the slightest pressure as she followed Greg up three flights of stairs. "We took it . . . because it was cheap," he puffed, "and there's a . . . handy storage area in the basement."

She preferred not thinking about what they had put down there. "Where's the van?"

"Sold it. Alex had the money angle all figured out." Approaching a door on the top landing, Greg pointed to one at

69

the end. "The john's over there when you need it." She hoped she wouldn't.

He walked ahead of her into the room. A mattress, two cardboard cartons, two floor cushions; Alex, eyes closed, was sitting in a yoga position on one of them. As Greg bent to kiss her, Irena looked off and around their small space. The scant daylight managing to come in fell on ancient flowered wallpaper, so pitted and discolored it was a relief to see part of it covered by a large calendar and an immense square clock. She examined this as they murmured, embraced, behind her. Someone with a penchant for dayglow paint had carefully blocked in rainbow roman numerals on a huge piece of plywood; the hands, enameled black and about eight inches long, had to be moved manually, she realized, for there was no cord attached or room for batteries. They probably changed it every hour.

"Hi, Rena." Alex was peering around Greg's body and waving to her.

"Hi."

"Grab a cushion." On his knees, Greg swung the little bag from the drugstore in front of her; Alex grabbed it and peeked inside. "Hey, thanks! But you better get your friend to give us a prescription for sleeping pills, too, or you'll have to scrape me off the ceiling. Want some tea, Rena?"

"If you're having some."

"Are you kidding? Liquids really fill you up. Greg'll make us some, won't you, honey?"

"For a fee." He kissed her again, then went to rummage in the carton that wasn't being used for a table. From the sound of it, there were innumerable bottles—vitamins, she supposed —inside.

"So." Alex tucked her legs under. "How've you been?"

"I've been fine—how have *you* been?"

"Okay." She nodded. "Doing okay." Glassy eyes, drawn face; Irena would have to take her word for it.

"I'm sorry I couldn't get here sooner. Aunt Eunice . . . you know." She ought to abandon that limp excuse.

"She been praying a lot? The icon in her bedroom must be so worn out," checking her wristwatch, "she's gonna go up there one day and see old Mary's backside instead of her face." Abruptly her other arm shot skyward. "Ho!" Down it plunged, then up and down marking four, three, two . . . "Thirty-nine! The lady's hit a big three-nine! Clock change, clock change!"

"And it's another mighty hour!" With a flourish Greg moved the hand ahead. "Give that lady a mouth-waterin', stomach-fillin' cup-o'-tea!" He bounded back to the hot plate, lifted the steaming kettle, and let the water pour from a height into each of their cups.

"Hey, you know what I want?"

Seeing Alex's eyes light up, she wondered what delicacy she would be yearning for if she were the one fasting.

"A jigsaw puzzle! Yeah! Babe, next time you go out, will you pick me up one? The thousand-piece kind, with a picture of . . . lemme see, the Maine seacoast! That's what I want, the Maine seacoast, a thousand pieces of wave breaking onto shore, some rocks, an island of pine trees, and a pizza." She fell off the pillow giggling; Greg guffawed and Irena laughed as if she, too, were lightheaded.

Their high spirits are transforming. Sitting on the hard-wood floor with them, Irena sees a sun-dappled glen. A jolly band of comrades-in-arms, clinking cups filled with strong, steeped tea. Down with the King—hooray for their Leader! Three cheers. More laughter, more talk, more piping hot mead. Let the sun fade away, over the trees, she basks in their warmth, the unity.

"Man, the only problem with this stuff is it goes right through you." Alex got to her feet; she started swaying. Both Irena and Greg scrambled up to help her. "No . . ." she was slow-motioning them back. "I can make it on my own."

"The hell you say." Rough but protective, Greg took her arm.

When they returned, Alex seemed even weaker and her face was alarmingly pale. Greg eased her onto a cushion.

"Is she all right?"

"Sure she is," Alex answered. "She is fine."

"Do people normally feel this way after fasting forty hours?"

"Greg, she wants to know what's normal."

"I heard."

"We don't know, Rena. Why don't you go out and check the encyclopedias? Under Hunger Strikes—Hourly Reports and Blow-by-Blow Descriptions of Normal People Who Have Decided Not To Eat for Perfectly Normal Reasons of Justice and Equality."

"Come on, Alex, don't make fun. I really want to help. I think what you're doing is brave and beautiful and—"

"Glorious and noble. Do not forget glorious and noble."

She was ridiculing her, the sarcasm was meant for the praiser not the doer.

"Uh, I got a few errands to do." Greg swept his jacket off a hook. "I'll see you later."

"Well, aren't you the sensitive one." Now she had turned on him, too. "Or is it hunger pangs?" He was ignoring her, leaving. "Yeah, that's it, I can hear your stomach rumbling from here! Be sure to eat enough for two, you mother!"

"Don't take it out on me, lady. Cop a Valium or something." The door closed on his hulking figure.

"Prick." A saucer went scooting over the floor. She hid her face in her hands. "Jesus, I don't know why I did that." When she lifted her head, her cheeks were mottled. "Guess he's right, must be nerves—Rena, see if you can find a Valium in that treasure chest over there, will you?"

She poked around in the carton searching for the right vial. Finding several, she brought one to Alex with a glass of water.

"Thanks." Her sister had to use both hands to hold the glass.

"Alex, is it safe to be taking all these pills?"

"They're legal, aren't they?"

"I guess so, but that doesn't answer my question."

"Reenah, stop being an old maid. Christ. Aunt Eunice has really done a job on you." She wiped her mouth on her wrist. "You get it yet?"

"Get what?"

"The job. You know, work? Independence?"

"Not yet. After everything that's happened, I . . . I just want to do whatever I can to help. But you keep pushing me away. Why?"

"What's there to do, Rena? You see anything for you to do? Before, you should have. The tank was rolling over Phil, you, me, all of us. But you just lay there, like Phil; only he had a pretty neat excuse. I'm the one who acted, this is my fight now, and I don't need you behind me jumping in at the last minute."

"Afraid I'll take away some of your glory?"

She made a noise of disgust. "Sure. That's what this is all about. Glory." The shake of her head showed how hopeless Irena's thinking was.

"Alex, give me a chance." She sat across from her on the floor. "I can't help it if you've always figured things out ahead of me. When haven't you acted before I did?"

Her sigh indicated this was futile talk but she would summon up patience for it anyway. "Look, this is between me and him. Just like it's always been. There's no need for you to come into it—there's no room, Rena."

"What about Greg? He's here; he's in it. You made room for him."

"You can't do what Greg does."

"Why not? I know Delos Street, I can make tea and go get . . . Oh." Lewd, superior, Alex's smirk cut her down to a fool. "Well, if that's . . ." She didn't know how to finish.

"What's the matter, a little incest too much for you?"

"No! I mean, that's stupid, that's Aunt Eunice's hangup—will you stop smirking! If you could just see yourself, sitting there like some . . . yogi, some sage with hidden knowledge the rest of us aren't qualified to hear."

"Nothing's hidden to those who look."

"Cut it out, Alex. Stop playing with me."

"I'm not." Her expression had altered. "Maybe that's your problem," she said seriously.

"What is that supposed to mean?"

"Make of it what you will."

"Damn it! Tell me what that was supposed to mean!"

"Nothing. Forget it." She scratched her nails back and forth along the floor, then drummed them rapidly.

"I'm tired of being told to forget things! You and Greg both think you're so damn superior. You're not, you just like keeping people in the dark—that way you have an edge, it's easy to get the upper hand when you're the only ones who see all the cards. It's cheating, Alex. You call it strategy, but I call it a cheap trick."

The wall was up when Alex gazed at her; she could see it blocking her eyes, making her face hard. "You better get your head together, Rena. One minute I'm brave and beautiful, the next I'm a games-playing cheat. Like the ad says, which sister has the schizophrenia?"

She pressed her temples; this was ridiculous, it was so far away from what she wanted. Why did everything have to get distorted? Her arms flopped to her lap. She stared at a floorboard until she was blind to it, hoping magic or Alex would turn things around, put them where they belonged. No luck; it was up to her to try, or wait for something that might never come. "Our wires always seem to get crossed, don't they." Alex made no reply. "We can't seem to be close and stay there without a whole bunch of static getting in the way, ruining it." Nothing in return; she forced herself to keep on.

74

"Do you realize . . . the last time we were really close, just the two of us, we had to smoke dope before it happened? That's not right." She felt the beginning sting of tears. "It's pathetic."

"All sisters fight, Rena."

"Do they?" Despite her brimming eyes, she looked up. "Alex . . . remember the phone call . . . when you said you loved me?" She searched for a trace of that emotion. Though the wall was down, Alex only nodded. "I love you, too. I do, Alex." A soft smile touched her sister's features, making them gentle, giving Irena hope. "Couldn't we learn to show it better? More often?"

The gentleness twisted, and Alex opened her arms. Gratefully Irena crawled over, to be taken in a sisterly embrace.

The phone rang at ninety-nine hours. "She wants you." Irena left her term paper in disarray.

Greg answered her knock. Behind him, Alex was rapidly pacing the room; she didn't stop when Irena came in, or even seem to see her. Hollowed, glinting eyes; fingernails bitten down to blood. As if her sister were in the best of health, Greg sprawled on the floor beneath the window and began picking out pieces of jigsaw-puzzle sky.

On the move, Alex lit a cigaret. "What's he doing, Rena?"

"Trying to put in a piece of sky."

"Wha—? Not Greg, him! Jesus, I've got eyes."

"Well it's hard to tell where you're looking, you're moving around so much. He was watching a football game when I left."

"You hear that?" she screamed at Greg from two feet away. He didn't bother to answer. "The bastard's watching a god-damn football game!" She kicked a carton out of her path. "He is really worried, isn't he? We are at the top of his list, aren't we?"

"Alex, it's like Greg's doing a puzzle—does that mean he's

not worried or involved or that you're not on his mind every second?"

"No, no! He's not budging, not giving one fucking inch!" Without stopping her frenetic pace, she popped a pill in her mouth, picked up a paper cup in passing, and drank; half the liquid dribbled onto her shirt.

Greg unfolded himself from the floor and strolled over to check the bottle she had taken the pill from. "Hey, you've had enough of these—you oughtta be on the other to bring you down a little."

She tossed the cup aside. "Forget it! I don't need that numb feeling, I need energy! I got to plan, I got to think!"

"Suit yourself." He ambled back to the window.

"Fucking right, I'll suit myself. With no help from you!"

"Alex, please try to calm down a bit." She looked toward Greg for assistance, but he was engrossed in his puzzle again, or pretending to be. "Do you want some tea? Should I make you some?"

"No I do not want some tea! I'm sick of it—listen," grasping her above the wrist, surprising her. "You've got to do something for me. You said you'd help, I remember, so you can't back out. Don't back out, Rena."

"Alex, I'm not, I just got here!"

She whipped around, crisscrossed the room, gnawed nails that weren't there. "Right, okay. Here's the thing. What we have to do is—" All motion in her stopped. The wall received a blank stare. Slowly her hands went to her head. "Shit!" She wheeled, pulling at her hair. "I lost it! I just had it! it was on the tip of my . . ." whirling toward the mattress, "goddamn tongue!" She lay on the bed in the position she had fallen.

"How long has she been like this, Greg?"

"Rena, I'm here, I can hear every word you're saying, so don't talk about me like I was some kind of idiot paralyzed patient."

"Paralyzed isn't the word—you're way too hyper. Maybe you should take something, like Greg said."

"No. Later, I'll take something later." She rolled off the mattress. "Willpower. That'll do it." Crossing her legs, straightening her torso, she breathed in deeply. Out, in, slower, deeper. The backs of her hands rested limply on her knees; her eyelids no longer fluttered but drooped.

Just watching, Irena started to relax, too. Alex's state was so dominant. The room itself seemed to be unwinding.

Her sister's eyes flashed open. "He thinks I'm a kid who's holding her breath. That's it. He thinks I'll have to open my mouth any second now. The pressure's all been on me—he hasn't started to feel it yet because he thinks it's just a dumb kid's bluff that'll be over soon. Okay. Now I understand."

Greg held a piece over the puzzle without attempting to put it in place. "So what do we do?"

"We . . . get Rena to tell him my lips are blue and my eyes are popping."

"What? Alex, I can't—they aren't! Anyway, I'm not talking to him."

"Reenah, will you use your imagination for once! You've got to give him vivid descriptions. Report everything. Make him see it—see me, starving. You have to, Rena; you're the link. You're going to force him to look."

"But what if he won't listen to me?"

"He'll listen. I know him. He needs to think well of himself, keep his good intentions intact. I mean it! In his schizy perspective he can justify it all. We have to play on that, trounce him with such a horror story, even *his* delusions won't be able to handle it."

"Alex, that's a long shot. Supposing he does listen, why should he believe me? He knows I'm on your side."

"He'll *want* to believe you, Rena. Sooner or later he has to find a way out. The worse I get, the easier that'll make it for him."

77

"Easy!" Greg pushed himself up from the floor, his anger jolting Irena but not Alex. "Wait a goddamn minute! Since when does he rate *easy?*"

Her sister's lips curved in a disdainful smile. "I got to let the little man back down, don't I? Take him by the hand and say, 'Here, little man, here's an opening. Why, there's even a sign that reads Exit Here All Ye Humanitarians.' Then once he's through—bam! A victory dance all over his little body."

"I don't like it."

The smile was instantly removed. "Not enough blood for you, Greg?" Alex's voice could freeze quicker than anyone else's. "Or not enough honor."

So he had confided in her. "You ball-breaking bitch." She could have told him Alex would use it. "Not these, lady," he was pointing at his crotch. "For five lousy days I been waiting on you. Get this, do that—who the fuck do you think I am, your water boy? There's a *real* war on, you know; I got better things to do with my time."

In two strides he was out the door. It slammed shut and bounced open. The room shook as he took the stairs.

Alex smiled again, unsteadily. "He'll be back."

"Why, Alex? What's in it for him?"

"Me, among other things. And I," she eased onto the mattress, "am my uncle's daughter."

"Meaning what? That must make sense to you, but . . ." She was impossible to follow today.

"Sex and aggression, Rena, the good old male imperatives. The magic word is war; he's got to fight one somewhere."

"But you said this was your fight."

"Yeah, well, I'm in the center." She lay back, looking very small, alone on the mattress. "You know how two men can fuck one woman, and they're really getting at each other? Same thing." She felt behind her for the bottle of sleeping pills, tapped out three, and swallowed them dry. "They don't see it, but I do. Let 'em screw each other through me, so long as I get what I want. Nothing's pure or simple." Weariness dragged the corners of her mouth. "Ever heard of a victor being the spoils?"

"No, and I don't think—your body's slowed down but your mind's jumping around too much. You need to rest."

She forced a weak laugh. "It's hard. Things are . . . shimmering." Her eyes were beginning to tear; she turned her face to the wall. "Oh God, Rena, I am . . . so tired. If only I could sleep."

The patch of forehead visible to her had an unhealthy-looking sheen. She knelt by the side of the mattress; tentatively stroked away the moisture. Eyes closed, Alex moved her brow underneath. "Mm, feels good. Stay with me?"

"Of course."

"Just till . . . I drop off."

"Ssh, give yourself a chance to."

She was quiet. The pills had to be working.

" 'Member nursery school? Best napper got a . . . gold star."

"I'll give you one if you'll go to sleep."

"Hot lunches. Smelled terrific, waking up."

"They tasted terrible."

"Did they? Creamed chipped beef. On soggy toast. Heaven."

"Sleep now. Please, Alex, sleep."

Her head rolled around and she stared up with wide-awake eyes. "Rena?"

"What."

"I'm scared."

She couldn't be. Not Alex. Irena had no memories of her ever being frightened. No image of her sister being afraid. The confession didn't fit. Yet she must have felt it, before she shut her eyes. Making Irena want to stay and keep watch, Alex looked so unguarded.

Like a child, legs slightly curved, loose fists up alongside her face. Small bubbles burst from her lips as she sinks fitfully into slumber. Such an innocent-seeming Alex; so young, curled upon the mattress. Perhaps real fear, instead of mere fright, comes with growing older, much as the puppy love of early years matures into full-blown passion. Knowing too much, and for the first time, having too much invested, she is vulnerable now precisely because she has lost childhood's true protection.

Alex had been right in saying Greg would come back. Whatever his reasons for being there, he played the role of faithful attendant gracelessly but well. Irena would have liked to feel at ease with him, yet she was always relieved when he took advantage of her daily visits to go out. Usually he left soon after she arrived; once she had managed to miss him. On the ninth day, hurrying up, she literally ran into him on the stairs.

"Just going to call you. Her Highness," he jerked his thumb toward the top floor, "is waiting."

"As I recall, Greg, Amazons were queens. You're responsible for some of that buildup."

"Is that right."

"I think so."

He had backed up a step when they collided, but now, half smiling, he came down next to her; there wasn't comfortable room for two bodies. "Speaking of buildup . . ." she was pressed against the wall, "consider, the common *man's*." Hard thrust at her groin. Lips clamped onto hers and a tongue muscled its way into her mouth. She tried to shove him away. Swerve her mouth clear. Free her hair from his hands. He took every effort as a challenge, a perverse invitation for more, all of her bruising, everywhere attacked. Gagging on his tongue, rammed harder and harder in the same sore spot between her legs, she blindly grabbed a patch of beard and yanked, ready to snatch it out of his face if he didn't stop. Muffled protest—body twisting just enough to give her knee room—jamming fast. She'd never done it before, was surprised it worked as he lost his footing clutching himself and she scrambled out of reach, up the stairs, escaping.

"You cunt!" hoarse screams bounced off the walls, "you frigid fuckless cunt!"

Running, tripping. The top-floor landing; the john. Only then, with the door bolted and the dismal light turned on, did she breathe. In gasps, her lungs frantic. Gripping the scummy sink for support, she saw that her arms were shaking, her whole body was. When she looked up, horrified eyes stared back, warped by smeared and wavy glass.

Crying does not make her clean—it will take years, streams.

She splashed rusty tap water over her face, trying to wash away at least the outer traces. There were no towels; using her skirt, she rubbed and rubbed, needing the harsh fabric. How was she supposed to act in front of Alex? Two hundred hours of fasting had taken their toll, and now neither one of them was at her strongest or most rational.

Muzzy-headed, she unlocked the bathroom door; walked across the hall; knocked, and let herself in to face her sister.

"About time you got here," hunched on the mattress, peering from an Army blanket wrapped around her like a hooded cloak. Burning globes in deep, discolored sockets glared steadily; they swiveled toward the clock. "Change that."

She obeyed, moving the long black hand forward to mark another hour. Without looking again at the gaunt old beggar woman, she went to the hot plate to put on tea.

"Seen Greg anywhere?"

". . . Yes."

"He doing what he's supposed to?"

"I . . . don't know, we met on the stairs." A mumble; she busied herself with teabags and cups.

"Stairs. What? Oh man, seemed like he left half an hour ago. You positive? These stairs?"

81

"Yes."

"Well, what the . . . hey, no, I remember, I checked my watch. You two sure must have found a lot to talk about. He should've been out there on the streets, you know."

Filling them too far, she brought over their cups. Her hand was trembling as Alex reached an arm out from the blanket to take one.

"Ouch!" Only a few drops had spilled. "What's the matter with you, Rena?"

"Sorry." She couldn't confront her; sat, looking at the mattress.

"Burned enough. Sitting here waiting for you, thinking he's doing his job, and the both of you are having a social hour. Can't rely on anyone anymore."

"Alex, please." She rested her forehead on her palm. "We weren't . . ." The tears were coming back.

"Yeah, sure. Miss Innocence. Didn't do a . . . well for God's sake, Rena, can't you take any criticism at all? Two words and you're—will you stop it! Jesus, I'm the one who hasn't eaten for nine goddamn days, I've got *some* excuse. Haven't I? *Haven't I?* God, okay. I'm sorry. I said I . . . ohh, I get it. Did he . . . ? Yeah, he did. That jerk."

"Alex, it was . . . awful!" She lifted her head to let her see how awful it had been, show her the ugliness.

"Rena, he was hot and bothered, that's all. I don't have the energy for it. I won't even blow him." She cackled. "Might be nothing left, you know?"

"He tried to rape me, Alex!"

"Rape! Haven't you ever had a horny guy on your hands before? You're making too big a deal out of it."

She couldn't believe what she was hearing.

"Don't look at me like that! You've been around—what's the worst thing that could've happened?"

"But I . . . didn't . . . want it to! Doesn't that matter? Doesn't that mean anything to anybody but me?"

Hostile silence. Alex was setting up her defenses; there'd be a heavy attack soon.

"Let's drop it." She was too tired, and they were both too unstable.

"*Fine.*" She threw off her blanket dramatically. "We've got important things to talk about, Rena." So that wasn't—she could put it aside as easily as the blanket. "Everything's come together. Everything! I've figured it out. I am *in touch.*" It was rabid, her self-obsession. "Visionaries—saints—fasted in the wilderness, you know why? So they could have the experiences I've had. I've *seen.* I *know.* And I've come back to tell. The meaning is here," tapping her head, "and here," fingertipping her mouth, "and you," the finger pointed at Irena, "are my witness. Take this down."

"What?" Her sister was sick—delirious from pills and lack of—

"Get a pencil and paper and take this down! You're the chronicler, you have to write down what I say or it'll get lost. Go on!"

A little frightened, not wanting to argue with her in this state, she got up from her cushion and scanned the room. "Alex, I don't see any . . ."

"Use Kleenex—a paper towel, do I have to think of everything?"

She started searching in earnest, poking through jackets and cartons. "Black and white, Rena, so the wind won't steal it. The sibyl had loose tree leaves, she wrote her prophecies on leaves." Alex might send her out for some if she didn't find paper soon. "That is poetic. I'm not interested in poetry, I am interested in power. I want you to write that down in capital letters, capital pee-oh-doubleyou-ee-ar. Get that, put it on top. Then write—"

"Wait a minute, Alex, I haven't found anything to write with yet."

"The present is a continuation of the past. Put it second. It's important, the present . . . did you get that?"

"No . . . wait . . ."

"When you look at it the right way, it's beautiful. The wisdom is right there but you have to take the time to look and most of us don't. Then next is a question. Who is the victim? That's third. You'd be surprised, but don't write that, just write who is the victim, question mark."

She gave up; it obviously didn't matter, Alex wasn't waiting or stopping for her. Sitting down again, she hoped her sister would be satisfied with total attention.

"Stimulus and response, that's what it is, Rena. Stimulus and response. You have to put conditioning next, conditioning, dash, trap. Conditioning is a trap but if you don't get that down you don't see it. Then it's pure logic. You write break the chain, because it has to follow. Everything leads to number five, *break the chain*." Her eyes fastened on Irena. "And stomp down hard. Hard!" They were glinting—her sister seemed lit from within, on fire and stunned by the spectacle of her own light. Not seeing an audience of one, but a reflected blur of upturned faces. Then something happened inside; her eyes dimmed. She shivered, and slumped against the wall. "Get me a pill."

Irena had to readjust, stay with her. "What kind?"

"I don't know, any kind." She was hugging herself.

"Alex, please stop messing up your system with those. Try doing without them—I'm sure he's on the verge. The plan *is* working, but you've got to give it time."

"Why me, God? Is that where he's up to? Or is he still dishing out the suffering."

"He's worried about you. Honestly. He can't believe you've gone this long without food. It's thrown him, I know he'll come into the house soon and tell us . . . but he won't apologize, Alex, don't hold out for that."

"Who needs his shitty apology?" She snuggled against the wall as if it were a pillow. "Victory, Rena. Even if it kills me and I have to crow from the grave."

"Don't talk that way. You don't know how frightening it is to hear you—see you. You don't have any idea what kind of

84

shape you're in."

"I can beat him. I can stop him." Her sudden grin was cockeyed, like a drunk's, coming and going for private reasons. "Old Agnes couldn't. Weepy old Aunt Eunice . . . No one. Like his father before him, and *his* father before *him*. Don't care. Just *one* man, once and for all." She rubbed her head along the wall. "Just one, then someone else another . . ." Turning slowly, she looked at her from under drooping lids. "And you'll get the benefit."

"Me? But you're doing this for Phil, for yourself!"

"You and all the dead weight like you. Not Aunt Eunice, though. Too late for her."

"Alex, you can't be putting yourself through all this for me! I don't want you to!"

"You wouldn't. But you'll get it. That's why the meek inherit. They just sit by, Rena, they sit it out, and live to take."

"No! I'm not that way, I've tried to prove it to you—let me prove it!" Back and forth against the wall, her sister was shaking her head. "Alex, I'm not dead weight. I'm not."

She stopped with a thump, arching, her chin high. The awkward angle made her eyes into slits as she stared down at Irena's face. Her lips moved. "Then promise me you'll carry it."

She didn't know what that meant, but, "I promise." She would do whatever it was.

"Don't let him forget, Rena. Ever. I'll haunt you for it if you do. Carry it. Be the witness, the conscience. Don't run away from it—*carry* it."

"I will!" She had vowed, given her word—why couldn't Alex believe her?

Her shoulders sank. "Do something else."

"Anything."

Her head lolled to the side. "Go home."

"But I want to stay here with you! Alex, you need someone —let me at least stay until Greg . . ." That, too, she would deal with.

"Do what I say."

"Please, don't send me away. Don't." She crawled onto the mattress to get closer, put her arms . . .

"Goddamn it!" Alex's hand flashed out and hit her between the breasts. "I told you what you have to do! Now push that carton of pills over here, get me a glass of water, and get out!"

In chaos, she stumbles across the room. Is compliance right or wrong? Reason is gone. Choice undone. Intuition a victim of tumult. Just follow orders. Then certainty is not in upheaval, dread not loose in the air.

"Better get over here quick." Tight, too high, his voice itself propelled her.

Racing downstairs, grabbing her coat, she ought to have known, the way Alex was . . .

"Irena?" Aunt Eunice, in hallway shadows. "The phone . . . what is it? What's happened?"

"I don't know—something." She had to go, get there.

"Wait!" Coat caught. "Let me go with you. Please, she may need me."

"No—I'll call you."

"But to stay here not knowing! Let me be of *some* use."

"Work on *him* if you want to help. Get him, make him see he has to change his mind." Before it's too late, she held back from saying, out the door. Before it's too late. The words pounded as she ran; streets, sidewalks, shortcuts, stairs.

She had to lean over, let the painful heaving subside. Too late; with everything still thudding and aching, she rapped on the door.

Greg opened. "It was just a cold—not even the flu!" Impossible to hide how frightened he was. "She didn't have to take the whole damn bottle!" She brushed past him. "I *told* her the stuff was twenty-five percent alcohol." He had piled

86

the blankets and all the clothes they had on top of her; only Alex's face and matted hair were visible. "Oh man, she's been shivering and sweating and sweating and shivering—I don't know, it must be some kind of shock or something. I thought she was sleeping after a while but . . ."

"You mean she's unconscious?"

"I don't know, I don't know, I think so."

What did people look for when they raised somebody's eyelids? Cautiously placing the tip of her thumb under an eyebrow, she pulled the skin up, and jerked her hand away from the eye staring creepily off to the side. "We've got to get her to a hospital!"

"No! She doesn't want that! The first thing they'll do is stick a food tube in her!"

"Then call a doctor!"

"No doctors! She said so!"

"Greg this is insane! She might be dying! What if she doesn't come out of this? What if she's dying?"

"No, no, she's strong, man! She's got willpower!"

"Don't be an ass—she hasn't eaten for fifteen days!" Spying the empty cold-remedy bottle by the mattress, she scooped it up and scanned the labels. "How could you let her take this on top of all those pills? For God's sake, Greg, she is not an Amazon!" She flung down the bottle. "I'm calling an ambulance."

"You're gonna ruin the whole thing! She made me swear I'd let her go full course, no matter what happened."

"Well she didn't make *me* swear to that. You let her die— I'm not going to."

He gripped her arm with much less strength than he was capable of, just enough to put himself in the clear and let Irena take the responsibility. "I'm warning you. If you pull her out, she'll never forgive you."

"Fine! she'll have to be around to do that. You and your perverted warrior mystique—why did you call me? To stand some sort of deathwatch with you? I won't be that kind of witness. If that's what she meant I can't be a part of it—I've got my own conscience to live with." She freed herself and crossed to the door. There was a pay phone on the corner.

A siren cries. Tires screech. Men hurry up the stairs. Men lift Alex onto a stretcher. Men carry her downstairs.

One of them lets Irena climb in the back of the ambulance. He inserts a needle into her sister's arm. It connects to a tube, which leads to a bottle hanging overhead. Fluid drops in the tube, trickles through, and enters Alex's body. Glucose, the man instructs: sugar.

The siren still cries, tires still screech, the man keeps feeding Alex. At last, her eyes flick open. They swerve and find Irena's. She forces a smile, attempting reassurance. But they sharpen. They glare. They slash to the soul, then cruelly close, leaving her impaled upon sheer hatred.

But she had to do it, she had been right to do it. Alex was on the critical list. Greg had wanted her to do it. Creep, he wouldn't admit it. She hadn't regained consciousness again. He wouldn't even come to the hospital. She was in intensive care. Coward. She had shouldered it alone. Why? She could have called the one person who would support her. No time then, but she had to tell her now, and lean on someone, hysterical or not.

Light-headed, nauseated by the hospital smell, she dialed. "Irena, where have you been? I've been waiting and waiting —he's done it! He said yes! Why didn't you call? I only had to poke him a little, he was ready to cave in—you're to bring Alexandra right home for dinner, I'm making her favorite— moussaka won't be too rich, will it? Would an omelet—I'll ask her, put her on. But you tell her, tell Alexandra her uncle has agreed to the funeral."

Whose? "When did he do that?" Before or after she had phoned for the ambulance? before or after she was responsible?

88

"Almost an hour ago! Why didn't you . . ."

The receiver fell out of her hand; she was reeling.

O Lord, Rotten King of Timing. Dear God, Inflictor of If Only. A day, an hour, a second down here . . . But the blink of Your eye takes human years—You have lost the earthly perspective. If ever You had it.

Upright on a leatherette couch near the gift shop, she waited for them, refusing to think about what she had done. Concentrating on the double entrance doors; their finger-marked glass, the creak of their swing, the people coming in and leaving. Counting one two three four, a flowered dress, a bandaged wrist. Other people had problems or they wouldn't be here, hurrying to family, friends; some even looking after themselves, with no one else to worry about, no one else who cared. Forty-three, forty-four. Did they sense their lives falling, weight and burden buckling their legs, crushing them beyond hope of rising? No. They all had a secret way of coping; they knew how, but they were hugging it close, not telling.

Her aunt pushed open the heavy door. The mechanical woman again, no life in her face or walk—and no master behind her.

Fury whipped her off the couch. "Where is he? Why didn't he come? How dare he stay away!"

"Irena, he can't. How can he face it? But he said the bills —whatever it takes—specialists, equipment, the best. He will pay for all of it."

"Pay how? Does he think his money is enough? Does he think money will get him off?"

"I don't know what he thinks, and I don't care. Let him deal with it alone, let him spend the rest of his life trying to deal with it, without any help from anyone. Alexandra, how is she? Have the doctors told you more?"

"She's critical—she might die, does he realize that?" She spun around and walked rapidly away, making her aunt catch up or get lost in the maze of linoleum corridors.

"The best—I must talk to someone, tell them spare no expense, do everything that is necessary."

"They're already doing everything! What does he think, some orderly's in charge and she's hooked up to a broken-down kidney machine? His money won't save anyone—it's useless."

"Sshh. We all know you did the best you could."

"I . . . ! Where were you? Where was he, goddamn it! Why didn't that bastard give in sooner?"

"Keep your voice down. Please. You mustn't think about it. It's out of our hands now."

"Oh, it's so easy for you not to think about anything when you don't want to! You just sit and cook and dust and pray, and leave everything else to God! You don't have to *think* anything or *do* anything—you've got a note from heaven excusing you."

"You sound just like your sister now."

"Good! I'm glad!"

"You're not yourself, I can't deal with you. I'm going to ask them to give you something that will calm you down."

"Why? so I'll sound like you instead? No thank you, I might rust to death." She slapped the swinging doors open, not caring if her aunt got through them before they sprang back.

The nurse at the duty station finished a sheet of figures before deigning to glance up. "Oh, Miss Lampros. Doctor was looking for you." She peered around her shoulder. "Is that the girl's mother?"

"That is the woman's aunt."

"I see. Well, the parents really should—"

"Check your records; there are no parents."

Too prim for words, she flipped through a box of index cards. "Ah, yes," holding one away from her by the top corner, as if it were germ-ridden. "Mr. Lampros. Is he here? In these cases Doctor prefers both—"

"Mr. Lampros preferred sparing himself, you'll have to—"

"Perhaps you ought to call him. Doctor feels—"

"Look, I don't care what Doctor feels, or how Doctor feels, or if Doctor feels at all! I want to know how my sister feels, so would you please page him or whatever you have to do to get him."

She pursed her lips. "Take a seat over there, please."

Aunt Eunice followed the instruction immediately, but Irena couldn't sit. She paced the waiting area, back and forth past beige vinyl chairs with unwelcoming metal arms. "Did you have to be so rude?" her aunt whispered. "She hasn't paged him. Look, the microphone's right there and she won't use it."

"She knows we're here." Normal voice, making sure the nurse heard.

"Then why isn't she paging him?" Still whispering, afraid she might offend but willing to goad Irena.

"How do I know why she hasn't paged him!" Loud. "Sadistic bitch." That was a mutter; even so, Aunt Eunice darted a fearful glance at the woman who was controlling their lives.

Every time the door swung open or footsteps padded along the corridor, they looked expectantly toward the sound, then had to try to breathe again, force their hearts back down. Ten minutes. Fifteen. Finally a man in surgical greens stopped by the nurse. They mumbled, she nodded toward them, he looked around, they agreed on something, and he came over.

Aunt Eunice got up, grasping Irena's sleeve. "Mrs. Lampros?" Wordless, she bobbed her head. "Sorry to have kept you." There was blood on his tunic; he saw her staring at it. "Emergency—a tracheotomy."

"Not . . . not on Alexandra?"

"No. Why don't you sit down? Please."

Fingers dug into Irena's arm but she remained standing.

He sighed. "That young lady of yours . . ."

"Her niece."

"Niece," acknowledging Irena, "did a very thorough job. Taken separately, neither the alcohol nor the pills would have been enough, even for someone in her malnourished condition. Had she ever tried anything like this before?"

"What? Tried . . . what?"

"Was she suicidal?"

"No! Never. Alexandra wouldn't."

"You're sure."

"Yes, she's sure! Alex was fasting and got a cold—everything she took had a prescription."

"An unfortunate combination," encompassing both of them, "but familiar. We'll list it as accidental, and you'll be spared an investigation."

"By whom? the insurance company?" She knew Alex had student coverage; her sister might not need one dime from their uncle to cover this.

"Well, the insurance people, certainly; I was thinking more of the police. I'm sorry that's all I can do to help. An hour earlier . . . I'm truly sorry. We couldn't save her. By the time she got to us, believe me, no one could have."

IV

Y O U   W E R E the last person who saw my eyes. I opened
them just for you. To show you. The hatred was for you,
Rena.

But I had to try to save you!

Why? Who asked you to?

Please don't blame me. Please—it was *his* fault. He held
out too long.

He had a right to; he was my enemy. But you robbed me
of victory. You did.

I didn't mean to! You were dying! that's all that mattered
to me.

I was winning. That's what mattered to me. I could have
stopped him.

If only he'd said yes before I called.

But he didn't, Rena. You've checked and double-checked;
we both know how it went.

Maybe . . . maybe the food didn't actually go in you until after he gave in.

But it did, Rena. You've checked and double-checked; we both know how it went.

No, Alex—in the ambulance, it was a guess, just a guess on the timing. And Aunt Eunice—she isn't positive about the exact second he said yes.

You can't escape it, Rena. Remember how I looked at you. I knew. You'll always see the hatred in my eyes. Always. If not for you my death would have served a purpose. You robbed me of that; you took away my meaning, undid everything I had done. You destroyed me, Rena.

No! I was trying to save you!

Who asked you to? I had a right to go full course.

Even if it meant *that*? Alex, you were unconscious, you didn't know what was happening.

Remember how I looked at you? I knew. The hatred was for you, Rena.

What about him? Why aren't you doing this to him?

It's up to you to hate him. He didn't see me then; he doesn't see me now. It's up to you to show him. Never let him forget; I told you that before.

I know—I'll be your witness, Alex. I promise. I'll hate him for both of us; I won't ever let him forget.

Do you think that will appease me?

I'll be doing exactly what you want me to!

What you *have* to do. That won't change the look in my eyes. You're always going to see it.

Alex, please, please forgive me.

The dead don't forgive unless the living do. Their last emotion is the one they feel forever. Remember what mine was? Hatred in my eyes. Hatred in my heart. For you, Rena. See my eyes? You will never find forgiveness there.

* * *

94

"When you were a child, Irena, I used to spoon you soup like this. When you were sick in bed, you used to like to have me sit with you and feed you soup. Remember? Take some, that's a good girl. And another, down we go, that's right. A little more, there's just a little left, open now. That's right. That's a good girl."

You aren't good. You're guilty, Rena. You took away my meaning. Undid everything I had done. See my eyes? Your guilt is there, reflected.

"Irena? Look, someone is here to see you."

"Hello, Irena. How are you feeling today?"

"You see, Reverend? She won't talk. She won't look at us. Do you think she even hears?"

"Of course she does, Eunice. A pretty girl like her with so much to live for. Why don't you leave us alone for a while?"

"Can you . . . she hasn't been to confession all year. Do you think maybe it would help?"

"We'll see, we'll see. Close the door behind you. Now then, Irena. You don't have to talk to me if you don't want to, but you will have to listen. That poor woman is very worried. Hasn't she had enough? You're young, Irena; it's time you put your problems aside. For her sake. You are the last child she has left; it isn't fair to do this. You're young; your life is ahead of you. Would it take so much to make her remaining years a little easier? Do you think she deserves such selfishness from you?

"I know what you are thinking. Why you? is that not right? Eugene, Philip, Alexandra—you feel the burden is too much to carry. But you have been elected, Irena. You must not deny the living and desecrate the dead. Your aunt needs you to help make her life more bearable. Your brothers and sister need you to pray for their departed souls. And, Irena, your uncle needs you to forgive him. God will judge him in due time. You must not take upon yourself God's work; you must try to understand, and find compassion in your heart.

"Now, why don't you talk to me about it, eh? Tell me everything that is troubling you; there is no need for you to carry such weight all by yourself. The church is here for you. Remember, through Jesus Christ you are redeemed."

Well, holy halitosis, just bring your blue-chip guilt and get reprieved. Tell the old fart where he can put his redemption center, Rena.

"No, Eunice, she did not speak. She laughed. Quite hysterically, in fact. Perhaps you should consider a lay counselor. If you wish, I can recommend a competent man. The church is magnanimous; if today's young people are blind to our eternal relevance, we love them nonetheless, and feel their pain. I assure you, I won't be offended if you call on Dr. Ammons."

Tell a shrink about me, Rena, and they'll really think you're crazy. Be on your guard. They lock you up and *he* gets off scot-free. You can't do what you have to in a straitjacket. Otherwise it wouldn't matter. They could throw away the key, I wouldn't care, I can visit you anywhere. You'd look around your padded cell and you know what you'd see. *These.* Staring at you from every wall. You know what you've done. You know, and no psychiatrist can help you.

"My name is Dr. Ammons, Irena. I'm a therapist, and your aunt has asked me to come and see you. She's told me certain facts; I think I know a little of what you're going through. But I'd rather hear it from you. She says you're an intelligent girl; that's good. I don't have to explain to you then that simply talking about a thing often makes it better."

Don't listen to that oily voice. Talking won't do anything. Talking can't change my eyes.

"All right, then, perhaps you'll correct me if I'm wrong— you can show some sign or other, you needn't speak unless you want to. I'll trust you to let me know when I'm on the right track, and if I am, maybe you'll start trusting me in return."

Ha! Why should you trust him? A stranger in it for the money, you could be anyone to him. I'm the one you trust—you can trust eternal hatred. You know it, Rena, you saw it fixed forever.

"You know, Irena, it's not unusual to feel the kind of torment I imagine you do. Because you survived a terrible tragedy and others didn't. Guilt, unworthiness—it's important to bring those feelings out into the open. To see that as a survivor, you're responsible for only one thing. Your future."

The past dictates your future, Rena. You are responsible for what you did. Your future is dictated. You are the witness, for as long as you both shall live.

"By bringing things out in the open, you don't clear your conscience so much as you learn to live with it. And then to live. Kept in the dark, things don't go away, Irena; they grow to monstrous proportions, until one day they bury you. Does that sound fitting? Isn't that what you want right now? To doom yourself so you can take your place with the others?"

You can never stand in my place! Never. I won't have it. You're a thief, you robbed me of my purpose. You're a killer, you cut me down before I went full course.

"Irena, you *can* live with your memories, if you accept them. If you remember, but with a difference. To accept the past you have to understand it, and allow its meaning to change. When you've done that, you've made it into something new; freed yourself from it. It's possible, and it's up to you. Lock yourself in, make your life nothing but a series of responses to what went before, or break loose so you can respond to other things, other people. It's work. But why victimize yourself for the rest of your days, when you can make something of your life instead?"

Just snap your fingers and live, baby, live! The philosopher king here is full of it. Don't let him seduce you, Rena. You don't deserve to be healed. You have no right to go on whole.

"Do you understand what I'm saying?"

Don't twitch an eyelid. Don't lift a finger or move a muscle. Not one sign. I demand it, Rena: no signs.

"Somehow, I think you do. In time, you'll want to talk about it. Right now, there are too many obstacles in your way. I want to help you get rid of them. And it seems to me, if you agree, we ought to tackle responsibility first."

No! That stays. Forever.

"We have to be very specific now. Do you think you could have saved your sister's life? That if only you had gotten her medical attention earlier, she would have lived?"

Is he ever on the wrong track. But you saw my condition, Rena. You could have done something about it sooner. I wouldn't have let you, but everybody else sees it that way. Everybody else blames you. They don't know what the real charge is. We do. *These* do. They're still here; they're not going anywhere. Neither are you, Rena.

"Now, it's natural to *feel* that, but I'm sure there's a part of you that realizes you had nothing to do with your sister's death. The controversy, as I understand it, was between her and your uncle; certainly, if anyone should have acted sooner, he should have. But not even your uncle can be held primarily responsible."

What! Who does he think he is! Watch it, Rena. It's a conspiracy—the men are closing ranks on you, protecting one another.

"Can you see how your sister worked to control her own death? She knew what she was doing; even if it was accidental, she did everything necessary to bring that accident about. You had no part in it; it wasn't your place to save her; you're inserting yourself where you don't belong. It was up to your sister to save herself—she probably could have, you know, if she had wanted to."

There! You've had it, Rena. He's trying to make you feel

better, but he's only made it worse—you don't have any defense at all now, he's just demolished it. You had no business butting in. He said so. He took it, Rena. Destroyed the thing you needed most. You know what it feels like now. Crying won't help; crying won't give either one of us relief. You see them. You know my eyes, my hatred, are inside your head and you're always going to see them.

"Tears could be a healthy sign, Mrs. Lampros. Very likely, something I said got through to her. If you would like me to see her again next week, I will. But I have to admit her unwillingness to talk severely limits any good that I can do for now. When she comes out of this temporary withdrawal, then I think a series of appointments would be beneficial."

"How long is temporary, Doctor?"

"That's up to her. From what you've told me, the trauma's been severe, but at her age I doubt she'll keep this up forever."

"Doctor, my husband . . . he refuses to go in there. Do you think that has anything to do with her behavior?"

"Do you mean is she employing some sort of emotional blackmail? It's hard to tell, of course, but it could be. You said she's been this way for how many weeks?"

"Three, Doctor. Three weeks . . . since the funerals."

"And he is in this house but he won't see her? It seems to me, Mrs. Lampros, that your husband is a man in need of counseling."

"Oh, he wouldn't! I'm sorry, Constantine would never agree to such a thing."

"Well, that's his privilege of course. But he ought to realize that sooner or later he's going to have to face her. And for her sake, as well as his, I recommend the sooner the better. I'll be glad to tell him that myself if you think it would help."

"Uhm, no, thank you, Doctor. I'll . . . I'll tell him."

She doesn't want a scene. How embarrassing if he kicked the doctor's ass right out the window. Got to save him from himself. Run interference for the fool. See how the victim keeps the ogre fed? He could beat her physically, she'd hand him the rubber hose. It's true—the same thing. Just meekly let the blows fall, then rush to salve his soul. You're going to be like that, Rena; unless you grab the hose.

"Stay out here, Eunice. I do not need an introduction like on your talk shows."

At last—the bastard's coming in! You know what you have to do, Rena. But hold your fire, I want to watch him squirm; I want to see him struggling to get out of it. Don't let him know you know he's here. Let him sit there by your prostrate body. A reminder that *I'm* lying in the ground.

"Irena. I know you can hear me. What I'm saying, don't expect me to repeat. So pay attention."

Right off, he's giving orders. Just wait, you'll show him things have changed.

"I am not here to beg."

Of course not—only women belong on their knees. He'll see. Let him do his big man act then fall—a long way down.

"I am not here for myself. What I suffer is my business. My agony is no concern of yours—I will not even ask you to believe it. You cannot believe when you have no idea what something is like."

Poor misunderstood baby! Nobuddee knows dee trouble dadum.

"But, this that you are doing does not make me suffer. Whatever it is, you are doing it to yourself, nobody else. I know Reverend Kourides preached to you about your aunt—what he said should not be taken lightly, but since Niobe and before, mothers have suffered. Your aunt comes from a long line, it is her heritage, she is Greek."

She could be a Jew or a foot-bound Chinese lady. He's romanticizing, Rena; dismissing her. You're supposed to think, though he won't condescend to talk of it, that his suffering stands alone; his suffering is unique.

"It is in her blood, she would not know what to do if God were suddenly to take away all suffering from her life. But she has her consolation; her charities, her church. She can find comfort. I, on the other hand, am not so lucky, I do not believe so deeply. But, I am not without my resources. I have my business, my brothers in the Society; friends. Some spurn me now, but a man cannot go through life acting on principle, misguided or not—and I do not say I was misguided—"

Good, because evil's a much better word, so is sick, warped, selfish brutal petty . . .

"—without offending people, or risking their misjudgment. A man, Irena, does what he thinks is best, and pays the price for it."

So does everyone! But a woman pays whether or not she's done anything at all, a woman pays just for being. Double-ex marks the spot—we're it, and we pay.

"I am paying, Irena, whatever you may think. And though I choose to deal with this alone, as best I can, in my own way, I am still a member of the community, and I have my resources. But what do you have? What are you doing? You lie here, brooding, making yourself sick. You should be back in school. Out meeting people. You are giving yourself no chance, no way of starting to forget."

Never! He'll see—you're going to rise up, Rena! You're going to show him. No mercy. No forgiveness. *No forgetting.* Ever!

"It is time this came to an end, Irena. It is not necessary. I do not accuse you of helping your sister in her foolish plan. No, I make no accusations but one. You are not sparing yourself. Why? There has been more than enough tragedy in this family; if there were a market for tragedy we would be millionaires. Do not add to it. I am not asking for myself or for your aunt, but for you. Get up; you owe yourself a life. What is over, is over."

No! It will *never* be over. Now, Rena! Pass it on—that's

what you're here for, that's why you've survived. See my eyes? Look at him, look at him and pass it on. Say it—you're my witness, Rena—say it!

She turned her head so he could see them. "I'll hate you forever for what you've done. You'll always see the hatred in my eyes. I will never let you forget this. Never. Every time you look at me you'll be reminded. Every time you see my eyes you'll know. I'm the witness. I'll always carry it. You'll always see what you've done. *Here*." Her voice was hoarse from disuse but she knew her eyes were speaking. His were shocked. She was showing him. And in her were vibrations of triumph—Alex was dancing, victorious.

V

It is tedious work, hating someone forever. Often she looks back upon that first time, and wishes she could recapture it. She fulfills her obligation, she embodies her sister's purpose—every night when he comes home, the witness is there, reminding; but instead of vibrating triumph, exhaustion and depression drag her through the days. Even when he is absent, Alex refuses to fade.

Too much is dead, too many have died; she must haunt the halls, and stare forth from living eyes. But the animosities must be safely kept inside. Irena must stay in, even though the air itself oppresses; not risk a public tirade, or people will say she is crazy. Day after day. She tells herself security offsets the suffocation. The walls are not really closing in. The house that has protected her since childhood, and been a faithful friend, has not become a tomb. It is the bulky old-world furniture, the blinds drawn against the sun, the doilies, icons, and incense that make it hard for her to breathe.

Things seem to lift a little bit when she no longer sees the web of Fate creeping over the family. She is confined, but not in that ancient structure—the Lampros house is made of brick and mortar, shaded by trees on a quiet street, with a roof and walls securely fixed. To assure herself, she walks around checking. A house cannot fall just because it is dismal and needs a coat of paint.

She wishes it were that easy, to brighten herself with a handyman's brush. Slipcover gloom. Do surface restoration. She could buy a new dress . . . but it would mean going out, to a store that catered to witnesses.

"I am not sick. I'm just tired."

"Then refresh yourself, Irena. If you can't go back to school yet, at least go for a walk. I promise you, you'll have more energy."

"Maybe I could drag out Alex's hiking boots, and rough it through the house. Would you like that, Aunt Eunice?"

"It doesn't matter what I would like. Obviously."

"You have such simple solutions. Eat, take a walk, keep busy. Pray."

"We all have to go on. You are not the only one affected. I don't like your setting yourself up, as if none of the rest of us felt pain, or had our own grief to live with."

"*Hubris?*"

"I don't use such glorified terms. I'm an everyday woman, Irena, no different than most. What you call simple, I call getting through, as best one can. I don't put myself above the rest of humanity."

"No, you play the humble sufferer very well."

"I don't *play* anything."

She's right, it's built in—it comes with the territory. Go on, tell her it isn't healthy.

"Now that I think about it, Aunt Eunice, I never have seen you play. It's strange. Do you?"

"Do I what?"

"Get giddy, frivolous. Romp a little."

"Me? Don't be ridiculous. Romp. That's what you should be doing, at your age."

Dressed in a pinafore, and braids?

"Sure. A little heartless romping—you'll have to forgive me if I'm not up to it."

"A young girl should be up to something, Irena. You're so serious—you'll get worry lines."

If she had it her way, you'd be silly forever. You're still not very useful. Hide behind me and you won't grow up, you'll just get absorbed in my shadow.

"I was . . . thinking of getting a job, before. What would you say to that idea?"

"A job? But your uncle . . ."

Can support his sister's daughter, thank you, what will people think? A woman's place is blah blah blah . . .

"I know what he'll say, I'm asking you."

"Your education should come first. There is a season for everything. That's why staying here all day like you do isn't right. When you have your own—"

"Kitchen to take care of, then it's right, huh?"

"Irena, there was enough of that tone of voice from your sister. Tell me, since you sounded so much like her, what would she say about the way you spend your time now?"

You can do both, Rena. Don't blame me for moping around, for sapping your strength with depression. Do it— get out. My witness should be a strong person. But you better be in the house when it counts. Never forget. Your first job is here—you can't get away from reminding him.

* * *

Terrible work, quelling the palpitations. Every day, for weeks on end, she has to increase her time outside by a fraction. Venturing into space that she knows. Then seeking her history of comforts. For a while she settles in at the library. Ensconced in a favorite corner—she could stay right there, forever building up her capacity. But, she is not destined to get off easily; after reading a bulletin board announcement she goes, unable to stop Alex from seeing it.

The small room was hot and smelled of nervous bodies. She filled out an application form, then waited for the test to begin, trying to look as composed as the others. Even if she wasn't, she was at least functioning; able to do what they were doing so far. And equally lucky, she supposed, that some grant had been late. The delay made two jobs available at the museum now. Plenty of people were after them, though. Alex didn't have to go on about the competition.

A trickle of sweat formed under her arm; it started crawling down her side. She wished a window were open. There was a peculiar buzz in the air, as if it resented being disturbed by strangers. Probably the heating system. She had to stop this about places, making the inanimate alive. But the motes of dust hovering so impatiently in the light did seem to be irritated by the crowd. They were used to museum artifacts and their silent attendants, not these foreign elements who scratched their pens hoping to belong. Watching the restless particles wait for things to return to normal, she wanted to reassure them, tell them they would have life the way they wanted it soon. Gratefully they would settle onto her shoulders, and rub up against her Snow White legs; she might be new to this atmosphere, but they could sense her empathy.

Asshole. Alex's comment made her blush; she nervously fingered her test booklet.

"All right, people." The secretary was young and employed; Alex slotted her into the category of early obnoxious. "Open the booklet to page one, read the instructions." They all

106

obeyed. "Turn the page, you've got twenty minutes."

It was easy: verbal comprehension, figure aptitude, ability to do detail, and a final section on spatial relations. She was double-checking the math when Alex said it was too easy. Everyone would do well, only the interview would count.

What if her sister's voice broke through then? "Sorting potsherds all day in a musty room" might be exactly what she had to make someone think she most wanted to do. Dull duties would even be a blessing; Alex might get bored enough to leave her alone for a while. If the work were interesting, she'd probably stay out of curiosity; but maybe Irena would be too involved to notice. Much. Just let her land one of the jobs without interference. Then she'd need Alex's help, to handle His Greekness, keep him down to a sputter about her working.

"Time's up, pass them forward, the cut list'll be posted at two."

"Computers," somebody mumbled.

"Nah, they just toss 'em down the stairs, the one on the bottom comes in first."

"No," a third one said, "this isn't school, man, this is a museum. They got trained mummies here."

She lost the rejoinder as they filed out. Among the bodies milling indecisively in the corridor, she took some comfort in the fact not everyone knew what to do with the intervening time. Most began drifting off when she did. But she was alone, heading toward the main gallery; perhaps they'd been in the museum more recently, or knew the collection so well they had no interest in browsing.

Footsteps clicking along polished wood surfaces, she entered the rotunda, and stopped. Natural light filtering from the dome was spilling over bronze—a burnished female body, awesomely high, on a rocklike pedestal. Exquisitely draped and winged as if poised for flight or just touching down. Headless, armless, but somehow complete. Radiating strength. Sensuality. The proud nakedness beneath her clinging gown

—modesty played no part. Her body, like her majesty, was a given, accustomed to tribute. She was the epitome—the great embodiment, conceived in classical Greece.

Glorious. Ceasing to think, Irena gives herself up to experiencing.

Minutes had passed without her; she was back, standing in the rotunda. If she had known this was here, she would have come time and again for the feeling. Not the prickles on her neck and shallow breath, which made her too aware of herself, but the spell. She had wanted it to last. To be totally immersed in her, or overcome by her—rooted in some way, she wasn't sure what the sensation had been. But she felt she had seen her before. Not here, like this. Somewhere smaller, more remote . . .

"She's even more beautiful in real life, isn't she?"

It startled her into turning; she hadn't heard anyone come in.

"Your name's Irena, isn't it?" She nodded, realizing his face was vaguely familiar. "John Kinsella. We were in Scofield's art-history survey last semester."

"Oh, yes, right. Hi."

"Hi." His smile stayed as his gaze reverted to the statue. "I can't see her now without hearing Scofield moaning in the background. Funny how he had his hands in his pockets the whole time she was on the screen."

That was where, but then the winged victory had been merely one of five hundred other slides she had to memorize. If it had been the Samothrace Nike, she might have bothered coming to the museum to see it.

"Too crass?"

"No." He must have been watching her out of the corner of his eye. "I was cursing my sophomoric snobbery just then. I'd forgotten where I'd met her—I'm embarrassed I needed reminding, but I'm glad you did."

"Good! Are you glad enough to have a cup of coffee with me? After reacquainting you two, I think it's only right." He grinned, encouraging her. "I'd let you buy."

She is waiting for palpitations, her standard panic signal. Strange. Alex is quiet, too.

"Okay . . . if you know some place close." Her sister must be testing, delaying; she remained on guard as they left the rotunda. "I have to come back later."

"Me too. How do you think you did?" He held open one of the glass-plated lobby doors.

"Were you there? I didn't notice you." Dumb, a slight. "I was awfully distracted."

He was laughing. "That's all right—my ego can take it."

Disconcerted, she kept her eyes on the wide granite stairs.

The coffee shop a block away was crowded. "Nice going, John," someone cracked as they passed a table. He pretended not to hear, taking her arm and guiding her to a vacated booth in the back. They sat across from each other; Alex, so strangely quiescent in front of the victory, nudged her now. Not bad.

Always slower to judge, Irena surreptitiously appraises. Long, narrow fingers rest upon the table; large knuckles, square-trimmed nails—an artist's hands? They look skillful. The blond hair there climbs up to cuffs turned neatly below the elbow. His plaid shirt fits, hinting at toned muscles, a cared-for, slender body. Bony nose and cheekbones; bush of sandy hair. She, too, likes what she sees, and relaxes, though she cannot meet his eyes.

". . . to get one of those jobs," he was saying. "The money's not much, but M. J. Leland is in charge of the project and really potent, tops in the field. Can you imagine discovering that winged victory at the age of thirty?"

"He did? God, *we* ought to be paying the museum for the chance to work with *him*."

"Her."

He had a very playful mouth. "You have a sly streak, don't you."

He shrugged. "The em's for Maggie, also known as EmJay.

Friend of mine was on a dig with her two years ago and fell in love for life. They say it's an occupational hazard."

"Well, it beats black lung." Alex; even though the rejoinder delighted him, she wanted to push her back. "The one in the museum—that can't be the original."

"Bronze cast. The original's in Athens. I'd settle for just seeing Greece before I'm thirty." He made a long-fingered tent over his cup. "I wonder if Leland'll be doing the interviews herself, or if she'll leave it to some assistant to screen the peons."

"Maybe it would be better talking to someone less high-powered. Assuming we make it that far."

"Hey," as soon as he looked up, she checked, "you scare easy." Gray-green. "The idea is to get to the great lady in person. There's another dig on next year, and it can't hurt to put a word in now."

"So it's not pure idolatry, huh?"

He grinned and rocked his hand.

She actually smiles. Two people do have to be hired. She knows the odds are against it, but Alex persists with visions of them, starting side by side.

Waiting through a week had been difficult enough. Did she have to be interviewed without one sign of approval? Now this assistant whose name she hadn't caught was taking her down to the lab, but for all she knew, everyone who scored high on the test would be given a tour.

He flicked on the lights. Half the room was devoted to a practical work area. Long counters, careful groupings of glues and brushes, leveled sand in low-sided boxes. Above, the shelving sagged under rows of pottery fragments in numbered plastic bags. Calipers, compasses, and instruments she couldn't identify, but which looked impressive, hung over a draftsman's table.

The other side held no trace of craft. The desks and counter tops were bare, the cupboards revealed nothing but supplies and record books. The indecipherable technical charts pinned on the far wall were intriguing, however. Multicolored, they surrounded a grainy photographic blowup of a woman in shorts and shirtsleeves, kneeling in the dirt; she was cradling a figurine, and smiling against the sun. Below, Greek-styled, WINCKELWOMAN LIVES! had been hand-lettered. Dr. Leland, she presumed; the assistant, choosing to protect an in joke or cult object, offered no explanation.

"Okay, that's the lab." He flicked off the lights. "I'll show you to Dr. Leland's office."

But she hadn't planned on an interview with the great goddess too—she'd lose it. The chance was real now. There was something here for her—real, just as her fear was, telling her she'd lose what she wanted.

The office was empty. He left her to wait alone, the heavy door shushing to a close behind him. The next time it opened, *she* would be coming in. How was anyone supposed to sit quietly, composed, like all the others must have done? She scanned a wall of pictures. Three people, arms intertwined, next to a fluted, uncapped column; two, before what looked like rubble. A series of etched old men whose names meant nothing to her. Sir Flinders Petrie, Sir Arthur John Evans, Heinrich Schliemann, J. J. Winckelmann. She peered at his caption: The Father of Archaeology, 1717–1768. What did that make Leland, the Mother? She returned to the picture of Schliemann; of course, he had excavated Troy—she knew that. If she'd only think, she'd remember who the rest were; they had to be fellow archaeologists, equally important.

Right beside this coterie, several diplomas charted Margaret J. Leland's climb to the top, by degrees, with honorable mentions and distinction. Obviously, she felt she deserved her place among the eminent. Irena wasn't sure what she thought of a woman showing her achievements so . . .

The door, with "Sorry I kept you waiting." A white lab coat. Passing by her, not looking up from an open folder. "Sit down." Still reading, feeling for the chair behind the cluttered desk. She could only see a bit of brow below her hair, dark brown, with gray strands the camera hadn't caught. "Smoke?" Tossing a pack forward. Snapping open a lighter.

Watching her use it, then hold on to it, rhythmically rubbing her thumb along the metal, she was glad she hadn't accepted a cigaret; it would have been too dumb, sitting there waiting for a light.

"Lampros." Finally the noted doctor looked up. Older than her picture—around forty?—the suntan made it difficult to tell. Unusually dark eyes; other than those, nothing special. "Any connection to the Lampros bakery on Delos Street?"

Here it came. "My uncle." Poor girl, such a tragic et cetera, nonetheless, can't have my project jinxed.

"Best baklava west of the Ionian." She leaned back in her swivel chair and smiled, crookedly. "I'm not sure the staff would forgive me if you weren't hired."

She couldn't be serious—everyone knew, even John had mumbled something about being sorry.

"That's one neighborhood I hope urban renewal never hits. Give him my compliments, will you?"

She tried to force her features into agreeableness; the thought of saying anything pleasant to him made her stomach churn.

Displeasure—with her because she—no, the look was directed at a stack of papers threatening to tumble off the desk. "Today, I think I'd trade places with anyone in business rather than have to mess with anal-retentive grant-givers and small-minded trustees." She pushed forward and ground out her cigaret. "I hate hiring good people with the understanding they may be out of work when the next budget comes in." Hand still on the cigaret, she glanced over. "Did Billy explain the job to you?"

"Yes."

"Under the circumstances I just mentioned," she sat back again, "would you take it?"

"Yes! Of course I would!"

"Why?" Her voice had changed. Hardened. Her face, the liveliness gone, was like a weathered mask; propping it on a stand, she folded her hands beneath her chin, and waited.

"Because, I think it would be very interesting."

Behind the mask, the eyes bored into her.

"I mean, the work you're doing . . . seems fascinating."

Nothing registered. Where was the woman who was supposedly so lovable? Just watching, not moving, not helping her at all. She had said "good people," she must have some . . . "Detail work—I'm good at that. Your assistant said the system was already set up but somebody on the site hadn't recorded things in the right places—everything's there, it's a question of sorting it out. I'd like to try—it'd be a challenge. Also, I like art—particularly art history—I like the idea of working here, around people who know more than I do." It didn't matter, she wasn't going to get the job; Margaret J. Leland, superwoman, hadn't activated an eyebrow.

When she spoke, only her lips moved. "Collating material for publication has nothing to do with art, nor is it in the remotest way fascinating. It's tedious but essential work. We're undertaking a significant reconstruction. While that's going on, you'd be off in a corner pulling cross-referenced data into shape. You might well think the other side of the lab interesting, with no chance to transfer there. I have a bare-bones staff as it is, and I don't want any romanticizing employee quitting on me."

"I wouldn't quit. And I assure you, I would not romanticize." Everyone else might fall all over themselves, but not her.

Leland was holding the silver lighter to a cigaret gripped between her teeth. What had John's friend seen in her?

113

Maybe John would be susceptible, too—good luck to him, trying to charm this woman.

The telephone buzzed. After answering with a curt "Leland," she changed again. Her face came to life, led by that smile crooking its way, making years disappear. She swiveled around, keeping her back to Irena for privacy. Low words radiated warmth. There was a brief lascivious laugh. Whoever was on the other end of the line certainly had provided, and was receiving, pleasure. The conversation closed on a murmur. Turning, she replaced the receiver, her hand lingering there while she smiled to herself, and shook her head.

"All right, Irena. Come in Monday at eight thirty." Her voice still held delight. "And bring baklava."

"You mean I've got the job?"

The phone buzzed again. "You needn't be so surprised—Leland." She listened intently. Irena didn't know whether to go or stay. An uncomfortable minute passed before the woman noticed and waved her off. "Wheelan, you fuck up one more glow curve and I'm going to come down there and kick in your kiln."

A throaty, cigaret laugh was undercutting that threat as Irena closed the door. Safely outside her office, she could have skipped down the corridor or collapsed against the wall. Before anything else, she had to find a bathroom.

On the way home it occurred to her: Alex hadn't spoken. All through the interview, her sister had been silent. Unless she was behind her small display of confidence and anger. No, it amazed her, but the voice had been her own.

Entering the house, she feels Alex reawakening. Her sister never sleeps here; every act and thought is shadowed. The price she pays for a faithful if difficult ally. A steadfast critic who toughens her up, prepares her for family battle. Always, each night, confrontation unites them; her accuser becomes a supporter then, doubling Irena's strength against the enemy they have in common.

Tonight, a *fait accompli* awaits him. In days gone by it might have been M'Lord, this loyal serf begs leave to plant a flower garden. Or, On bended knee, O mighty liege, I ask of you a favor: my tapestry is finished now, I would step outside the castle. No more: the age of groveling is over.

She knows everything he will say, on top of supporting his sister's daughter, and blah-blahing a woman's place. Has she forgotten her education? The money he has spent? Not that he begrudges it—a little learning is only right. But this archaeology—what good does it do a wife? Naked statues and obscene urns—what kind of work is that? And this bossy lady *doctor*—did she wear a wedding band? So. She must be one of "those." Never mind what he means—she cannot go!

But I am supposed to bring baklava! the old Irena might cry, like a child deprived of a party for which she was to make the fudge. No more: the tearful years are over. He will see when she faces him, and reminds him without mercy. He cannot keep this female in jail or tell the witness what to do—the accused is not the judge. Let him waste his breath objecting; the eyes will overrule.

"I'm surprised, Irena. He didn't make much of a fuss—I think the fight has gone out of him."

"You talk as if that's something to grieve about."

"It makes him old before his time. Who can be happy about that? He sits too much now. Your uncle always held himself tall, he never used to sag. I don't like to see him this way."

"How you can have even a twinge of sympathy after what he's done—he doesn't deserve any compassion. Especially yours."

"You are so hard lately. It's sad to see a beaten man, no matter who he is. Life, that's what's draining out of him."

"Poor Uncle Constantine, there's nobody around to oppress anymore. Except his wife, and she's gone along with it for so long it's too easy—there aren't enough kicks to keep him going."

"If I were to shut my eyes, I would think Alexandra was in this room, not you."

"Alex is in every room of this house, Aunt Eunice. If he's sagging, it's because he can't get away from her."

"And you? Can you get away from her?"

"I don't want to! He's the one who wants to—he'd like nothing better than to forget her and what he's done. I won't let him. To the grave, he's going to be reminded."

"Enough graves—you should just hear yourself. It isn't right; it isn't healthy."

"I suppose *you're* right, you're healthy. Taking his side—it's like breathing with you."

"Your voice—everything. She has given it all to you, hasn't she? Your sister has left you a legacy."

"Yes! Alex didn't just close her eyes to that tank rolling over the family, and you can be sure I won't either."

"They were harsh, angry eyes. Always at war with something. Is that what you want for yourself? You used to be such a gentle girl."

"You mean docile. I have absolutely no respect for who I was."

"That's a pity, I'm sorry she's gone. I want to know, with other people, do you meet them with anger now, too? Or is it just us, your uncle and me, who get the full benefit of your hostility?"

"I don't . . . I haven't been around other people a whole lot lately."

"The ones at the museum, I wonder if they'll appreciate such treatment."

"Why should I be hostile to them? I don't even know them."

"Because it spreads, Irena. Once you fill yourself with it, it spills over and falls onto everyone, you can't pick and choose.

Your uncle couldn't. Your sister. What makes you think you'll be any different?"

"At least I feel something. Where there's hate there's life."

"We are back where we started, no?"

"No! Alex didn't like that comparison and neither do I."

"I am sorry I say things you don't like. There has been too much not liking in this family for too many years. When will it stop?"

"When you meet someone likable, it stops."

"Oh, so there are such people. This boy you are seeing tomorrow night—you will be working every day in the same place?"

"Every day, five hours a day, Monday through Friday, Aunt Eunice."

"Kinsella. That is a Catholic name, isn't it?"

"Don't worry, we'll be on opposite sides of the lab, I won't catch anything. Talk about not liking—you're a fine one to set yourself up. We all hate someone, don't we?"

"I do not hate Catholics. I simply would prefer that my niece not marry one."

"Aunt Eunice, we are going out to celebrate our jobs—the plan is to eat—but I promise, if I find an engagement ring in the antipasto I'll send it right back."

Start the whispered rumors. Drag out the black. Just let them share a pizza, and in no time flat, ten babies will be born to them, then baptized on the head. So get those whispers going. Put on mourning black. She has made a date for dinner with a Roman Catholic!

"That *xenos* is coming here to pick you up?"

"No. I'm meeting the 'foreigner' at Romano's, okay? I wouldn't want him exposed to the paranoia in this house on our first night out."

*　*　*

117

It was a cozy place, dim enough for the plastic plants to look real by candlelight. Classically Italian, not a trite touch was missing, from the candles wedged in tallow-dripped Chianti bottles down to the red and white checked tablecloths. She wouldn't have had it any other way.

"I'm glad you like it," John said. "Just don't expect me to pick up the table in my teeth after dinner."

She laughed. "Wrong nationality."

"Yeah, but I thought you might be used to it after dating Greek guys."

"No, they only twirled their big black mustaches and danced in a circle after dinner. You're saved—checked napkins won't do."

"I could handle the dancing part okay, but my mustache comes out sort of skimpy and red-looking. Not attractive."

She liked him as he was. "Men are lucky they can change their looks. I remember my brother couldn't wait to grow a mustache—he was only about twelve. Shaving bare skin every day—he got a terrible rash, no one could understand it. Then my aunt started finding strange little teeth marks all around the edge of his nightstand."

"Ambitious kid." The enjoyment faded. "Which brother was that?"

"Gene. The oldest." Instead of John's face, a powdered one. "When they played taps . . ." She blinked it away. "Trust the military to get it backwards—it should have been reveille, the soul rising to angelic trumpets."

He smiled sympathetically, and held out a finger to catch the dripping candle wax.

She had been drawn to his hands from the beginning. Now she wanted to reach over and touch one, apologize for having made him feel awkward. She couldn't, though Alex would have; in fact she was prodding her to, urging her hand forward.

She grasped her wineglass. "I was wondering, will you lose a student deferment when you take this job?"

"Nope." He tilted his chair precariously onto two legs. "I don't have one."

"But how have you managed to avoid being drafted?"

He rolled his eyes suggestively.

"Oh come on, tell me."

Bringing the chair level, he lifted their bottle of wine to see how much was left, then carefully portioned out the remainder between their glasses. Raising his, he smiled at her over the rim. She half smiled in return, puzzled. He sipped his wine; still looking at her, waiting, it seemed, for something she should be doing or saying.

"I'm sorry." She had no idea what he wanted. "I didn't mean to get personal."

"If we're going to be friends, we should get personal. We ought to know about each other. For example. I'm a coward." Curiosity may not have been the reaction he expected, but it was all she felt. "No way am I going to face it over there. I don't trust student deferments; I had to be sure, short of saying goodby to friends or toes, that they couldn't get me. It took one stunning earring and a pair of bikini briefs—black mesh." He checked again; she was still curious, wanting him to go on. "During the physical, I fantasized myself into an erection and let my hand graze the doctor's. Moved a little closer, and it was all over. Some people thought it wouldn't work, but I didn't even have to take one of those stupid psych exams where they ask you if you've ever wanted to fuck your mother." His hands flew up. "Mercy!" They dropped to the table, he was simply John again. "The only problem is, they code reasons for deferment—it's permanently on record for anyone who wants the information. Maggie Leland couldn't care less, but she is not your typical employer."

She didn't understand why he had hesitated to tell her. It had only been an act, he wasn't really . . . If he were, why was he taking her out to dinner? Maybe friendship was all he wanted—all he was capable of with a woman. But he didn't seem . . . would she be this attracted to someone who was?

"Irena," he ducked his head and looked at her from under a creasing brow, "I play it both ways. In case you're wondering about that too, and I can tell you are."

"Oh." She nodded several times. "I see." But she didn't, quite.

"Like your ancestors, you know?"

Not really. She never visualized the truth behind the stories, preferring to think of ideal love blurring sexuality. Now, given John's "confession," she wants to look more closely.

What of Achilles and Patroklos—fabled warrior companions, sharing battles in the field, making love within their tent—what if either lived to marry? No woman could have won them from their passionate commitment. Like Socrates' being in love with Alcibiades' beauty. What chance had wife Xanthippe against that young man's glory? Confined at home with children, perhaps a slave or two, the butt of dinner-party ridicule—no wonder she became a shrew. High-class whores really were better competition. Men favored them with gifts —even serious conversation. But hetaerae plied a trade in which the heart did not exist. That, man gave to man, holding women undeserving.

So, in turn, did women burn with love for one another? Did they seek and find the bliss they wished in loving female union? Unless a Sappho or a slave, their opportunities were few. Some religious rites induced their lust and frenzy—but why were maenad revelries invariably "disgusting?" If ideal love was limited to male behavior only, then reality was a privileged sexual practice reserved for boys and men.

It didn't matter if times had changed. She had no knowledge of what it was actually like, how someone lived that way. John was so open about it, he must have assumed she knew more, and understood.

"Hey. Say something, will you? I'd sort of like to know what you're thinking."

It didn't seem right pretending to a sophistication she

didn't have. "I'm wondering . . . how it works. I mean, do you have any preference?"

"It depends on the mood I'm in."

"That sounds like . . . the people who satisfy your mood might get hurt. After the mood is over."

"I don't think I spread hurt around more than anyone else. Less, probably. I never promise commitment, or make long-range plans. All I'm interested in is a joyous union. There's no harm in that."

"What about emotional involvement? Or is what you do— is what you want just sexual?"

"I've met people who enjoy impersonal sex, or say they do. I don't. I have to like someone first. Then it can happen— when you make love, you do love. Bed is the best place for emotional involvement—you have a chance for openness and honesty there you don't get elsewhere."

"But what about after? Don't you have to deal with that?"

"Irena, if people can't just meet, and enjoy, without complications, they shouldn't say yes in the first place."

"But, John, people don't always know ahead of time how they're going to feel. It sounds so . . . limited."

"But it's not! Everything's compressed—it's immediate, intensified. You're alive."

"I don't know . . . your way doesn't seem to open up much opportunity for getting to know someone. I mean, ideally, people share a variety of things over a period of time —they need that, don't they? for a sense of . . . wholeness?"

"I'm not talking about one-night stands, Irena, though they have their place in the scheme of things. But cramps and diapers and mortgage payments and ulcers? Who needs that? Let's do the laundry together, it'll really turn us on, then you fix the dry rot and I'll mow the lawn—no thanks. I like my way better."

Bim-bam thank you ma'am, or sir. They hadn't talked about the physical part. "They must be very different experiences."

"What, mowing the lawn and . . . hey, no." He reached across and pressed her hand. "I apologize, they are different. And each seems to make the other that much better. But don't get me wrong, I'm not constantly jumping from one bed to the next." His hand was warmly enclosing hers. "Honestly, I'm not promiscuous in any real sense. I try not to use people; I try to act ethically. But why should the mere fact of someone's sex determine their desirability? Love is love, right? The world could certainly use more of it—I'm just doing my patriotic duty."

Phil would have said that. John accepted, even reveled in, what was repugnant to most. His choices didn't bother her —why had the thought of somebody old been more distasteful? Clutching her water glass with her free hand, she gulped, trying to wash down shameful traces of that earlier reaction.

"Listen, I didn't mean to come on so strong. You're easy to talk to. I might have overdone it."

"No, I'm glad you told me. Really." She was able to smile. His was the only presence with her now.

He squeezed her hand, then began slowly letting go. As his fingertips trailed down her skin, she saw her fingers sliding, spreading on their own. Meshing with his; locked, joined, swaying in the candlelight.

Alex bets he is a super lay. Irena says shut up, just go away.

Their order arrived; impossible to eat one-handed. Each of them watched the waiter arrange their meal on the table, taking his time, then bowing at their smiles of appreciation. She wouldn't be able to cope with it all unless they changed to a safer topic of conversation.

John's appetite seemed to be stimulated; he was well into his salad when she thought of something to say. "Do you know much about Maggie Leland's project?"

"Not as much as I'd like to. I'm sure looking forward to getting my hands on those fragments. It's amazing how they can reconstruct something on the basis of a few key pieces.

Of course I won't be working on the big one—three semesters of sculpting and ceramics don't make me an expert." But his artist's hands were skillful. "I'll be given some of the small finds, though, the figurines and jewelry and such."

"What's she after? She said the reconstruction was really important."

"It's going to set a lot of people on their ears, if she's found what she thinks she has. The way I understand it, she's discovered an underground chamber on the mainland that was used by a female cult. Which wouldn't be so unusual, except they were ruled by priestess queens who worshipped a pre-Olympian goddess. Which makes them, literally, an underground matriarchy. If she's right."

"She must have found something awfully impressive to go out on that limb—people have tried to prove it before."

"Well, from the shape of the tomb they expected to find royal artifacts, and did. The strange thing is, they're native to the area, but most of the religious ones aren't. None of that's been verified yet, but you don't need lab tests to tell the amphorae are 'female.' Even when they're in umpteen pieces, like the queen's she's brought home. Once they've reconstructed it and decoded the iconography, she'll be able to buttress her theory."

"On the basis of a single funeral urn? That's confidence, I guess."

"She'll have to put together a lot more than that eventually. But linked to some of the small finds we'll be identifying and dating, it'll be a major piece in the puzzle. Then more excavating for more proof. I think she's up against it, though. Look at the grant being late and throwing her off schedule. A group of women who successfully defied all the institutions of Greece for hundreds of years—digging that up doesn't exactly endear her to the power structure."

"What makes her so sure the chamber isn't just a burial spot for the wives of kings?"

"It's too vast for that, and the mixture of finds is too odd.

123

She thinks a hidden resurgence—a revival of an earlier way of life—accounts for the peculiar mix. If a Bronze Age cult *was* intent on preserving pre–Bronze Age relics, it could have used the chamber as a repository for its heritage, a sort of museum in addition to a place of burial and worship. It's possible, and really exciting—we're lucky to be in on it."

"Maybe those women knew they'd be destroyed and wanted to leave some kind of testimony. The thing that gets me is how they could have gone on for so long without anyone knowing about them."

"Knowing and telling are two different things. If Leland's fighting people in this day and age who don't like the idea of ancient matriarchies, imagine what the male establishment back then thought of them. Every urn was smashed—there were shards and ornaments all over the place."

"I still don't—if they were self-contained and lasted for hundreds of years, there had to be men in the group. They had to reproduce themselves."

"Sure. Why not go outside the system to mate, or bring in males for fertility rites and then sacrifice them to the earth goddess? Or keep a male population of slaves—maybe their own sons? Leland won't have a chance at knowing any of that until more of the area is excavated. Which is why she has to reconstruct and publish as soon as possible, in order to get funding for the next dig." Quicker and more adroit than Irena, he was twirling his last forkful of spaghetti.

"John, how did you manage to find out so much? All I heard about were site registers and find tags from some assistant. The eminent Leland didn't say anything at all."

He looked up; his amusement always started in his eyes. "I asked her."

"Oh." In her office or over coffee? Stupid, Maggie Leland had to be at least fifteen years older than John. "What did you think of her?"

"In the flesh?" It played around his mouth now. "I thought

everything my friend said about her was true. What did you think?"

"Mixed, I guess. Tell me what your friend said and I'll tell you if I agree with him."

Mischief, everywhere. "Didn't I mention my friend was female?"

She swallowed. Never had she felt so naive.

"Irena, we're going to have to do something about your innocence."

But too many eyes are watching. Not his so much as Alex's, judging her performance. Exposed to evaluation, her body is self-conscious and not free.

"Please . . . don't." He was nuzzling between her thighs. "I can't . . ." Fingers curling in his hair, she tried to lift his head. "John, please stop—I'm sorry."

Her knee was kissed. "Don't apologize." Lips skimmed over her abdomen, then left. He was lying alongside, "It's all right, I'm not asking you to rush your pleasures," smoothing a tear she had tried very hard to hold back. "Don't feel pressured. Not here," touching her mouth, her cheek, the moisture clinging to her lashes. "We have time. Don't worry." Fingertips traced her brow. "You'll pass this way again, won't you?"

She wants to be in this bed again, oh yes, there is nothing she wants more. Her arms go around his shoulders; she clutches at his back.

She hadn't come the first time, but he had, trying to take her along with him, finally letting go. She wanted him again, drawing him down onto her, hoping he could tell.

She wants to make him happy. He enters with a moan, oblivious to her smile. Accepting all she can offer. Climbing, on his own.

Coming out, he kissed her breasts; rubbed her flank. She was content.

His eyelashes fluttered against her neck. "I know you didn't make it tonight." She was about to protest when he rolled off her and sat up. "That's okay, it happens. I won't view it as a slur on my manliness, if you'll promise me you won't pretend. This is the place," he patted the bed, "where honesty has a chance. Please don't fake it here, ever."

"I won't. I didn't. But John . . ." Didn't he know how good he had made her feel? Even without that, her body was suffused with pleasure. "I . . ." she hid her face in his side, "loved it."

"Yay." He slid down to hold her. "You've got great potential, lady. Anyone ever tell you that?"

Her head moved back and forth against his chest.

"No?" He massaged her neck. "Then that's our discovery. You and I have a lot to explore, Irena."

Later, in her own bed recalling every moment, Irena hears a snicker: great potential, lady. Be quiet, she tells her sister, or the whole thing will be ruined. He patronized you, Rena; and accusing you of faking sure put the blame on you. It was not an accusation! Irena hotly denies, he was just asking me to promise. Otherwise, Alex replies, you would naturally be dishonest; acting so glad no one had discovered you before—mentors to the virgin, Rena, always want to be first so the lady avoids comparisons. Alex, he knows I've had experience —why must you undermine? You didn't even come. That's not everything! Why settle for less? I'm not, just don't interfere in the pleasures I find—I like being close to him. Partners in joy, well isn't that grand; it won't be mutual, Rena—he's a man. Thank you, I noticed that tonight. Okay, have it your way, but don't cry to me when the guy's heart and mind start destroying that sweetness and light. I won't if you'll just leave us alone; please stay out of this, Alex, I don't want your warped perspective. Too bad, she says, totally unsympathetic; you can shut me up if you really try, but you are stuck with me forever.

Sleep was the borderline kind so fitful and close to waking.

It must have been deeper in the morning, but she was instantly alert at the sound of her aunt coming back from church. Tensing, she waited for her uncle's footsteps to follow. Hangers jingled. The closet door creaked shut. Blessed absence; maybe he would be gone until evening. Usually she had to rely on Alex to get her through a Sunday; if he stayed away, she would have time for herself—a whole day in which to think about last night.

It had been a long time since she'd hummed in the shower. She entered the kitchen on the same melody. "You're in a fine mood." Her aunt was sorting old clothes into boxes; Irena no longer kept track of her charities. "Did you have a pleasant evening?"

"Very." She went for the quickest diversion. "Where's Uncle Constantine?"

"Meeting with the board and Reverend Kourides. When did—"

"What are they plotting now?" Popping two pieces of bread in the toaster, she hoped the topic would last through breakfast.

"I shouldn't be saying anything about it yet, but . . ." Her aunt beamed over the boxes. "Eugene's going to have a window."

"What do you mean, Eugene's going to have a window— what does that mean?"

"Two panels, high on the left as you walk in. For years, the stained glass has needed repair Your uncle is seeing to it."

"Oh is he." So a priest in his pocket wasn't enough. "Paying the bill entitles him to a bronze plaque, I suppose. What's it going to say, Aunt Eunice? 'The generosity of Constantine Lampros . . . in memory of . . . he gave his life et cetera?' What are Phil and Alex getting, new toilet seats for the Sunday school john?"

"Irena! Your uncle is giving to his church—the best craftsmanship, the finest art. You should be proud of him, and glad

127

for your brother. To honor such beauty—what is wrong with your uncle offering that to Eugene?"

Alex jeering, going to buy off God? "Nothing, I'm sure a testimonial in bronze will be very effective. They can even engrave the cost of the repair work on it so everyone'll know what a great and good man he is."

"That is *not* why he is doing this. You won't grant him an inch. The man can do nothing right in your eyes."

"Mine aren't the only ones." Piling her plate of toast on top of her coffee cup and saucer, she walked away from the conversation. She didn't want her morning sullied further, another minute and she would have accused her aunt of having been bought; once again, as usual; this time for the price of a stained-glass window. Thumping up the stairs; how could she be expected to share anything from her life with a woman like that? Nearly losing her wobbly load, she kicked the bedroom door closed and set her breakfast down near the bed. Climbing back in; no one could blame her for shutting her out. Settling the pillows. She reached for the coffee and cursed. It was no good having reveries if they were going to come tinged with guilt.

John was already there when she arrived on Monday, bearing baklava, unsure about that and everything else. Even though one of the pottery assistants was explaining a procedure, he broke his concentration to flash her a brilliant, leg-weakening smile.

She sank onto a chair just as Maggie Leland strode in, carrying a batch of photographs. "Kelly." Spoken so quietly Irena didn't know which person she was addressing, but the assistant left John and went to her. "Get the find tag info and pull out this, this, and this," pointing to separate pictures. "I want them sent to the lab for spectrographic analysis right away." Taking the top three photos, he frowned over each of them, then slowly nodded agreement. Leland had been watching his reaction. "How much do you want to bet they came from Anatolia?"

"Two doughnuts?"

"Oh come on, you're supposed to be the gambler in the group."

He tried to control a grin. "I'd have to be a fool to bet good money when your intuition is showing."

His response rated the cigaret laugh. "Too bad I can't footnote it—think what we'd save on lab reports. That cult originated in Asia Minor, all right, and the metal in those ornaments is going to help prove it." She looked around. "Where's Haynes?"

"Here!" Skidding in, he flung himself onto a desk, swung one leg over the other, and leaned back, theatrically casual.

Leland strolled over to him. "Been here long, sailor?" He broke his pose laughing. "Get your artistry in gear and hang this up somewhere, Billy. I want to have her watching us." She moved on as he held the photograph at arm's length and whistled. Making an immense production of his assignment, trying one place then another, he ended by tacking the photo onto a cupboard door above Irena's desk; stepping back, he glanced from it to her and winked broadly. She thought he'd say something before sashaying away.

She stood to study the picture more closely. It appeared to be nothing more than a rock wall. But then she made out two eyes peering from the surface; a line curving like a necklace; beneath that, two faint half circles, suggesting breasts.

"What do you think?" The voice was right behind her.

Unexpectedly close, asking her opinion—she couldn't turn around. "What is it?"

"A dolmen deity. An underworld goddess of death and fertility."

"Was she in the tomb you excavated?" she asked the cupboard.

An indulgent sound. "No, she's from Spain—they've only been found in the giant rock-cut tombs of Western Europe.

She and her sisters are known for the oculus motif, but that's a pedantic phrase that doesn't do them justice. The force in those few lines—it's been refined right out of her elaborate descendants. She *is* the rock, the cave. Imagine being in that presence, the awe she must have inspired."

Like being held, or seen into. The power of suggestion, probably.

"What's this?"

Forced to follow the voice, she saw Maggie Leland prodding at her pastry box. "It's . . . baklava," she said weakly.

The woman's large dark eyes shifted; her mouth started to twist. Something sarcastic was coming, Irena knew it and bent her head, prepared to be humiliated. "Thank you." When she dared to look, Leland was halfway across the lab, murmuring something to an assistant that made him slap his brow. "I forgot! Jesus, I'm sorry, Maggie." "It's not the end of the world, just do it now, then start Lampros on those registers, will you?" Moving on toward the drafting table, she didn't see him melt.

The head draftsman was a woman not much older than Irena, pretty in a pallid way, with an angular dancer's body. She was greeted by her first name as Maggie Leland leaned over her shoulder to pick up a pair of calipers. So brown in contrast, her hand found the base of Carolyn's neck, and rested there while they checked a measurement together. Irena made herself look elsewhere, only to catch John looking at her. His bright eyes veered from her to the two women to her again, then rolled as they had in the restaurant. She felt her cheeks grow hot. She didn't know what to make of any of it yet. The current resonating through her was too new; different.

V I

WHATEVER WAS GENERATED then stays with her. That is, during working hours. It takes a few days for her to accept she is charged, functioning on a different level. Perhaps it is the past itself that inspires, for she only has to enter the place and it happens. Suspicious at first, she no longer waits for the rush to subside, or calls it beginner's enthusiasm. It is there; in her. And she suspects the others have it, too, for as the weeks increase, so does her sense of connection. After one short month, there is no questioning it—the lab, the people, her work—nothing around her seems foreign.

And her competence amazes her, though she tells herself anyone can flourish when treated with respect. Everyone is a colleague—even those who have been on digs before do not lord it over the rest, but share what they know during coffee breaks and lunchtime conversations. Of course the tone has been set; the example is there to follow. Maggie Leland makes each person feel vital to the project.

When she enters the room, the atmosphere is heightened; a sense of creation envelopes them then, no matter how small their assignment. Working alongside, inspiring dedication— somehow she is one of them yet someone apart and higher. Not that she fosters the separation. It is Irena who thinks she emanates the magical and earthy. It is Irena whose vision convinces, like any other convert's. A tongue-tied acolyte in Maggie Leland's presence, she fervently hopes the results she achieves will speak, and be an offering.

"I told you." John's most mischievous grin flashed up at her from the pillow. "Everyone wants to please the potent lady."

"And have they?"

"What do you mean?"

Astride him, she trailed tips of hair across his face. "I get a funny feeling sometimes that she's biblically known everyone in the lab except us."

"Yeah?" He thrust his pelvis upward and she felt him stiffening inside her. "I know everyone would jump at the chance." He lifted himself to run his tongue along her breast-bone. "Including you."

"John!"

"Oh yeah," his voice was husky, "most of all you. You'd like it; I've seen the way you look at her." He eased her over. "How you follow her around." He started, deep and slow. "Come on." She closed her eyes, knowing he was watching. "Admit it."

"No."

"You want her." Teasing strokes.

"I do not." Tormenting her with slowness.

132

"Liar." He took her hand and added it. "You want to get in bed with her."

"No I don't!" She pulled it back.

"Yes you do!"

"No!" shaking her head from side to side. Something, a coiling in her groin, a piercing hum not heard but felt, and it was climbing, coiling. She wanted more, wanted him faster, urging him with her body.

"Say, I want her."

"You." He knew but wouldn't do it. "Please faster."

"Uh-uh." She was burning, taut, her hips were straining up to his but he wouldn't give it to her. "Say it. Tell me you want her."

"John, please!"

"You want her don't you. All over you and in you. Don't you."

"Faster!"

"Don't you. Say it. I want her, say it."

"Please!"

"Tell me, say it."

"John!"

"Say it, say it, say . . ."

"Yes goddamn it please!"

A trip release. He is plunging, plunging, and she is shooting to a place where life convulses. Mind apart, she cannot see, is somewhere else, eyelids fluttering while greedy loins milk waves of pleasure and will not stop until the last drop has gushed and rolled within her. Jesus, she vaguely hears, oh Jesus.

Spent, he lay on top of her. She was idly stroking his back. Let Alex interfere now. Her sister had been quelled, she couldn't come here anymore. But she would later, at home; her own bed was still open territory. Here, with John, she was safe; freed.

"I love you." She hadn't meant to say that; the words were

out before she even knew they were on the way.

His mouth was motionless against her cheek; he wasn't asleep, he had heard. That was all right; she didn't need to hear it from him. Not yet. She dozed under the weight of his body.

When she awoke, he was propped up on one arm staring at her. Silently, he offered her the last sip of wine from his glass. She refused, needing nothing. "Lady, that was worth waiting for. I think we ought to celebrate." He hopped out of bed. Naked and unselfconscious, he padded over to the little icebox in the corner; she watched, enjoying his body, not embarrassed to be looking. Cautiously carrying two full glasses back to the bed, he noticed her frank appraisal; it registered immediately. He held the wineglasses up higher to see himself rising. "Down, boy. Down. I want to have a drink with the lady first." He shook his head, "Mind of its own," and handed her a glass. Sitting cross-legged on the sheet, he clinked a toast. "To many more."

The organ responsible was right before her. She gripped it lightly, "Thanks, boy." The wine was cool and perfect.

"He can't take all the credit."

Looking down at her own bush of hair, dry now and tightly curled, she raised her glass. "Thanks, girl."

She felt him swelling within her grasp; moistening, thickening. His hand covered hers and gently rubbed her knuckles. "Tell me about your crushes on girls when you were younger."

"I didn't have any."

"You must've. You want to make love to a woman."

It jarred her airy pleasure. "No I don't."

"Sure you do. That's what did it. What turned you on. The idea." She tried to draw her hand away but he held it down, cupping her around him.

"That's not true, John. I only said it because you wouldn't speed up and I thought I'd go out of my mind if you didn't."

He tapped the bed with the base of his glass. "Honesty, remember?"

134

"I'm being honest! First you accuse me of wanting someone when I know I don't, then you accuse me of being dishonest for denying it." He was spoiling both the act and the aftermath; everything she had felt was being ruined.

"I'm not accusing you. I just think you're not as in touch with yourself as you ought to be."

"Look, bisexuality is your trip, not mine. You're projecting. Why is it so important to you whether or not I'm *yearning* to go to bed with some woman?"

"Maggie Leland is not *some* woman. And what's important is your knowing yourself better. I may be projecting a little, but it seems to me you're protesting a lot."

"Hey," this time she tapped the bed, "honesty works both ways. It was your turn-on. You were the one getting off thinking about the two of us doing it."

"Let's prove it, then." He took their glasses and set them on the floor, giving her a chance to withdraw her hand.

"I don't have to prove anything." She had no desire at all to make love now. "If you were right, I'd be all hot and bothered just talking about it. And I'm not, I assure you— Don't." He was trying to press her down from her sitting position.

"Okay!" Before she could move, he climbed on her lap and hunched himself forward until his cock was only inches from her mouth. "Do it."

Struggling to back up with no place to go, "I don't want to, dammit!"

"Why not? Any straight woman would." Knees were pinning her arms and it was so close to her lips she could barely turn her head aside. "What's wrong? It's a part of me, isn't it? You said you loved me, didn't you? If you love a man you've got to love this." He was trying to force her head around, digging his fingers into her cheeks, squeezing her lips together like a fish.

"Stoph!" forced from the throat. She couldn't thrash him off, she was trapped, twisting. Straining, "Dhone!" bodies

135

men stairs, resisting, every muscle fighting to . . . The hand eased up. Miraculously, the weight lifted; the springs jounced. She hid her face.

"What do I care? Guys give better blow jobs anyway."

She heard him walking across to the bathroom; shutting the door. Crying, she curled onto her side, and hugged herself for comfort.

"Where have you been?" He had let her come into the house with her key, catching her off guard. Arms folded across his barrel chest, he stood by the bannister. "Do you know what time it is?" She knew nothing; the bus ride, the slow walk home in the night air hadn't cleared up anything. "No niece of mine comes home at three o'clock in the morning! I'm still in charge of this house—you live under my roof, you conduct yourself decently! I know about that Bulgar, that Turk Kinsella. Where did you go with him you don't come home until three o'clock in the morning? You come back here! you answer me!" Her arm was grabbed.

Irena looks down. Black hairs, thick, on a hand.

When would it stop? Always, some man was laying claim to her; grasping. Brutalizing. "Please let go of me." She was too tired to confront him with her eyes. She didn't care anymore, she had no desire to remind or fight; all she wanted was to sink into her bed, alone.

Something makes him release her. Limp and weary, she does not analyze how she gets away from him.

Walking up the stairs, she needed the railing for support. "I forbid you to see him again! I forbid it!"

His voice calling after her makes no impression.

Dropping her clothes on the floor, she crawled into bed wishing everyone would just leave her alone.

But they don't, even in sleep. Clutching fingers. Insistent demands. Where is Irena? They have ripped her to shreds. In her place, in the space she once occupied, Alex stands

holding two crying eyes. I told you, she whispers, I told you
I told you! she yells. Grinning with malice, she motions her
close. Come here, little sister, no one's through with you yet.

Mocking victory. That's what they should call her, there on
her pedestal under the dome. She has nothing to do with her.
There is no immersion; she is not overcome, but separate.
Unrooted and mocked by glorified bronze, idealized strength.
Eight feet of it, draped; not a mere statue, missing a head.
Once she had arms; once, she embraced.

Her limbs are lethargic as she leaves the main gallery. She
has only made things worse. The contrast is even stronger
now; the absence of wings more dispiriting.

Dragging down the basement stairs, she told herself the
high had to leave her sometime. Life was bound to overtake
her eventually; she had been a fool to hope it might work
the other way. The polished wood floor turned into cork tiles,
and she thought how appropriate it was for her footsteps to
be muffled. No heralding the approach of Irena Lampros, who
had not found a sanctuary, who had not been transformed.

Rounding the last corner, she saw John pacing outside the
lab door. Her body weight seemed to increase as he came
trotting up the corridor to meet her. "I've got to talk to
you." He fell in step imploring, "Please. I never should have
let you go like that. Have coffee with me after work. Let me
explain, apologize properly. Please—for our sake." All day,
she might have to withstand this; make an effort every time
he asked, keep finding the energy to resist. Better, easier to
give in now, and spare herself. "Irena?" She nodded, once.
He squeezed her arm and was about to kiss her cheek, when
Maggie Leland walked out of the lab.

"Good morning!" He said it with embarrassing brightness.
Eyes lowered, Irena slipped past them and into the workroom.

What she wanted was to lose herself in numbers; unemotional, pure. Movable from register to register, having proper places where anyone could measure an event. She tried. Consistently. But it would never be one of those mind-absorbing days. The air crackled, unnerving her. There was too much tension around. Not just hers, or John's—his could have been deflected. It was Maggie Leland's.

She supposed it was because the reconstruction had neared a crucial stage that Winckelwoman was everywhere, checking, correcting. Paying attention to every project but the one she cared about most, the funeral vase taking shape across the room. Calculating the height, curvature, and rim diameter seemed to have taken more time than actually matching and joining the upper section. Soon they would be down to the key meander, and it was there, in the decorated band, they hoped to see matriarchal secrets revealed. So close yet still needing to take such care—Carolyn had said it was "EmJay's way" to handle strain by heightening her interest in everything else.

"Christ," now she was reaching past Irena for the Small Finds Index, "some days I wish I'd gone in for humps and bumps archaeology." Coat sleeve, brushing along her wrist. "I could be in a chartered plane winging over ground configurations instead of . . . ah, here it is. Wrong grid, John!" Taking the card with her; unsettling the air where he was hunched before a sand box attempting to sort out a figurine. Wrist still tingling, she saw her touching him. Bending over his body, placing her hand on the small of his back. Keeping her strong brown hand on his white-sweatered back; such a thin layer of fabric between the palm of her hand, the flesh of his back. Soft skin, her hand and his back; firm, his back and her hand. Touching. Knowing that back; feeling that hand, touching . . . Her wrist. It was burning, rubbed red. Bewildered, she looked at her fingers as if they belonged to somebody else.

Nerves and fatigue, that was all. Everything was out of kilter today. She forced herself to work. Concentrated. Despite figures jumping off pages and magnified sounds. But now the dolmen deity was staring at her. She knew without looking. Last week, smoothing and retaping her on the cupboard door, she had sensed appreciation floating from the goddess, an eerie acknowledgment. Ever since—she glanced at the stone idol. Just as she thought; directly on her.

An Earth Mother's gaze. She tries to decipher the eyes, the visage. Archaic, rock-hewn. An Earth Mother Age? Hard to envision women. In command, of themselves most of all. Hard to believe women. Respecting their own image. Powerful mirror. Hard to accept, affirming.

If only she could link into the person she might have been then. Find a residual trace, an ancient memory she could capture and build on. The heritage had to be there, waiting. Those women in the tomb had managed to resurrect it. Re-create themselves somehow. But they were many. In union. She was just one, on her own. And her senses were playing tricks again. She blinked; the necklace moved down, was no longer a smiling mouth.

"Paying homage?" Maggie Leland held out the index card for her to replace.

Instead of adding to her turmoil, something, like space, was clearing within it. She took the card, not able to glance above the tanned fingers but capable of speech. "She grows on you, doesn't she? Every time I see her, she seems to hold more." Filing, she listened for her moving away; when the woman didn't, she looked up at the deity again. "She changes a lot. I don't think anything surprises her, she just . . . knows."

"Maybe because she created herself out of Chaos."

To herself, she mumbled, "I wonder how long that took."

The response was equally low, a sound merely.

Perhaps it was feeling understood that kept her talking. "Is it true she demanded human sacrifice? It doesn't seem to fit." The goddess she could face was elemental, hard yet nurturing, not really rock at all.

Leland was striking a match, her hand flashing in the periphery of vision. "I don't know for sure. Probably. As the eternal cycle, all life came from her and all life returned to her. Whoever died in her service would be reborn with higher powers. Very likely, they thought of themselves as chosen people rather than victims, honored stand-ins for her son-consort."

The necklace was definitely a necklace now. "So it's honor and death, even with her. I thought she was wiser."

"Don't overlook the positive side of the cycle. Her capacity to create was much more frightening. It was *the* power her male successors had to lay claim to. I imagine the patriarchs who came along sacrificing innocent young females every time the wind didn't blow right were a very frustrated bunch."

"But they—or people like them—overthrew her. How could they capture that kind of potency?"

"The question is, why did they want to?" A rustle. A smoky current—she was waving goodby to the staff. "Again, I'm not sure. But people bent on conquest don't worship fertility and the land, they can't afford to revere what they're destroying. A warrior population pushing for dominance must either defile the nonsupportive myths and idols, or coopt them." Leaning against the desk—so near, her thigh seemed to give off heat. "On the surface, not that hard to do, the tactics go back a long way. To survive, the goddesses had to become devious. Some of them infiltrated the new regime, others went underground for the duration." Pulling an ashtray over, stubbing out her cigaret—she'd leave unless . . .

"Does that mean we'd have to join a resistance group to get in contact with them again?" Veering, she could see the lower half of her face; a smile changing it.

"Good idea. But something has to be done about the fighter image." A hand, rubbing her chin then disappearing, sliding into a pocket. "If we hadn't lost so much, we'd know how to translate positively, into creation rather than destruction. But we've become so literal. Giving birth, for instance.

A violent act uniquely ours, and about the only valid one allowed or accepted. Suppose we don't choose that path, or it doesn't suit us? We have to do more than resist then, we have to discover and legitimize—make the connection in other ways." Her body shifted. "Anyone who realizes that early on, and gets into the process sooner, is lucky. One needs a head start and a good push, so many are against it." She stood, removing herself from direct view. A slight movement —her lab coat, would she reach out now . . . "Enough. Your friend's getting impatient over there."

Hands firmly in her pockets, she strolled away. Depriving. Why? What was it about her Maggie Leland didn't like? There had to be some reason why she was the only one among them the woman never touched.

John held the lab door open for her. "What was that all about?" It closed with a thump.

"Earth goddesses."

"Resident or ancient?"

She let him hear her exasperation.

"Sorry. Guess I can't complain, can I?"

"No." They left the museum. For the first time, she'd been able to talk to her. She would have liked to be alone now, slowly taking the steps without another presence but the one she'd been in.

"The lady's really gotten to you, hasn't she."

It halted her. "If you start that again, we can say goodby now." She moved onto the second tier, not caring whether he followed.

"Hey." He skipped ahead and turned around below her. "Do you think I'll be able to say anything right today?" Concern, open and genuine, made his face look boyish. So innocent, waiting for reprieve.

"Just don't make me feel like a character in a porno flick, John."

"I never meant to do that to you. You know I don't see

you that way." People were passing close by, crisscrossing the wide stairs. "We can't talk about it here. Not properly. Come on," holding out his hand. Beseeched, she took it, and was helped down the steps as if she were an old lady getting out of a carriage.

The courtly manner was maintained during their walk to his apartment. It felt strange. She wasn't some damsel in need of wooing, the delicate female, incapable of deciding when to step off a curb to cross the street. Sullied one day, lily-white the next—it was unreal, sheer role-playing. Maggie Leland had treated her like a person; why couldn't John? He didn't even realize what he was doing, or if he did, that she resented it. But then, why should he be expected to? Until last night, she had been willing to be what he wanted.

"What are you thinking?"

". . . This and that. It's too bad, we haven't had a real talk since our first evening in the restaurant."

"But we always talk—before, during, and after. With one exception, and we're going to get that cleared up."

"Then what. We're never out of bed, and when we're in bed, what we talk about is bed."

"I didn't notice you complaining before." She was surprised by the hurt in his voice. "Don't let what happened last night ruin things between us, Irena."

"So we'll spend the 'before' part talking about it, then go to bed and . . ."

"Not unless you want to."

"What if I didn't? What if I didn't even want to mention last night, I wanted to discuss . . . I don't know, Minoan art, or—"

"Earth goddesses? I'm sorry I can't compete with Maggie Leland's fund of knowledge."

"Who's saying you have to? Must you create sexual competition when it doesn't exist? In bed, out—you keep moving me around like some kind of mindless object in your fantasies.

142

Wherever and however it suits you."

"Irena, you are not a mindless object to me—I'm no jerkass football player who thinks women are pieces of tail. Next thing you'll be saying I don't respect you, the old sophomoric worry about the guy not respecting the girl if she 'puts out.'"

"This isn't guys and girls, John. It's us—me. I *am*. I exist, I'm here."

"I know that! And I *saw* the effect she was having on you, I didn't make it up. Words seduce too, Irena. Believe me, if anyone knows how erotic the interchange of ideas can be, Maggie Leland does. She's got that game down to a fine art."

"John, she was not . . . playing with me. I asked her some questions and she answered them. As if I were an equal." Worth the time and mind. "Hard as that may be for you to believe." It was for her.

"Phooey. You're not equals, she's your boss and she knows a hundred times more than you do."

"Well, she made me feel like one."

"And I haven't? Christ, one lousy slip and I'm forever tainted. You'd think all that joyful sharing we had meant nothing."

"Am I saying that? If you'd get over your fixation you'd—"

"You're the one who's fixated! And I'm jealous—me! the guy who doesn't believe in jealousy. You were right, it *was* a turn-on. But actually seeing the two of you together . . . man, I was wilting. Threatened. There was no way I could break that up and get you to notice me."

"This is hopeless. You imagined what you wanted to see. Nothing happened—it was just a conversation." Nothing; her neck, her back had waited; it hadn't come. "We're not getting anywhere, there's no point in my coming in with you."

He was unlocking the door to his apartment. "We'll sort it out. We have to." The bed was made, the room tidy. "Have a seat—I'll make coffee."

Aside from the desk chair, there was one low canvas sling, or the bed. She should have chosen the desk chair, the sling gave way so much she was nearly on the floor. Legs too high, trapped there, she watched him nimbly moving about in the cramped kitchen area.

Taking his freedom for granted. At home, not needing room or affirmation. Not seeing what he has.

"It's not just me I'm concerned about, Irena." He put away the dish towel. "That friend I mentioned on Leland's dig still hasn't gotten over her." Like a chill, it stiffened her. "Not that they had an affair. Leland said, 'I rob graves, not cradles,' and that was that." Tossing over a floor pillow, he plumped in front of the sling. "If they'd done it, maybe Ginny wouldn't be so hung up on her now. That can be a real power trip—leave someone dangling, they can't let go."

"And if someone gloms on to you like a leech, you can't shake her off. But that wouldn't be her perspective, would it."

"You're pretty quick to attack someone you've never met."

Too much seesawing—she didn't have the energy for any of it. Whatever had been gained in the lab was gone. "You're right, this is a stupid discussion. I'd better go, John. I'm exhausted and we're all at odds and evens. Nothing's sortable today."

Back came the boyish look, entreating. "Don't go. Take a nap here—I mean it, I've got reading to catch up on. Lie down for a while. It can wait." She could barely remember the original point of controversy. "Come on, Irena, I'm trying, at least meet me halfway."

"John, I have to sleep, really."

"Fine!" He got up and headed for the bed.

"But this seems so weird—are you sure you don't mind?"

"Of course not." The spread off, he was drawing down the blankets.

She didn't think she could have made it to her own bed. Undressed to her slip and shivering with fatigue, she climbed

144

between fresh sheets. John pulled a blanket around her shoulders, then withdrew. No gentle kiss or light caress; he seemed to know even that would have been too much for her to bear. She fell asleep appreciating him.

When she woke up, he was reading in the canvas chair. Undetected, she watched his arm as he turned the page, his jaw when he sipped from the mug of coffee. The afternoon sun was slanting on golden skin and shadowed muscles, backlighting his profile, highlighting the finest hairs on his forearm. He swung his leg around the frame, unknowing, his thigh, molded to taut white denim, inviting.

"Hi," she said softly.

"Well hello." He put the book on the floor. Coming over to her, he gingerly sat on a tip of sheet. "Sleep well?"

"Mmm." She stretched luxuriously. Her hands landed on his shoulders, and slid down his arms. The look this brought made her smile. Rising to meet it, she held his face and kissed him; then again, full-tongued, deep, hands moving under his sweater. Pushing it up, squeezing flesh. She dropped down to suck his nipple into her mouth; rim it with her teeth; rub both, tongue each. Aggressive, excited by it, she wanted in a way not known to her before. She was going to take him, unclasping his belt buckle, she was going to make love to him, grasping his zipper, she was commanding, she was ascendant, and she was going to control it all.

Unquestioning, he lay back and let her pull off his clothes. Her slip and pants followed as he kicked away the blankets to stretch full length in the middle of the bed. When she braced herself over him, his arms went around her neck; again she entered him, and the surge of power made her hips gyrate with excitement. She wanted all of him to know it, running her nails over his body; forging wet trails over his chest, his belly, with her open mouth. She rubbed the hard muscles of his thighs, kissed his knees, his ankle, biting as pleasure cries came down to her. He was spreading, there for whatever

145

she wanted. And what she wanted was possession. Moving up, she bit along his hip bone, slid one hand under him and the other between his legs, gripping the tight muscles behind and the thick pulsing one in front. She raised her head . . . and lowered her mouth full onto him. His gasp, his clutching at her hair. She pumped. Building, quickening her strokes, she made him talk out, tell her; pleas and curses, priming her, bringing her closer to the verge. Closer, coiling—urgent, rhythms fierce, she scrambled up to straddle him, thrust herself down onto him and feel that charging high feed into hers. Lunging, ramming, she rode him for every ounce he had, before he fell away and she was alone, on her own exultant course until the last spasm ended.

When they kissed, a thin film of sweat lay between them. It caused a plopping sound as she lifted her breasts off his chest.

He pushed a damp strand of hair away from her forehead. "I sure hope I'm around the next time you wake up from a sex dream."

"Yeah? I don't remember having one."

"Well, something was responsible for that other than my breathless good looks."

Making a basso voice, "Did you like it, baby?" Laughing, she rolled onto the sheet, and tucked a pillow under her head. The air felt cool on her body; the recollection of strength made her smile. She didn't know why that commanding desire had taken hold of her. It seemed enough, for now, to know it as a potent first, a memory that was hers to draw upon.

"So," his mouth played over her ear, "what's your opinion of Minoan art?"

"Fabulous." His arm lay across her rib cage; she raised it and checked his watch. "God, it's past five. I've got to go."

"I don't want you to."

"But I have to. They're expecting me." She started to get up; he held her back.

"Irena, about last night . . . I want to explain."

"All right, just let me wash and then we'll talk, while I'm dressing. I *have* to get home, John, I'm sorry." Disentangling herself, she left him on the bed.

As she came back from the bathroom, he sat up and pulled the sheet to his waist. She had never seen him pouting before. "What's wrong?"

"Nothing." He bunched the sheet closer.

"John, you're carrying the reversal too far." She stepped into her slip. "I feel like a businessman going home to the wife and kids after an afternoon's romp with his mistress. What's the matter?"

"Forget it."

She had no idea how to handle this—where was Alex? Banished, needed. She buttoned her blouse. Zipped her skirt. Strapped on her sandals. There was nothing more to do but comb her hair; she did it slowly, through continued silence. If that was the way he wanted it—spying her purse, she walked over to the kitchen counter. Leave, or make one last effort? She went back to the bed; when she sat on the edge, he turned his head aside. "I have to go now. Will you tell me what it is?"

"You've got to go—go."

She tried to control her resentment; once again, he had brought her down from a high. Why did he have to do that? "John?" He wouldn't look at her or speak. Without words, she rose from the bed, and let herself out.

Don't cry to me when the guy's heart and mind . . . But on the way home, she makes an appeal. She has no right to advice—Alex refuses to offer guidance. It is only in the house that she counts—let Irena pay for restricting her. If her lover's hostility lasts a few days, so what? Her sister's is eternal.

Futile, hoping it might have abated. The sentence stands, the judgment is fixed; Irena cannot escape it. Forgetting at times only makes coming back more brutal, especially when,

147

for a while at least, she relished a sense of mastery. An illusion, a dream—nothing but wish fulfillment. For her, reality means being chained to a ghost, and chained to a gross man's conscience. Doubly tied; inextricably linked. Condemned and condemning, both. No point in trying to break away—the eyes would only follow.

Approaching the house, she stopped to let the full weight descend on her. Feet dragging, she climbed the porch stairs. Dinner was being cooked, she could smell it, going in. Chicken.

"Irena?"

"Yes!" She went into the kitchen. Her aunt was at the stove managing to turn over a batch of crisp pieces and avoid the sputtering oil.

"You're very late. Will you set the table for four, please? Use the good silver."

"Who's coming?"

"Your uncle Theo."

"So he and Uncle Constantine are buddies again. That didn't take long."

"And why not? Forty years of friendship don't disappear overnight."

"Over nothing," she muttered, shoving back the drawer.

"How was work?"

"Fine."

"Where have you been since two thirty? I thought you were so tired you were going to come straight home."

"I changed my mind; visited a friend."

"Oh? Who?"

"One of the kids from work." She slapped the linen napkins into place.

"That boy, John Kinsella. You have been seeing him a lot?"

"Some."

"Does he live at home?"

"No."

148

"Is that where you were today? In his . . . apartment or room or whatever he has?"

"Aunt Eunice, do you mind—I'm a big girl now."

"I'm well aware of that." She lifted the dripping pieces onto paper towels. "Maybe that's why I'm asking."

Noisily getting out the plates, she was damned if she would submit to a third degree.

"You don't have to tell me times have changed, Irena. I just hope . . . you're being careful."

She was closer to being amazed. Staring at her aunt's back, she couldn't think of a reply that wouldn't be an admission.

"You and I have never discussed these things—your uncle would be shocked." She opened the oven door and slid in two full platters. "Somehow, I always thought you girls would know what you had to when the time came. Osmosis, magic —something would take care of it." Pouring the frying pan grease into a can, she carefully watched its progress. "Not very intelligent of me, was it? You might even say, cowardly." She actually tittered, pushing the can into a corner. "You could probably explain it all to me, now."

Impossible—inconceivable, her aunt in the missionary position, let alone . . .

"I'm sure your sister could have. If she'd ever talked to me. I think," she began wiping between the stove burners, "what I'm trying to say is," taking her time, rubbing at spots, "I'm here, if there should be . . . any problems, or . . . well, problems."

Like pregnancy, abortion—naming was too dangerous; it brought things home. "I can take care of myself, Aunt Eunice. Thanks anyway."

For the first time since she had come into the kitchen, her aunt looked her in the face. "Can you?" Her eyes were moist and searching. "You're lucky, then. Maybe . . . I was asking for my sake, as well as yours."

Her need was so palpable, Irena had to turn away. She

149

started sliding the water glasses nearer to the plates. "Is there anything else you want me to do toward dinner?" She knew her aunt hadn't moved, was still hoping for something from her. But the prom days were over; she didn't need help on what clothes to wear, or how to greet a boy on her first date, or any other girlish thing Aunt Eunice might be capable of counseling her about. She listened to her digging in her apron for a tissue. That shoulder she was supposed to lean on was sure to be quivering now.

The snuffling subsided sooner than usual. "Some ladies dropped by this afternoon." The voice was shaky, but she had retreated to the sink and seemed determined to show self-control. "They're organizing a mothers' march for peace." Potatoes tumbled and thumped onto the counter; one fell on the floor. She used the moment to steady herself as she picked it up. "They asked me if I would join them."

The least she could do was acknowledge her aunt's effort, "And?" sit down temporarily.

"I told them my husband wouldn't allow it." The peeler flashed; rapid, angry strokes. "They offered to talk to him for me—said they were used to confronting that problem. I said obviously they didn't know my husband."

Lucky for them. "How did they handle that?"

"Oh, it didn't daunt them in the slightest. He's just the sort of man who has to be reached, they said. Had I ever stopped to think that everyone who makes a policy decision about the war is somebody's husband? Frankly, I said, I hadn't. Well, they said, it's time the wives and women of this country did something about it. I didn't say what I felt about that. Look, they said, if opposing the war means opposing our husbands, we'll do it, in the home, in the streets, where-ever we have to. We *must* support one another in this, we *can* make changes in the world—they were getting very heated. Really, they were doing a good job. I wanted to write a check, to help, but they said . . ." She stopped peeling. "They needed . . . me." She gazed at the wall, her lips moving. Then she briskly shook her head, and scraped. "If it isn't a massive demonstration, no one will listen. Nothing will change."

"So how did you leave it?"

"The way I leave everything." Bending, she picked out a pot from the cupboard. "I thanked them and told them I'd think about it. Which I will, right here. Right through their marching in the streets without me." The faucet gushed. "No matter what they say, they don't have to live in this house, with him."

"But they have to live in their own houses, with their own husbands—maybe it's not that different."

Using both hands, she lifted the heavy pot and set it on the stove to boil. "I've never believed in confrontation; it's a little late in the day for me now. Perhaps that's a poor excuse, but it's the only one I have. There's been too much destruction in this family because of that war—I can't face any more. I won't risk it."

"Well, it's a good thing some people aren't afraid to put their bodies on the line."

"I don't hear you offering to march in my place."

"I'm not a mother!"

"You're a woman. I believe that's what you were indicating earlier."

She bowed her head, watched her finger create patterns on the tablecloth. Alex had been the activist—she had left all that to her, let her do enough for two. What was *her* excuse? A sad one, selfishness. "People whose own problems aren't sorted out don't have any business tackling the world's. They ought to get their life in order first, don't you think?"

"As you get older, Irena, you'll realize your life never quite manages to be ordered as you would like it. Which doesn't leave much time for the world." She began dropping chunks of potato into the boiling water. "It would be nice if we

151

could accept that without feeling guilty. Just live with what little we can do, and not burden ourselves with what we can't."

"Those women today—they might do a lot, together."

"Pah. The president of this country isn't going to listen to them any more than your uncle does to me. Maybe they'll feel better for having tried, but that's all."

Checking her aunt's profile, she had an odd sense of unfamiliarity. "I never saw you as a pessimist. A fatalist, yes, but not a pessimist."

"What have I got to be optimistic about? You were my last hope, and look at us."

"Aunt Eunice, I won't take the responsibility for that—you can't live your life through me, it isn't possible—it isn't fair."

She turned, empty-handed. "Is that what you think I want to do? Did I ever say such a thing? May the Lord forgive me if I did." Her body seemed to shrink as her eyes traveled from item to item in the room, up the walls, to a corner of the ceiling. "I'm tired, Irena. Tired beyond belief. The last thing I want . . ." Her hands weighed the air. They fell to her sides. She tried to force a smile, but her mouth, a bitter curve, refused. "Live *your* life, when I can barely get through my own?"

Averting her face, Irena touched napkins, plates, the silverware. This wasn't a confessional; she didn't want to hear it.

Once again, her aunt is requesting. Look at me, my domain is hollow. Give me some reason for being. Lift your eyes and realize I am more than a shadow. Why is it so hard for you? See me, Irena; make me real. Be glad that I am alive; let me for once in my life rejoice. Reach for me. Show me. Say, I understand. I see you. I know you, you are a person like I am.

She wished her aunt would move, do something; not just stand there mutely exerting pressure.

The front door opened. Uncle voices, their heavy male tread. Back bent, Aunt Eunice returned to her post at the stove, then snapped into action. Heavy with guilt, surreptitiously watching, Irena knew the vibrations of men in the house had reprieved her.

It was part of the human condition—being guilty meant being alive and only death brought escape. It would be egocentric to think the hounds singled her out while letting others get away. Even her uncle—all she did was constantly remind him of what was on his trail. Inevitably, people were hunted down, driven to earth for their misdeeds. Hunted or haunted.

Universality wasn't very comforting, though. It wasn't even true—at work she was struck by an exception so glaring it hurt.

John was free. At large, doing whatever he pleased without remorse. Ignoring her—it stung in public, it would have been sufficient. But it wasn't enough for John. He was being reprehensible, and she was the one paying for it. At least Billy Haynes had the decency to glance at her now and then. Not that he would have stopped anything; obviously he loved being blatantly seduced. The rest of the staff saw what was going on, too. But they were at liberty to smirk or look quizzical or shrug it off—they weren't being tormented, they didn't have to be impassive. She thanked God Maggie Leland wasn't there with her knowing eyes; it was the only mercy shown her.

Unable to manage nonchalance, she had to settle for phony composure and get through the morning pretending to be immersed in site data. When lunchtime came, John and Billy disappeared. She didn't want to think about where they had gone or what they were doing. Nor could she face a convivial half-hour break. The lab empty, she brought a cup of coffee back to her desk, and opened another register, trying for real absorption.

153

Men didn't need much time or space. She peered at an illegible figure. They could do it almost anywhere, standing up even. Deciphering, she copied a long column. They didn't have to bother with diaphragms and foreplay, or moods. Three numbers had to be erased and entered again. Everything out front—no guessing, no leaving each other stranded, not knowing if . . .

"What are you doing here?" Maggie Leland paused with her hand on the door; it swung shut as she walked to the drafting table. "Everyone's having a giggle in the lunchroom."

"I . . . needed to catch up."

Leland searched through the pottery diagrams, all her attention going to them. Irena wanted some—no, she didn't. She had to *work*. Too aware of the woman's presence, of being alone in the room with her; the silence, so noticeable it hummed. Prickles of heat stabbed at her skin; could Leland sense she was blushing? She swallowed; the noise seemed inordinate. She moved; her chair creaked. Cautiously, she turned a journal page and winced at the awful ripping sound it made. Her cheeks felt even hotter as she scanned the headings.

There had to be a mistake; she started to cross-check, panic mounting. Back and forth she flipped, not wanting to believe. How could she have been that careless, that stupid? All morning long she had been transferring the wrong figures— entries for an entire level had been misnumbered, it would take days to get it right. Days! "Oh God." Her face went rigid and tears fell out before she could stop them. She wasn't good for anything! She was an idiot, sobbing like an idiot.

"I knew the job was tedious, but to be bored to *tears*." A box of Kleenex thunked onto the desk. Standing close—she could feel her there. "If this has to do with work, Irena, it can't be that bad. What's the problem?" Shielded by tissues, she shoved the journals forward. Pages were turned rapidly, then carefully as Maggie Leland sat on the edge of the desk, and discovered stupidity. "Well, it's not a royal fuck-up. Paste in some overlays with the correct figures and you won't have to recopy the whole thing." She hadn't thought of that; of course not, it was too smart. Everyone knew how to handle things but her. "Okay," the registers were pushed aside, "it's not just work." Underneath, a quiet offer to listen. But not to comfort, to rub her neck or . . . hold her in her arms and . . . tell her, give her . . . Instead she stood, put *more* space between them. "Would you rather be alone? If so, you can leave the lab to the rest of us and use my office. Here's the key," held so Irena could see it, glinting between her fingers. "Take it, the others will be back from lunch soon." More than the key, the hand that held it; how take the object and not . . . her fingers trembled against the woman's. Forcefully Maggie Leland took her hand, pressed the key in her palm, and wrapped Irena's fist around it under her own hand—but it didn't stay—it withdrew completely. "Go." Desperate, she looked up.

Give me, her eyes, her face are pleading. Please. While the tears are streaming. Give me what you have.

The woman read her; she knew, acknowledgment was clear in her eyes. Dark, vivid, they stared straight into her. For seconds, a minute. Then, helpless, Irena had to watch them abandon her. Why? "Is there someone you'd like me to send down later?"

No! With a furious look she accuses, then runs, leaves the room, flees the one who refused her.

Hurrying down the corridor; impatiently attacking the lock; throwing wide the door and shoving it shut. She flung herself onto the small office couch. Leland knew! She had to. It was a slap in the face—total, absolute rejection. Why? What was so wrong with her?

She had done something to John, she didn't know what but she would, he had his reasons. When he was through making her pay they'd talk—John was approachable. But not Maggie Leland, oh no, she was the great bitch goddess who liked having people grovel in front of her. Who loved being adored so she could see people making fools of themselves before she turned them away. So superior, she never needed help, she never needed anyone.

Tears and revilement, yet she listens for sounds, hoping the door will open. On whom, her arch-betrayer? Wild ideas attack and retreat, chaotic notions of wanting a mother, seeking the teat.

"No!" She beat them away, pounding thoughts, approaching hysteria.

Fighting the rising tantrum, she strives to choke it back down, along with the concept of child. To get a grip on her self, gulping for air, and drag that self up. To breathe, to become Irena.

How long before she heard gasps, separate, controllable? The cushion under her face felt uncomfortably wet. She sat up, was wiping her eyes and chin when something . . . Her hands stilled on her lips. No wonder she had been told to go; have her breakdown someplace else. Maggie Leland didn't want dependency, drooling adoration. She wasn't anyone's mother, she hadn't chosen that link. Irena's behavior had probably disgusted her. It couldn't have attracted her. And she wanted it to. Because she did adore her. She did. She sat back. She more than adored her. Her hands dropped to her lap. She hiccoughed, smiling. It was a relief, admitting it. Finally. Without embellishment.

"John, you bastard."

Why wasn't he here? They could talk honestly now. John knew—underlying everything, he knew and he was her friend. That's what she needed, why she had been so hurt this morning. He had taken the friend away. Cut him out, left her. Not for Billy—he could have had Billy without inflicting loss. Instinctively he had known it was the loss that counted.

"You jerk, John, you didn't have to do that."

He was important in her life—it wasn't necessary to show her that as well as everything else, she knew how much he meant to her. But, did he? She was a specialist in insecurity;

she should have *seen*. John needed reassurance from her; he deserved it—without going through contortions like this morning's.

"Blind bitch."

She would still be totally in the dark if not for him. And her sexuality would be there with her; tamped down, repressed. He had released it. Freed so much, that it was flying everywhere, even toward a woman. No—not true. It had landed there. She might as well admit that, too. Why not admit it? Say it. Go ahead, say it.

"I want her," she whispered.

The sky does not fall. The earth does not open. God does not smite her. But her face is on fire, and the place between her thighs is pulsing.

She wanted Maggie Leland. In every way she could think of. No childish crush. No yearning for a mother—one person trying to fill that role was enough. Was it Alex, then? some kind of sister-fixation? Years ago . . . I'll be the man and you be the woman; I'm the doctor you do what I say. Kids' games, they didn't mean a thing. She remembered Alex calling the typing teacher a "dumb diesel," and her agreeing she belched like a train. She had hated that woman's touch. What was it about Maggie Leland? Who was it she wanted?

Earth mother sister friend lover self? She has never questioned wanting John, why must she question this?

It didn't matter who. She wanted *her*. To know *her*, be with her. *Be* with her. Sweet luxury, to be.

How does it feel? Kissing her mouth . . . caressing her breasts . . . pressing bodies, naked, together . . .

She shivered. Her stomach had cramped, she was discharging, and incredibly sad. It was hopeless. The woman wasn't interested in her. How could she be, when Irena had nothing to offer. Nothing to give that she could possibly need.

Maggie Leland, deity, resides in the empyrean, above the merely human. Yet Irena has seen her, time and again, immune to adoration. She must get love from somewhere.

Maybe her lovers are peers, not subjects. They walk the same earth—ground Irena touches. If she would let her down from the sky . . . Place her back in the lab, then imagine the scene that might have ensued—the risks that would have been taken—had the woman been confronted with comforting a *woman.*

What had she seen instead? A little girl crying her heart out. She slumped against the cushions. A kid letting emotions interfere with work. Immature, undisciplined, weak-willed . . . she'd never be able to undo that image. Even if she apologized and owned up to totally incorrect behavior, she couldn't . . . be hearing footsteps.

Bolting off the sofa, she smoothed her clothes, ran her fingers through her hair, grabbed wads of Kleenex. There was a soft knock and the door opened just as she found the wastebasket.

"Hi, Irena." Carolyn. "EmJay thought you might be needing this." She put Irena's purse on the couch. "She asked me to tell you to leave the key with the secretary."

"Oh. Thanks—I didn't know it was so late. That was some break I took." No sense in coming up with an excuse. "I guess . . . everybody's gone."

" 'Fraid so." They had avoided looking at each other directly. Both braved it now. "Irena, I don't want to butt in . . ." She was quickly given permission. "Then if it's any consolation, John's known for this sort of thing. I mean, he can't help it, that's the way he is. Basically an all-right guy too many people say yes to. He's as self-indulgent as the next person, but I don't think he wants to be cruel."

"I know. And there were reasons. I'm just embarrassed everything had to be so conspicuous—including my absence. It's not going to be easy tomorrow morning, showing up as if nothing had happened."

"Oh listen, don't worry about it. We were busy—EmJay seemed to be finding fault with everything, we didn't have time to gossip. The kids won't want to make an issue of it, why don't you let them and yourself off the hook and forget about that part?"

Because she wasn't good at forgetting. "I'll try. But even if I can't, thank you. You didn't have to, and it's nice." Someone cared; she felt better.

"I know what it's like—any voice in the wilderness, right?" Hoisting her shoulder bag higher, she smiled faintly, to herself. "We keep thinking no one's out there with us. It's hard, noticing friends where you don't expect them." She cocked her head in a small, self-deprecating gesture. "My wisdom for today." Raising a slender arm, "See you tomorrow," she turned to go.

She even moved like a dancer. "Bye." So vivid, Maggie Leland's hand on the base of that neck; she wondered what other advice Carolyn could have given her.

Putting her purse on the floor, she began smoothing the couch. Tomorrow, she would have to apologize, and try to erase an image. Tomorrow, she would work extra hours to make up for the lost time. She could drop by John's now to straighten things out with him, but Billy would probably be there. So, she'd have to do that tomorrow, too. A piece of bedraggled Kleenex lay wedged under a cushion. She tossed it; tomorrow would be hell.

Yet she feels anticipation exciting her. Locking the door; leaving the key. Her step grows buoyant; she waves, passing the gallery. It strikes her as odd, walking out, how the burnished bronze looked bereft, alone in the light.

Arms loose and eyes closed, she stood next to her bed, testing. She hadn't been ready for any of the day's punches. Why didn't she feel off-balance? All that shooting from one emotion to the next revelation—she wasn't reeling, or even tired.

The phone rang. Calmly going to answer it, she somehow felt sure the caller was John.

"Hi, do you want to talk?"

It wasn't the tension in his voice so much as his actually being on the line that made her suddenly want to sit down. "Yes, I do." Not waiting to take the phone to her room, she sank cross-legged to the carpet.

"Can you get out? come over?"

"It's pretty late. I don't know."

"What about my coming over there and picking you up? We could go for a walk."

"Ha, brave spirit. My uncle's home. He hasn't thrown anybody out of the house in at least two months—you'd be a prime candidate."

"So I'll put a brick in my purse. Half an hour."

He didn't hear her laugh. Shaking her head at the receiver in her hand, she put it back, then leaned against the wall. To match his courage, she would have to go downstairs and prepare the way.

They were in the living room, the happy couple, he stuffed into his chair, glaring at the tube; she sunk in hers, staring at a dreary portrayal of life in living color which was no less dreary but at least more colorful than her own.

"John's coming over and we're going out for a walk."

Her aunt darted a glance at her uncle who raised his head in disbelief. "At this hour?"

"It's only nine forty-five."

He had to be tired—his rage wasn't up yet. "Did I not forbid you to see him?"

"You can't forbid me to see him. I work with him every day, what's the difference if I see him at night?"

"Plenty! At night is a date. You cannot date him and I don't tell you that again."

"People aren't dating anymore. Anyway, this isn't a date. It's a conversation. Are you trying to dictate who I can talk to and who I can't?"

"People don't date anymore. Then what do they do? You think I believe just talk? That a boy and girl get together, at night, for *conversation*?"

"I hardly expect you to believe it, since you haven't talked to your own wife in thirty years, but yes. And neither Alex nor I think you have any right to set yourself up as the guardian of morality."

"Don't bring her into this!"

"Why not? She's listening. She's here. She sees you."

"Shut your mouth."

"Like Alex shut hers the last time you did your forbidding act?"

"Irena . . ." her aunt's hands wavered in the air, "please."

"Please what? Let him rule my life? Roll over and play dead because if he had his way I would be?"

"Irena!" It was pathetic, her shock.

"I've seen what his rule has done—so have you, but you want to forget. You want to go on pretending nothing has happened. Well, I can't. And I won't."

"Irena, I will tell you something." His voice was ominously subdued. "You don't like the way things are run here, you can leave. You eat my food, you sleep in my house, you run up bills every month for me and my checkbook to take care of. You don't do me any favors by staying here. You think you can take, and use, and then spit on me? The hell with you. You don't like it, say goodby."

"Constantine . . . Irena, he doesn't mean it."

"Yes, he does. And he's right. I *should* pay for room and board here, the next check I get I'll—"

"I don't need your money, I don't need your disrespect, and I don't need you to tell me I am right. To your aunt, you can start showing some consideration. Me, just leave alone. I pay for your keep, but I don't pay for the other. Not to you; not anymore. I'm through with your craziness; let that *xenos* deal with it. Go—get yourself and your problems out of my living room." He turned back to the television set; her aunt, distraught, looked from him to her wondering what to do; her hands fluttered and fell to her lap. She watched the screen as Irena retreated to the kitchen.

She cannot take much more of this. Alex tries to come in, but she shuts inner doors on her presence. Her chin sinks to her chest. She has to find *some* release from this psychic guerrilla warfare. Pressing her head, squeezing her eyes. She tries, but cannot seal her mind off.

I'm through with your craziness. Tell a shrink about me, Rena, and they'll really think you're crazy. A series of appointments would be beneficial. When they lock you up in a padded cell, you'll still be seeing *these*. Go, take your problems someplace else. Tell a shrink about your craziness, you're crazy . . .

Was she? She worked, held down a job alongside normal people. What kind of lunacy would allow her to function outside the house but not in it? Mistakes didn't mean madness—she could handle other relationships. She would prove it—tonight, with John. Tomorrow with . . . She had learned things today that would help her clear away the mess she'd made. She would take care of all the false impressions, handle every one of them, and prove she wasn't crazy.

The doorbell sounded. Grabbing her sweater and purse off the kitchen table, she rushed to answer it, to open the door but block John from the house.

He looked freshly scrubbed for the occasion. "Well?" A leather shoulder bag was raised for mock inspection. "I'm ready."

"How about if I spare us the encounter—would you mind?"

"Fine with me. Unless it'll make things worse for you when we get back."

"No, we already had our pleasant scene." She closed the door behind her and pecked his cheek. "Thanks for offering."

"Welcome." The living room curtains parted; he waved as they went down the steps. "Where'll we walk to?"

"Doesn't matter. There's a park about six blocks from here."

"Is it safe?"

"For two people ready to swing their purses? Sure."

162

Not touching each other, they struck a good pace, their togetherness slightly forced but promising.

"This is a nice neighborhood."

"Swell if you own two cars and go to the right church. Another aunt and uncle live in that house on the corner, but I rarely see them. Big feud."

"A common family trait."

"Yeah, I never have to apologize for anything, I can just chalk it up to genetics. Brown eyes, blind spots—not my responsibility, I was born that way."

"You too, huh? Hear it all the time." He lifted his chin and shuddered as if shaking back a long mane of hair. "Darling, I was born this way, the minute I saw those blue booties on my delicate feet I said, tacky tacky, whatever happened to tasteful pink?"

Amazed at the transformation in his voice and body, she had to laugh but felt uncertain with it.

"As opposed to . . ." swaggering, thumbs in his belt, "I don't kiss 'em, I just fuck 'em, I'm a guy," declared so gruffly it made her laugh harder and feel more unsettled.

"You're in a wild mood tonight."

"Not really." He slumped, a little further from her side. "Just acting out some confusion."

"It's been a weird day."

"Tell me. Think we can sort our way through this one?"

"I want to. Very much."

"Me too. I'm not sure we're aiming for the same thing, though. What do you see for us?"

She walked, looking down. "Being close."

"How close?"

It would have been nice but too soon to touch him. "Very close. Like loving friends are."

They came to a curb; crossing, he held his shoulder strap instead of her arm. "I hear the word 'friends' and I start to wonder. Do you think if people are just friends at heart they can turn each other on the way we have?"

"I don't know. Sex and friendship never came together in my life before—we were lucky, having both."

"Past tense I notice."

"Well, you made it pretty clear this morning you didn't want me as a lover or need me as a friend. The second part hurt—it doesn't have to go hand in hand."

"Are you saying friendship is all you want, then?"

"That's some 'all,' John. The person you took away was precious, and I'm not talking about Billy. The loss I felt had nothing to do with who you chose, but how. I missed *you*." He was silent; she peered at his face, saw the frown. "John? Doesn't that matter much more than jealousy?"

"It should. I'm not used to being a shit—it's thrown me. Everything's upside down, and for all I know I'm trying to land on the ceiling. I ought to be apologizing right now but—"

"Not unless you'll accept mine, too."

He stared at her, "For what?"

"Not showing you. Leaving you feeling insecure, not seeing."

"After the numbers I did on you? You're too much, Irena. Don't be so quick to take the blame—I was the one at fault."

"We both were."

"No." A smile, flashing, signaled desperation. "You going to rob me of absolution? Let a guy confess—I've been trying to for days."

He hadn't escaped the hounds; she had only imagined it. He had no idea how well she understood. His need for forgiveness was a priority now for both of them. He mustn't be rushed, though. Wanting to intone I absolve thee, she kept quiet, and waited.

His face was turned to the houses lining the other side of the street. "That time in bed, when you said you loved me?" It required no response. "I told myself, 'Well, the lady's just come, it's an involuntary reaction, it's gratitude, she doesn't mean it'—anything to keep from panicking. But I did anyway.

164

I was afraid you were getting too involved. So—it was a reflex, I didn't think. I just brutalized. To stop you. Which made me feel real good about myself." They entered the park, and still he kept his face averted. "I knew it was overkill. So much for gentle John. But the reason—it wasn't enough, something else had to've been frightening me. I circled around it a long time after you left—remember, I'm a coward. Eventually I got a hold on it." He nodded, as if acknowledging an unseen witness who could have told him all along. "My own neck. I was the one getting too involved. That's what had really panicked me. I was trying to stop myself, by debasing you." Shaking his head, he whispered, "Jesus."

"John . . ."

"Once I realized that," his voice surged to prevent hers, "I felt relieved—free almost. I got real excited about telling you and making everything just fine. I even worked out a neat scenario for the next day. I'd apologize, reveal all, and you'd fall into my arms, overjoyed at discovering your rapist-*manqué* was really Prince Charming in disguise. A Treat for Sleeping Beauty—how does that sound?"

She slipped her arm around his. "John, you don't have to . . ."

He pressed her hand against his side. "I was practically peeing when you agreed to take a nap—I'd get to act out the whole damn fantasy! But then, you woke up. And I felt . . . someone had gotten there ahead of me."

"What do you mean? I wasn't awake one minute before I seduced you—you can't possibly believe I was faking that!"

"No, it was real desire. But different—you were different. I needed to talk afterwards, be reassured it was really me you wanted, but all you had in mind was washing and getting home. So I acted like a kid and pouted, hoping Mommy wouldn't leave her little boy. The charming princelet."

That bit of sarcasm would have to wait. "Who did you think I wanted?"

"The great goddess, of course."

"Why?"

"I don't know, I can't pinpoint it . . . something about the way you took me. I was convinced you'd been dreaming about her and I got the benefit."

"That's not very flattering to either of us." Passing a dim pathway slanting off to the center of the park, they continued slowly on the circular one. "If you were right, how could I have done what I did? I mean, frontal assault—there's no way I could have been fantasizing or pretending you were a woman."

"I guess not. That's the trouble with love—people feel *very insecure* flip-flopping between the top of the world and the bottomless pit."

"Where were you this morning?"

"Level ground. Hitting back—evening the score."

"Does Billy know that?"

"Irena, Billy's been cruising me for months. He got what he wanted."

"So did you."

"Yeah, it was great. But it didn't work. I still love you."

The scored-upon could only laugh. "You mean your love for me is so strong it survived an afternoon's orgy with someone else?"

"I wish you minded, even a little."

"I mind a lot. How was I supposed to intuit all that? Instead of helping me to understand, you taught me a lesson—a harsh one, John. So we've each been callous and hurtful—can we call it quits now, and go back to loving?"

"Go back how? where? You haven't really said you love me, too."

"But I have! What do you think I've been doing since we left the house?" She thought she had been showing him so clearly. Saying it before had been simple—bed was the *easiest* place for emotional involvement. "John . . ." Tugging on his arm to make him bend his head, she kissed his jaw, his cheek; the springy coils of hair above his brow.

166

He clutched her waist briefly, then pulled away. Walked ahead, his dejection evident. "It's not the same—we don't feel the same way about each other. If we did, you'd care about what I did this afternoon, not just this morning."

She went a few yards before replying. "Maybe you're a better teacher than you realized, and I bought your theory."

"Good times and noninvolvement," he derided. "It's a shitty theory when the other person's applying it and you can't anymore."

"That's not the one I'm talking about."

He halted. His hands went to his hips; he sighed, his eyes shutting. He was berating himself and wanted it observed. "God, Kinsella." He looked at her. "So it really is Leland." She nodded. His mouth twisted and he turned to stare at the trees. "Serves me right." He crossed his arms, then looked at her again, from an angle, a sly half smile parting his lips. "Can I talk you out of it? I talked you into it." She shook her head. He lowered his, and butted his boot against a clump of grass.

"You didn't, you know. You just saw it a long time before I did."

"Terrific. I had to open my mouth."

"I'm grateful, John. There's so much you've set off in me."

"Neat. I always wanted to be a catalyst. Got it confused with catamite, I guess."

She wouldn't let him reduce any part of it. "Someone must have helped you see yourself once. Wasn't that a special time and person for you, too?"

He shrugged, dismissing a comparison, refusing to be consoled.

"We can still be together—we can be even closer. We just . . . can't be like we were."

"Right. Wouldn't want any incest, would we? Two sisters, bumping—"

"Don't." She had to push her back, eyes and image—it made her dizzy.

"Well, I'm not ready to be your brother, Irena."

"I don't want that." Not in pieces, not cold forever; she couldn't bear it.

"No, you just want a nice little faggot friend who can hold your hand and listen to your love life. Or am I supposed to coach you, too? 'Go on out there and do it, honey!' Don't mind me standing here on the sidelines like a stage mother crying joyfully into my hanky."

"Stop it, John." She was shaking, trying to deal with it and failing.

His hands flew up. "Lawsy, Miz Scarlett," falsettoing, "I don't know nuthin' 'bout birthin' no butches." He skipped to the side and batted his eyelashes. "Why, John, ahm not one of *theyem*, am ah?" Rigid, pressing his chin against his chest, "You are," he intoned, "what you *eat*. Think about it."

"I don't understand why you're doing this!" Her legs had no strength, she couldn't get away.

"The lady," he announced in a phony radio voice, "wants to know why I am doing it. The lady," he paused, and coldly aimed his eyes at her. "Can go fuck herself," he said quietly. "It'll be good practice."

"*Why* was it all right coming from you, but now that I've admitted it it's horrible?" Anger was cramping her so she couldn't stand.

"Do you think it's horrible?"

"Oh, for God's sake, John!" She was thrusting an arm around, searching for support.

"What do you want from me? How do you want me to be? You think jilted lovers do cartwheels and become instant friends? All right, *friend*—go after her. Go ahead, and good luck! Leland isn't available to you or anyone else who works for her, otherwise she'd have taken Ginny—*Ginny* is a very sexy lady."

Feeling the rough bark of a tree behind her, falling against it, she scrapes her palm. Welcomes pain that is brief. Only physical. Which is it? her left? stinging in several places?

Yes, her left. It must be bleeding. She imagines scratches will mark it tomorrow. It will have tightened by then, be stiff; but she will bathe it, and treat it gently.

"*Shit.*" From a distance. "Irena, I'm sorry." Nearer. "That was the lowest blow of all."

"It doesn't hurt now." Throbbing a little, probably beading, turning into tiny strings of bloodred beads.

"Then you must be some kind of Amazon, I—"

"Why did you say that?" She stared at the face too close to her. "Take it back! I don't want you to say that."

"But it was a *compliment.*"

"No it wasn't!" Why not? Didn't she want to be like Alex? wasn't that what she wanted?

"Okay, I take it back, I'm sorry. I wish I could take it all back. Irena . . ."

At his touch on her shoulder, she moved away from the tree, "I'm going home," sidestepping past him. As fast as she could. No one could get her there. The wounds were old and well known—no fresh damage was possible.

She heard him coming up behind her on the trail. Padding alongside. "Irena, it was you or me."

"I wasn't threatening you."

"You were from my point of view. I can't let your needs take me over—I can't stand *lovingly* by and watch someone else get you—it's self-destructive. I'm not a martyr, Irena. I'm a survivor. I went against every instinct I had, opening up to you. It's dangerous being that vulnerable—I had damn good reasons for my policies and I should've stuck to them."

"Yes, you should have. You were much nicer when you were charming the pants off people. *I* didn't ask you to stop being the golden boy."

"The role doesn't age well—I can't go on playing it forever. Maybe I saw the chance to step out of it, with you."

"I wouldn't worry, John. You displayed a very impressive repertoire tonight."

"Yeah, well, there's safety in numbers."

Unwilling to respond to that, she left the park, keeping up her pace, wanting to get the remaining blocks over with as soon as possible. He must have felt the same thing; their breathing, their shoes hitting cement, were the only sounds between them until they reached her corner.

"About work," he said, slowing their progress. "Don't expect anything from me. If you do you might get hurt again, and then it'll be your fault, not mine." No more fault; she was sick to death of being responsible, forced into determining blame. "Just protect yourself, that's all I'm saying. Any way you have to."

"I'm supposed to pretend you're not there, is that it? John Kinsella doesn't exist."

"Whatever works for you, do it. Things'll ease off in a while."

They came to her drive; he stopped at the foot of it.

"What're you going to do in the meantime, John? inflict more of your *numbers* on me?"

"No." Shoving his hands in his back pockets, he squinted down the street. "Whatever I do, it won't concern you—I don't like not liking myself."

"So you don't want anything to do with me."

"I can't have what I want, and half of it, just that without the rest, seems grotesque right now." He faced her; under the lamplight, she could see his eyes filming, but it was too late. "I'm sorry."

"So am I." She couldn't react to another fluctuation; she was out of responses. Unable to give him anything, barred from receiving anything from him, she turned and went up the drive. The moment her key entered the lock, he walked away.

Leaving her with no one. Abandoned again; no lover, no friend. Not even her uncle waits up inside; the enemy has retired, taking his wife. Only a lone hall light greets her. Even Alex, aware of her betrayal, is silent. No comment, no words of abuse or I told you so, no fervent reminders.

She refuses to come when Irena summons her fighting spirit, then pleads for it, needing to arm herself for tomorrow. Brushing, undressing, climbing in bed, all she can hear is an echo, a taunting male voice saying Leland is not available. She punches her pillow; she must find a way, there is nothing, no connecting without her. Thrashing between the sheets, she searches for strength, for sleep.

The night offers no rest. Strange fitful dreams beset her. Shadowy scenes, a stifling interior, a lamenting female figure who beats her fists on soft throbbing walls; creating a fissure, she tries to squeeze through unaided, to the help outside embodied in light that beckons yet stays at a distance; crying, the figure increases her efforts, yearning for light though it hurts her, pushing to reach what thwarts her, bleeding and blinded by shimmering rays, unable to see whose hand it is, the person who could be releasing her.

No mistake. No imagining. Maggie Leland *was* avoiding her. Maybe she didn't want to embarrass Irena over yesterday. Or maybe she herself was embarrassed—she could sense an intense need to talk and was steering clear, never even looking in Irena's direction. Either way, it let her watch without being observed, her heart thudding so strongly she peered once at the veins on her inner wrist and expected to see her pulse, the narrow blue branches pumping.

Everything in her was beating triple time, yet the hours were crawling by. At two thirty, the others would leave; if two thirty ever came, she would get her chance. The one that had to count and would, provided she could wait, sit still. Survive.

How can Leland divine her plan and disappear before two thirty? Must Irena track her to an office, trail her through the corridors? She is not equipped to play huntress—she will only get herself caught. Better stay put, catch up on work —do what she was hired for. No one need know she is praying, promising anything if only . . . When everyone leaves, she tries willing her back. Useless. She has no control over people.

Through with pasting in overlays, making up for lost time and stupid errors, she sat back. The amphora across the room meant so much to Maggie Leland, it was the best thing to look upon in her absence. Shaped now nearly to the base, the funeral urn had proven a regal artifact. Black silhouettes of mourning women slowly marched across its belly, their postures of lament ritualized yet starkly eloquent as they transported a queen to her grave.

Pulled, she rose from her chair. Reverent hands, sheltering, had placed the urn deep underground, in a place kept secret for thousands of years. Approaching, she wondered if they'd really known, had the faith or foreknowledge that other loving hands would someday unearth . . . resurrect. Tentatively she reached out, and stroked the vase where it widened in a beautifully proportioned curve, like a woman's hip, swelling, beckoning one to touch. She closed her eyes, caressing.

"Am I intruding?"

Her fingernail gashed across wet plaster. Horrified, she gaped at the plaster of Paris under her nail—the ugly scar on the vase. "I've ruined it! My God, I . . ."

"Excuse me," moving her away and bending to survey the damage. "Better get me a palette knife." Her hand was already out, waiting for it. "Hurry please, it's drying." Mobilized, she ran to a counter cluttered with implements— which was the stylus, which the knife? Gathering them up in a cluster, she hurried back with the instruments and Leland yanked the palette knife from the bundle. The others clattered to the floor. Irena knelt, retrieving them while the urn was saved from disfigurement.

Rising, she watched her performing the restoration. They had spent all day building up that section to match the original ones surrounding it; the inner surface near the wire screen had dried, the wound wasn't too deep, but Leland had to be careful or the curvature would be off. She operated as if her fingers needed no command; agile, brown; compelling Irena to stare at them. "Okay." They rubbed bits of caked plaster from each other. "The rest can wait."

"But it looks perfect."

"It isn't. That plaster under your fingernail will have to be replaced before it's perfect again."

The guilty nail; she focused on it through a blur. "I'm sorry —it was so careless, I feel horrible."

"Don't. That sort of thing happens. We've all messed up a piece before."

"What if you hadn't been here to fix it?" Her body recoiled.

"What if I hadn't interrupted you? What if the sky falls on it tomorrow? It's a chancy world. Look at it this way, you've learned what a palette knife is."

She didn't dare raise her eyes to possible mockery. "You must . . . wish you hadn't hired me."

"Must I? Why?"

"The stupid mistakes I've been making." A jagged crack in the cork tiles, the tip of her shoe, tracing it. "That scene over the registers yesterday—I apologize. I shouldn't have let things get in the way of work. I . . . want to thank you for letting me use your office."

"It was empty. You've made up for the time today, so let's forget it. As for making mistakes—perfection is best left to the gods, who are themselves notorious for muffing it. Don't be unnecessarily hard on yourself. You're good, despite difficult circumstances."

"There's no excuse for emotions interfering." Her shoe— she scraped it back, kept it still. "A person should have will-power," shifting her gaze from the floor, up to the woman's hand.

It entered her lab coat pocket to draw out a pack of cigarets. "Indeed a person should. But sometimes there isn't

173

enough." Her nails, trimmed quarter-moons, circled the lighter. "It's not a crime, it's not even a weakness. Some things take too much from us, that's all. A person who realizes that, can seek help before having to scream for it."

Meaning that's what she had done; screamed for it. Wheeling around, she went to the counter and picked up one instrument after another.

The voice alone followed her. "Irena, do you have a friend —someone you can talk to?"

Sure. Alex, John. All her friends were dead or gone; the magnificent Leland certainly wouldn't offer.

"If not, there are counselors—the right one can . . ."

"You mean a psychiatrist, don't you?" Then she *was* crazy.

"Do you think you need one?"

She tensed, "Do you?" waited, facing a shelf of fragments, for the answer.

"I'm no judge. I know there've been times when I thought I needed one."

"You!" Turning, finding a focal point where the lab coat formed a vee across her neck. "But you're so together. On top of things." She ached at her laugh, watching her throat move with the sound.

"I must have a good twenty years on you. I ought to have learned something from them."

"Did you? Go to a psychiatrist, I mean."

"No. Things happened. People, opportunities—no one's luck stays the same, the trick is to be receptive to its changing."

Afraid of showing too much, she went back to the instruments, touched each one searching for a charm, a way to keep her there. "How old were you, when things . . . started happening?" Perhaps the wood-handled tool with a metal loop on the end of it was the lucky one; she picked it up.

"About your age. I stopped letting the world make me feel guilty, and decided I had a life to live. Just that alone seemed to open things up for me—the decision itself freed a kind of force. Which sounds magical, I know. But you'll find it. You don't know what you're capable of yet; what you can do; what your powers are."

She was gripping the tool so hard her palm hurt. She couldn't hold it in any longer. "How do I find it?" She had to look at her—had to. *Now.* "What if I need a witch to show me?" saying it right to her. "What if . . . I know who she is, but she won't? She has rules, she won't get involved?" She had dared to do it and energy was pouring through her— she was challenging, meeting those eyes full on.

They shifted away from her. "There'll be others."

"No there won't, not for me." She would make her look up; had so much strength she could make her do it.

"Of course there will," hiding, lighting another cigaret.

"But I want this one."

The woman's hand descended with the lighter; her head came up. Her eyes held Irena's, then entered to grip her heart and send it coiling through her groin. But very slowly, almost imperceptibly, the head was shaking, no.

She couldn't—she didn't mean it. "Why not? Just tell me why, give me a reason."

"I don't have to. Look elsewhere, Irena." Moving, trying to break the spell, she went to a desk and stubbed out her cigaret.

It didn't work. "You're afraid, aren't you?" Amazing.

"If you like." She crossed to her worktable. Started filling her briefcase with papers.

"No, I have a right to know." She walked halfway to her. "I'm entitled to honesty. You of all people can't deny that."

"Why me of all people? Get me off that pedestal. I don't belong there and I detest it."

"So you're not responsible for being put there even when you see it happening."

"I'm responsible for my own actions." She snapped the briefcase shut. "And I've never done a thing to encourage you." She was leaving, heading past her to the door.

"Wait a minute." She actually did—dizzying surge, she could say anything. "How come you touch everyone in this room but me? Why does everyone know the feel of your hands on them but me?"

"That kind of logic is, if you'll forgive me, perverse."

"Then why am I standing here when I ought to be running away humiliated? What signals was I getting without realizing before?" She went even nearer. "I'm not imagining— why did you send them if you don't have the courage to act on them?"

Leland glanced away, anger showing around her mouth.

Anger couldn't stop her. "I saw your eyes. Eyes don't lie."

"Listen to me. I do not seduce young women anymore than I hang around school yards offering candy to anything in pigtails."

"I'm not a child. And it wouldn't be seduction."

"Irena, I cannot . . . give you . . . what you need."

"What about you? Don't you have needs?"

"Yes! There," pointing toward the vase, "is the love of my life. You cannot compete."

She looked at the amphora, hoping her anger had peaked, not knowing how to break its momentum. "I guess you're right, that's pretty sophisticated taste. I mean, a funeral urn —I wouldn't even know how to get one interested in me, let alone . . ." She shrugged, turning back to her.

Leland arched her fingers over her brow; she couldn't suppress a small smile. "I've never seen you like this—what on earth has gotten into you?"

"You have."

"Lord." She stood there, one hand holding the briefcase against her hip, the other rubbing her forehead. "How do I . . . Look, I'm not comfortable playing the part of older woman. I've no desire to be sage or mother or tutor or anything else. You are too young, you want too much, the intensities of youth are too consuming."

"So only lukewarm middle-agers have a chance with you,

176

right?" She tried to inject a tone of ennui into her voice. "Oh, an arm is all I want, thank you. A toe? Well, I don't know, maybe later, after I apply for social security."

She was openly grinning now. "Will you *stop?*"

"Will you touch me?"

The sharp intake of air thrills her. She closes her eyes, knowing. It comes—the caress. Firm fingers, on her cheek. Sliding to her hair, going through, their pressure increasing. The back of her neck—oh bliss! If this were all, she would settle for it, just please let it last forever.

They couldn't be gone. Her eyes flashed open. She was yards from her, "That shouldn't have happened," grimly speaking from the doorway. "Tomorrow, I'm leaving to meet with more money men. I'll be away a week, and when I get back . . ." Her face already relayed the message. "I want you either to have talked yourself out of it . . ."

"Or?"

"You won't be happy continuing to work on this project."

"You're telling me to find another job."

"It's up to you."

"The clerk *did* romanticize, and now she's a threat."

"To my work, possibly." Turning—the briefcase, she must have held on to it even while . . .

"The high-powered executive, attaché case and all. So busy wheeling and dealing he hasn't got time for love. It doesn't matter to him anyway—women are second-place, they're not important. They just drain his energy and make foolish demands. Good luck, *Doctor* Leland—I'm sure the money men will welcome you."

Her immobility was frightening; halfway out the door, she neither moved nor spoke. Then—no word, no glance—she disappeared. And Irena couldn't take it back.

That was it, forever. That was how she had handled—what she had proved. She had gone too far. Lost everything.

Facing an empty doorway, she tries to comprehend.

How could she have lost everything?

Nothing breaks through. Nothing in buzzing space, once called a mind.

It couldn't have happened, and if it had, then not to her. Not to Irena, rubbing her stiff left hand. She wasn't lost and surrounded by nothing; rubbing and wondering. It wasn't her looking down, blinking; seeing red marks on her palm, vague slashes, no pain. An end; nothing.

VII

LIKE A SNAKE, it weaves through the weeds of her sub-conscious, making its way toward rational thought. She senses it there, yet is unwilling to cut it off. Let them con-demn her for not summoning more strength. Too young to have none left—what do they know? How much loss can a person withstand? And why must she bother to try? Pointless to go on overcoming each day, as if anyone saw or cared. Everyone she loved has proven to her her existence has no meaning. Every last soul who meant something to her has shown her she does not matter. Futile to think she will. Not in the barren world she alone inhabits. The landscape blasted of hope. Unending desolation—no one can alter it. No one but she can kill that view.

"What's the matter, dear?"
"Nothing."

"Is something wrong with the food?"

"No."

"I thought you liked lamb done this way."

"It's fine, I'm just not hungry."

"Well, try to eat some anyway—it's a waste if you don't, this recipe doesn't stand reheating."

Irena pokes at the food on her plate.

"Irena, don't play with it."

"Sorry."

She manages a forkful. The piece gets stuck, forms a lump in her throat, refuses to go down.

"Try water—here, sip slowly. There, better now?"

"Yes, thanks."

No matter that the lump has swollen. Her throat is blocked and aching. Her eyes have started tearing. She insists that she is eating.

"Jesus God! How can a man eat in this house with that snuffling going on? Leave the table, Irena."

Pushing back her chair, she obeys.

"I'll bring a plate up to you later, dear!"

"Stop humoring her, Eunice."

"But for days—like before, I'm afraid it will be like before."

She could have told them this is different from then, when vigorous shock took over. She was shattered before; the cracks zigzagged through, and pain-racked nerves were exposed. There is violence in pain; force. The body fights back; the mind struggles to save what it can. But despair has no vigor. It lies like a blanket, and under its weight, life has no light or air. When it becomes too heavy to lift, the dead-prone soul succumbs. Resistance is out of the question; the choice is to suffocate slowly, or accede to a quicker end.

Stripped of spirit and not missing it, Irena calmly locked her bathroom door. She turned on the faucets. Watched the hot water pouring into the tub, the steam rising. Serenity was in that vapor; it seeped through her pores, cleansing; she felt peaceful inside. A fresh packet of razor blades had been waiting for her. Carefully she unwrapped one. She had read somewhere that the pain was hardly noticeable if the water was steaming hot. She stepped out of her clothes; not even shivering. By stages she lowered herself into the bath. So hot; her skin was the color of watered-down blood. A water-color wash of red, not like ink this time, streaking blue from a letter, but real, it would be real red on her hands. Her own; she was willing. Closing her eyes, resting her head on the rim, she allowed herself a long, luxurious moment. Then, she slid the blade off the porcelain; sank her left wrist under . . .

Do you know what you're doing?

I'm coming to join you, Alex.

Like hell—I won't let you quit.

You can't stop me.

I can. All you want is revenge.

You're wrong, this has nothing to do with vengeance. I just want to end it.

Bull. Don't lie to me, Rena. You want to make her sorry. You can't hide it from *me*. You want those goddess eyes to brim over. Your idol's not made of rock. Don't lie—I've noticed.

That isn't true—I'm tired, that's all, I can't anymore. I can't finish what you started.

You and your half-baked attempts. I bet you botch this one. I can just see the mess, you gagging and having to clean it up later. Listen to me. I know what you want and I've got a grand idea.

It's too late for advice—I've already made my decision.

You want to walk around with scars on your wrists so everyone'll know you're an ass? Listen. Instead you stay in the lab, and when everyone's gone—God, this is great—you pick up the urn, the love of her life, and—are you ready for this? Rena, you *smash* it.

Alex!

She'll never get over it. Guaranteed.

181

But the urn—I couldn't, I'd feel like a murderer!

It won't kill her to dig up another.

That's not what I mean.

The urn's just a thing—it's not alive, you are.

It *is*, in a way.

You're such a romantic. Take charge of your life and fight for a change. Don't follow me here—zero in on your target.

I am. Soon I'll be just like you are forever.

God but you're dumb—you can't imitate me. You're missing my flair for tactics. You don't have the edge, the fire I had, my all-consuming purpose. How many times must I tell you? Stop being afraid, and start being your own person.

How can I, with you dictating my every move?

You sure make it easy. You're not much of a match. No wonder I never respected you.

I don't care about that anymore. I don't care about anything.

Not even the feel of her hand on your face?

Ah don't.

The way her fingers caressed you?

Don't, Alex, please.

The touch of her hand—you said, "last forever," remember?

It didn't.

Too bad. What do you think you'll feel in the grave? The slash of that razor blade on your wrist, that's what you'll feel forever.

Don't! It's not supposed to hurt.

Reenah, the water's already gotten lukewarm. What're you going to do, refill the tub and start the whole thing all over? Jesus, that'll look stupid. Get out; dry yourself off; my plan's a beauty.

No.

Rena, the touch of her hand—remember? It's not the only hand in the world.

For me it is.

Then goddammit go after it!

I tried and she turned me down.

Christ, what impressive perseverance. I guess you don't really want her.

But I do!

Obviously you're not in love with her.

But I am!

Then what do you think you're doing? Is she some kind of necrophiliac? can you see her kissing your corpse? Rena, look at your body. Imagine hers—the pleasure. I never wanted like that in my life; I'd even lost the hope.

There's none for me now, either.

You've got more chances. Do you realize what I'd give for those?

Nothing. You didn't care when you had your own.

How dare you claim to know me! You're not fit to come here—you haven't earned it at all. You're not supporting a superior principle, you're still horning in on my act.

Once you're dead, Alex, one reason's as good as another.

Then go ahead kill yourself—see if I give a damn. Take that razor and shove it, you coward—asshole, shit! Go ahead do it! All because of some woman, you can—

Alex, didn't you do it over a man?

Shut up! You have no right to judge me—who do you think you are?

Not my uncle's daughter—only you qualified for that.

You'll never be what I was! Not in a thousand years! You're belittling what I stood for—you can't undermine my past! I had reason—logic—behind me, not soppy schoolgirl emotion! You're not acting in protest! You're not holding out to the end! I had a higher purpose! I was fighting a war! I . . .

I aye eye. Blustering sounded so funny. He he hee. She and Alex were hysterical, hollering and hooting like idiot sisters. Breast-beating! wrist-slashing! "Here she is boys, here she is world!" cackling and flinging drops of bathwater. One more overkill kid! Struggling to rise for a bow, she lifted herself, slid back; lifted and bowed into crawling over the rim. Bent double, she clutched at a towel. Stumbled patting idiotic pieces of her, hitting the wall whenever the convulsions became too much.

Even when she was dry, and in bed, the weepy laughter spurted out of her. Her gut ached; her sinuses pounded. Her arms flopped on the sheet. She had botched this one, all right; instead of blood now, she had life on her hands.

The back of her head. Down to her neck. Along the line of her chin. Retracing the path, her hand has her body remembering. Chills. A plummeting stomach, sweet surging through the limbs. Irena faces her image. Maggie Leland is returning today. Like it or not, this woman will be there, working.

Five minutes later she was skipping down the stairs. From one moment to the next she couldn't sustain being womanly, whatever that meant. She thought about going back up and slinkily descending, theme music playing while she smoldered with sensuality, the promise of passion in her animal grace.

"What's so funny?"

The only way she could share it was to give her aunt a bear-hug goodby, leaving her in shock. Poor Aunt Eunice; she still hadn't gotten over the huge breakfast Irena had eaten. Maybe she was bouncing too high from despair, but being a little manic was a nice kind of craziness compared with the other.

At the lab everyone seemed affected by the knowledge Leland was in the building. Irena hadn't been the only lethargic one during the week; now the staff couldn't speak without teasing, their voices lighthearted additions to the sounds of work. A good, invigorating tension—whenever she glanced up, she met someone, like her, wanting to smile. Even John forgot himself and grinned at her once.

By the end of their shift she hadn't made an appearance, so they hung a purple bow around the neck of the completed amphora and trooped out, pleased with how pleased she'd be. Irena decided to leave the museum by a side exit. It meant passing her office. She had no expectations or plans for confrontation. Today she had simply gotten up and gone to work, excited but not desperate, not driven to apologize or pursue. It was a victory of sorts; no strategies distorting things this time, no threatening tactics or risk of loss. If she could just maintain it, not ruin it by having to talk about it, Leland might feel easier about her. Chalk up last week's encounter to temporary insanity. Diet deficiency, the full moon. Sunspots.

She hadn't let herself hope the office door would be open. But it was and Leland was sitting at her desk, a hand shielding her eyes. Before the impulse could be squelched she had knocked on the jamb.

"Yes." The voice was flat.

"I'm sorry to interr . . ." The head lifted. Her face was shocking—haggard. Irena would never have believed Maggie Leland could be drained of vitality. "You look *exhausted*—didn't everything go okay?"

"I am. And it didn't."

She took a step into the room, wasn't stopped. "What happened?"

The woman tried to rub away some of her weariness. "What I should have anticipated but wasn't ready for." Her hands slid to her temples and stayed.

"Can I do anything? Get you some coffee?"

Her eyes closed in denial, then opened to stare vacantly. If she wanted to be alone, wouldn't she tell Irena to go? Looking that beaten—maybe she didn't have the energy to dismiss her. It probably didn't matter whether she was there or not.

In the corridor a faint noise was swelling into the voices, laughter, and clatter of an afternoon art class. Questioning, Irena read assent in the slight movement of her head. She shut out the racket but not herself. Prepared to leave when asked, she perched on an arm of the sofa. Her presence seemed to be accepted. She wished she knew of a way to help. "Do you think . . . if you told me what you weren't ready for, I'd understand?"

"It's not difficult to understand. Unfortunately, it's all too simple." A quick, bitter smile, and she dropped her hands to the desk. "They're perfectly willing to fund my project. Generously. Provided Robert Marcotte's put in charge of it."

"Who's he?"

"An eminently respectable, thoroughly incompetent old man who does not know a dig from a doughnut. But, man is the definitive word so that hardly matters. More than his prestigious name, and his affiliation with a prestigious university, it's Dr. Marcotte's prestigious genitals that equip him for the job."

"You mean they won't fund it unless a man takes over?"

Affirming the absurd truth, she nodded slowly.

"But why?"

"Why." Her laugh was humorless and did nothing to ease her. "The usual. A woman can't *master* money and men. Even if they admire *her* budget, consider the working crew— the common laborer just doesn't have the proper respect for a female boss. Even if she's proven they have, there's the question of international cooperation among professionals— the men's club where so much can be settled informally. Even if . . . and so forth. What it comes down to is, I do not urinate standing up."

"But how could those men, after meeting you, possibly pretend who you are and what you've done doesn't matter?"

"They weren't pretending."

"But it's your find—your discovery. You're entitled to it!"

"Apparently not." She picked up a pencil, twirled the point against her thumb, let it fall. "Marcotte's made a career of coattailing. He's never done an original piece of research in his life. But I don't care if he's the greatest archaeologist since Schliemann, I'll be damned if they'll have it their way."

"What are you going to do?"

"I don't know yet. I don't know. God." Her hand moved unsteadily across her brow. "It never stops. I've had to be twice as good and I still . . . Damn!" She pushed away from the desk, swiveling her chair so that Irena couldn't see her struggle. "The thought of him poking around in there," she faltered. "Scraping and emptying, like some . . . senile gynecologist. That cave is mine, it's a part of me. I'm supposed to just . . . lie back, and submit." Her head drooped; so vulnerable, the bending neck. "Violated. By a gang of sanctimonious . . . They've done this to me and I don't know what to do with my rage, the degradation."

The instant Irena heard her choke she was moving, around the desk, behind her chair, reaching out. "They *can't degrade you*. You *haven't been degraded*." Her hands sheltered surprisingly narrow shoulders. "You haven't, you can't be." Squeezing, feeling flesh and bone, her fingers tried to be messengers of strength.

"Oh damn," barely audible, she grasped for them, held on. "I'm so tired, fighting everything." Her hands slid up to Irena's wrists, "Damn," and she sank back, letting Irena see.

"Please," her own eyes began blurring, stinging, "don't. Don't," she was kissing her hair, kneading her shoulders. "Please," murmuring into her neck, "don't, Maggie," thrilled by the name, tasting her skin. "Maggie." Dazed.

She bends round the upturned face. Salty lips, soft and

receptive. She wants to sink into her mouth yet expects to be rejected. Instead a hand cups her head and presses her even closer. In disbelief and gratitude, she enters.

It was happening, to her.

A slow withdrawal. Her hand trailed down the woman's arm as she moved to kneel in front of her. They were still there under her closed lids; touching the lashes, she winced and wiped the beads before they could drop. "Maggie?" Incredible still, her name. "Please don't think I was taking advantage."

They opened, glittering and almost black. She felt probed; unable to translate. Puzzled by their narrowing, as if from pain. But they were coming toward her.

There is no doubt in this kiss. Irena opens wider, wanting her deeper inside her, wanting all of her inside her. The woman responds, abandoning. Giving herself up, Irena is taken. Then released to the world in stages. She wants where she was and seeks it again. Immersed in her, the sensation is freedom.

She couldn't believe how free she was to lay her cheek on Maggie's knee, and clasp her thighs. She felt her hair being stroked; it was real, had to be stored, instantly memorized. Every moment. Why couldn't they last forever, starting as they died? Her face was caressed; bringing the palm to her mouth, she tongued the heart of it.

"God." The hand was taken away, not far, to her hair again. "I've got to get *some* work done today. My 'attaché case' is bulging."

Holding her wrist, she lifted her head to check. "Please, can't you erase that? It was ridiculous, you have to erase it."

"I don't think so. I hadn't realized I needed reminding, but you and those gentlemen certainly made it clear."

"No—you're a beautiful woman." How could she make her see what was there, miraculously, before her? "Beautiful," stroking the shadows under her eyes, too taken to implore further.

188

"And you," moving the fingers to her lips, "are a sweet beholder." She kissed them, then firmly put Irena's hand down. "Enough of this, sit over there. I have got to get a grip on things."

She nearly tripped getting to the chair she had been interviewed in. Maggie swiveled back to her desk, and pulled a thick stack of papers from her briefcase. Watching her sort through them brought back the first time she'd sat across from her. So different now, yet the attraction had started then. It had been there, hidden among the tensions of trying to land a job. Maybe Maggie had known.

"Are you nearly through collating the registers?" All business, she might have been looking at that same folder.

"Almost."

"Forgive the cliché, but how well can you type?"

"Very."

"Have you ever worked on charts or graphs?"

"A few, for term papers."

"Good, then you shouldn't have any problem transferring to another job."

It stopped her breathing.

"It'll mean leaving the lab. Changing your hours." Unaware the first blow had stunned, she kept on, "You'll have to, I'm afraid." Rummaging in the case, totally oblivious. "The pay'll be the same." Callously leafing through more papers. "Can you rearrange your schedule? Afternoons would be better." Pushing away a stack, drawing a single paper to her. "It's your decision. But let me know soon, all right?"

There was no reply she could make.

"Irena?" Finally. "What's wrong, what is it?" Was she blind? "Well *speak*."

She couldn't.

The final blow was her laughter. "O ye of little faith." She laughed again, but regretfully. "Ah me. It doesn't last long with you, does it." Her look seemed to confirm something serious. "Irena, the job you're on is almost finished. If you want to keep working, you can move into the typing end of it without startling the budget minders. There's a redecorated closet down the hall some people call an office. It's best if you work on the report when I'm freer, which means afternoons." A smile almost appeared. "They have a tradition of ending in evenings."

"Jesus." She hid her face. "When will I stop being such a fool?"

"Soon I hope."

"I'm always having to apologize for some stupidity."

"No, but you think you do." Her chair squeaked as she eased back. "It's hard, learning to recognize trust. I had my opportunity when you closed the door on that art class."

She raised her eyes from the desk legs. "Did you know what would happen?"

"No. Nothing would have, though, if I hadn't trusted my needs and what you would do with them."

She felt dizzy—like someone realizing she'd been spared a car crash by changing her route at the last minute. "Maggie, what if I hadn't walked by your office?"

"I wouldn't have looked for you, Irena. You had to sort out your side of it without interference. So did I. It's been an extraordinary week of confronting. I don't think I really knew I'd done the sorting until you came in . . ." she let the smile out, "and I stopped being so damned disciplined. Denial's good for the soul up to a point; after that, it starts to have a hollowing effect. Which sounds so much like halo, one risks mistaking the two." Her self-mockery ended; she was revealing what lay beneath. "Sainthood is not what I'm hungry for."

Slack-jawed and helpless to hide what that look was doing to her, she pressed down on the pulsing. Her body arched. "Maggie . . ." She swallowed, not able to talk either.

"Sorry."

She cut off the current, reached for her cigarets.

Relief for a moment, then *all* of it hit. "Maggie! What if

I'd agreed with you last week? I might have been gone by now, I might have . . ." Never known—committed—or listened to Alex and smashed it—been dead to this, either way. "What if you'd come back and I'd . . . I wasn't here?"

"I'd have closed myself up, and done what I could to heal without you."

"But I almost—it scares me to think I . . . where I'd be if I . . ." Destroyed—no chance of being saved. "Maggie, I . . ."

"Come here. Bring your chair around." She did, grateful to have the horror breaking; to be nearer. Maggie took her hands. "You're actually shaking. Irena, it doesn't do to bedevil yourself with 'what ifs.' I didn't know if you'd be here, but you were. And this happened. *This*," she pressed tightly. "This *is*. If you'd come to the office in almost any state but the one you were in, I couldn't have dealt with it. If you hadn't given, if I hadn't gone—doesn't it seem a waste of energy worrying about all the things that could have happened but didn't?"

She nodded, afraid she'd still bedevil herself, despite the waste.

"Then accept." Maggie let go of her hands. "And try to put some of that energy into trusting, or we'll cause each other unnecessary pain. I wasn't aware you were misinterpreting me—there'll be times when I won't be aware again, when my mind's thrumming. Not to mention everything else." She picked out her lighter from under the papers. "I thought you knew. Should I have said thank you?"

"Maggie, if John or Carolyn had dropped by instead of me, wouldn't you have talked to them?"

"Is that what we were doing?" She smiled. "I told you before, you don't know what your powers are. You saw the change in me—where did you think it came from?"

Her own smile leaps and pleasure rushes inside her.

That shadowed pain returned to Maggie's face. "You should do that more often." Leaning forward, raising a finger, she traced Irena's mouth. "So much beauty, waiting . . ." Her eyes went from feature to feature. "Let it out, Irena. I want to see it with you."

She has no experience with lover's fears—how they work at undermining. But she learns. She *does* deserve this. It can indeed be. Some fantasy or dream is *not* clouding her mind, obscuring the claws of reality. See? Insidious fears just need to be firmly told they are nonsense. Then for days and weeks one can go around beaming. Not even chanting I am awake, not sleeping, I am alive and not dreaming. Freedom wins, for the moment. The present is hers for the taking, and she accepts the gift almost as if she really were meant to have it. For a while at least. It is hard to keep the past and future from intruding. Especially when a person in love has Irena's history.

"Irena, no. You didn't."
She rubbed her lips against the soft fullness of Maggie's breast, "I did," and peeked up at the underside of her chin.
"Of all the . . ." Maggie slid away, got out of bed; put on her robe. She had first seen her in that white terry-cloth robe four weeks ago, yet the intimacy still moved her. Maggie was lighting a cigaret, striding back and forth, then out, to the kitchen for coffee. She was obviously angry with her now. But then . . .
She lay on her back and saw them coming into the apartment. Maggie making her a drink before going to shower. Leaving her, nervous, wandering. Eyeing stark white walls, the art collected. One after another, prints, oils, artifacts, all striking expressions of kind and acquirer. Then, the nude, the small pencil sketch signed Always, Carly. Irena's stomach turning over, that body possibly being Maggie's. Not knowing, wondering who was Carly. Telling herself not to be

stupid, she wasn't the first. But needing to retreat, to a table, the carved amber stone on top; picking it up as Maggie appeared in the doorway. In a white terry-cloth robe, her tanned skin framed and glowing against it. The stone clunking onto the table. A carpeted hallway, Maggie ahead, the striding gait she had never followed before.

Her bedroom. Robe a blur, then lamplight casting it yellow. Embarrassing clothes while Maggie unmade the bed. Shivering, forcing herself not to cover her breasts, wishing her body were the most glorious one in the world, closing her eyes in silence recounting its imperfections.

Sensing her nearer, her being mere inches away. "You're lovely." Hands, soft as the voice. Reality: those hands caressing her body. Looking. Seeing she had never been so wanted. And wanting, wanting to touch her, with the freedom to there, beneath her collar, and there, over her breasts, there, along her rib cage. Each touch pushing aside the robe. Then moving and knowing, their bodies naked together. "Maggie!" every part of them meeting, "I'm so happy." Lips on her neck, muffled "I want you to be." Being drawn down to the bed.

The first touch of her tongue—she had never—wanted it on and on but her tongue—she couldn't hold back, had to let go of, release the unbearable pleasure. Then more, surprising, Maggie staying and knowing, bringing more and more. Until she was clinging to her, thanking and kissing saying "thank you thank you" out of control, just kissing, crying, speaking. Then the taste of herself on her mouth, and she was frantic to give her pleasure, share where she had just been. Give anything to give, get her lost in identical pleasure. Mouth sliding down her belly. "You don't have to." "But I want to I want to," and doing it, what she wanted. Kissing her there as if there were lips, entering her secret mouth, wanting her to come, to feel the unbearable pleasure but afraid she would lose her not know what to do. "Right there," help exciting the desire to bless, "yes right there, like that . . . yes don't stop . . ." and she was coming to her. Irena was free to have her.

But now, she was angry. Striding, smoking, swallowing coffee.

"That was a heartless, totally selfish act. You realize that, don't you?"

She watched from the edge of the bed. "It seemed a good idea at the time."

"Good idea!" The cup and saucer rattled onto the bureau. "Don't play dumb with me, or yourself. Your life is all you have. It's all any of us has. If you ever try that again . . ." She paused in front of her. "I won't even mourn, Irena. I'll despise you for it."

"Maggie, don't. At least try to understand how I felt."

"No." Turning away, striding. "Self-pity and despair aren't unique. You are. You're the only Irena on earth for all times. How dare you even think of destroying her."

"She's not much. I mean, you make me feel like I am, but—"

"Stop it. I am not responsible for your sense of worth or your happiness. You are." She jabbed her cigaret into the ashtray.

"Why are you so angry with me? Look . . ." She held out her wrists. "Not a scratch."

Maggie looked from a distance, then came over. Her palms slid under Irena's wrists; her thumbs rubbed the veins. As she gazed at them her expression saddened. "If only these were as precious to you as they are to me." She raised them to her lips. "They have to be. You must make them be."

"Maggie." She threw her arms around her waist and buried her face in terry-cloth. "I love you so much."

Gently both hands touched her hair. "I know. But you don't love yourself enough, and I can't do that for you."

Hugging her with all the strength she had, wanting to

194

make her forget; she relaxed the pressure, and began pulling the robe open with her teeth.

"What are . . ."

But her mouth was already there and her hands were going down and up under the robe to bring her even closer.

Holding her later, she knew she would never mention the urn. Even in search of forgiveness, she wouldn't risk the abhorrence; or survive the loss.

Hands behind her head, she looked at the robe hanging from its customary hook on the back of the bedroom door. It pleased her, knowing the robe's place; the clock on the bedside table always on the second shelf; the pre-Columbian mask that had a tendency to tilt above the bureau. She guessed it was a form of possessiveness, loving this room and everything in it; loving the fact of knowing it.

"Maggie? Tell me about Carly."

"What do you want to know?"

"Were you lovers?"

"Yes."

"Is that you in the living room?"

"Mmhm."

"What happened?"

"Stretch marks come with age, I'm afraid."

Unclasping her hands, she lightly slapped the thigh beside her. "Come on, you know what I meant."

"She had a chance to study with one of the best lithographers in the country."

"Where is she now?"

"New Mexico, last I heard."

"How long ago was that?"

"When I heard or when she left?"

"Both."

"About four months and five years."

Sliding over, "I don't understand how anyone could leave you, for anything," she nestled against her shoulder.

Maggie opened her eyes, stared without blinking at the ceiling. "When the timing's right, and it's the right thing to do . . . you will."

It made her rise. "I will what?"

Maggie pressed her back. "Understand."

It threw her when the assurance wasn't there for her. Unreasonable to expect it constantly; still, she couldn't help feeling put out and hurt.

" . . . can't be happy about that," Maggie was saying. "Sharing the same house all these years, and never once bothering." She brought over the teapot. As she slid onto the kitchen chair opposite, her robe revealed the shadowed contour of a breast; lovely but not there for Irena right now either. "We often seek revelations from each other, yet she's been there your whole life and you don't ask her a question or give her a moment. Of your time; yourself. I find that very strange."

"But I love you! And you just said an hour ago you loved me."

"Don't you have any love for her?"

"I guess so—sure."

"Do you think she realizes that?"

"I don't know. Probably not."

"Yet you've told me she loves you. She must show that."

"In her limited way."

"Limited. By what? I'm curious, when you do deign to talk to her, what tone of voice do you use?"

"Oh . . . bored, impatient. Maybe condescending—but not all the time. Mostly I'm just . . . remote."

"I wonder what would happen if one day you were to talk to her as if she were real. As if who she is mattered to you."

"Be fair, Maggie! It takes two—I'm not *real* to her, I'm just another person in the house she can feed and cluck over."

"And she's someone you've dismissed without ever knowing. Doesn't that seem a waste to you?"

"I don't want to hear about recipes and church gossip! Jesus. Or how much she's suffered because of him and how awful he is—I know how awful he is. Next thing you'll be asking me to talk to *him*!"

"No. You can't help him out of his trap. It may be different with your aunt."

"Look, if she's trapped, she let it happen—she's never even tried to free herself."

"Why? Do you know? Can you tell me what it's like to be her?"

"I think so."

"From her perspective or yours?"

"Okay, okay. Point made, you can stop lecturing."

"Irena, I thought I was talking to one woman about another. I'm sorry to hear I was lecturing a brat."

It made her get up from the kitchen table and thump, barefoot, to the sink; wash out her cup. Tying her robe tighter, she left the room. Maggie made no attempt to keep her.

A blanket absorbed the tears. She wasn't trying to stifle them, only the sound of them. When they stopped flowing naturally, she forced out more, but none of them were the good kind that gave relief. The source was drying up completely, leaving her with no knowledge of what to do next.

Sitting upright, she massages her brow, and wonders what Maggie is doing. Cursing? The maternal pit was so easy to fall into. Inevitable, given the years between them. Is she berating herself for lashing out the moment she was seen there?

How can Irena go to her, stripped of her image as child? Overcome instantly, spring full-blown, appear as the woman she can be? No magician can help her . . . intuit what Maggie is thinking . . . then change the way she is seeing.

The direct line into her thoughts had been severed. Somehow she had to link in—not guess, *know*. She tried relaxing. Tried tensing. Tried willing herself inside. Her muscles ached; nothing seemed to be happening. She sagged. If she didn't simply go to her, by the time she got home she'd be torturing herself. Anxiety would keep her awake all night, she wouldn't be able to wait until tomorrow but would have to, only to suffer more because sorting it out at work would mean emotions interfering, which would make it worse. She was damned if she would make it worse.

Tying her robe even tighter, she padded out of the bedroom.

Maggie wasn't in the kitchen. She found her sitting in the dark, on the far end of the living room sofa, her profile dim against the moonlit drapes. She didn't move when Irena came up to her.

"Maggie, I want to know why it's all right for you to use my powers but not for me to use yours. You *are* older than I am, you *do* know more than I do. Why should either of us be threatened by that? I've got a lot to learn, but I am learning. Some day I may even catch up to you." She waited, then took a step nearer. Maggie blindly stretched out her hand. Taking it, she brought it inside her robe, guided it over her breasts, wanting to show her, make her know. "They're full, Maggie. They aren't a child's. Feel what you do to them." She circled the palm on her distended nipples, and exulted in the cessation of breath across from her. "Do you love me?"

The choking told her first. "Yes."

"Then will you please . . ." From pulling her up, she was suddenly pulled, Maggie's mouth bruising her, biting, swallowing her saying "Maggie, take me, I want you to take me."

She did, there on the living room carpet, her hand driving so hard Irena wrenched away from their kiss gasping.

Waking up, she was full of her. The moment her eyes opened, she caressed the sheet. Her own bed wasn't a lonely place this morning. She had her here, not just in reverie but physically, in the sensations still between her legs and up inside her; the tender areas on her body, her mouth; the smell of sex vague yet heavy. She smiled. She had succeeded in keeping her with her, carrying her right home and into bed, purposely not showering in order to have her here now.

She ran her hand over her hipbone. How did its shape and flesh feel to Maggie? Seeing hers, the beautiful curve with its flattened slope when she lay on her side, drawing her, marveling, mouth touching, the taste. Her body rebelled. She would have to stop this and get up, or stay and do something quelling. Her hand fell to the sheet. She got up; she was prepared to lose some reminders, but not override them.

Twenty minutes later, a well-loved woman disguised in jeans sauntered into the kitchen and tossed an innocent "Hi!" to her opposite in a flowered housedress.

"Irena, what's happened to your lip?"

She prodded the swelling, pretending to diagnose. "Cold coming on I think." She hoped Aunt Eunice wouldn't want her own examination.

"Have you taken two aspirin?"

"Not yet." The wall got her smile as she pulled out a chair.

"Here, I want you to drink your orange juice, the vitamin C will help." Irena accepted the glass without argument. "Well! I'm glad to see you being sensible."

She swallowed the last of the juice. "That was good, thank you."

"There's more!"

"No thanks, that was just right." It never failed. She buttered her toast. If she gave another inch, her aunt would try to take another mile; but this morning, she could afford it. "What are you doing today?"

"Me?" She turned from the refrigerator to stare at her in surprise. "The usual. Why?"

"Just curious," munching her toast. Drinking her coffee, "How's the bazaar coming along?"

"It was last week. We're meeting tomorrow to discuss what to do with the money."

"How much did you make?" She was aware of her aunt's gaze as she went to refill her cup. "Want one?"

"No, finish that and I'll make fresh. About six hundred dollars. Irena, are you feeling feverish?"

"I feel fine. There's enough for two—are you sure?" She held up the pot.

"Well . . . all right." Nervously she wiped her hands on her apron as Irena got out another cup, filled it, and brought them both to the table. "Goodness," she was even shy, taking a seat, "I'm used to having my second cup on the move."

"You wouldn't have to if you didn't spoil us by making every meal from scratch."

"You haven't been eating many of them lately."

"I'm sorry, I won't be home for dinner tonight either."

"Theo's coming. He'll be disappointed."

"He eats here an awful lot. Don't you get tired of the way the two of them carry on?"

Into the cup she said, "He's a good friend."

"Of yours?"

The question startled her. She set down her coffee. Her cheeks were surprisingly pink. "Theo's family, he just . . ." she lowered her eyes, "gets a bit too liberal sometimes. With his hands."

"You're kidding!" She was genuinely laughing. "I never knew that."

"Don't tell your uncle. It only happens now and then, when there's been too much ouzo after dinner."

"What does he do, sneak up on you in the kitchen?"

"Oh, no," she couldn't look at her, "I just have to remember not to bend over when I'm near his chair." They both giggled. Irena was sorry her aunt had to cut hers short. "Beryl's been dead a long time. He should have remarried."

"So he's lonely, Aunt Eunice. That doesn't mean he has to goose his best friend's wife."

"Irena!"

She ducked her head. It was tricky, figuring out which thread could be followed for how long; she took up the next. "Would you remarry? I mean, if something happened to Uncle Constantine . . ."

"At my age? Certainly not. I'd have to be a fool."

"But lots of women do at your age. Anyway, you're not that old—there must be tons of women older than you who go out husband-hunting."

"Well, I'm sure they have their reasons. It all depends on what you're accustomed to, I suppose, and whether or not you want more of the same. I know I'd use what time I had left differently."

"How?" She realized she had no idea what her aunt would say. "What would you do that you don't do now?"

Picking up a spoon, she stirred her little bit of coffee, cautious about confessing. "I'd . . . travel," she risked, clinking the spoon against the rim of her cup and laying it aside. "I've always wanted to. We could have. But I've never been able to get your uncle away from Delos Street. Always some excuse for not leaving the business—as if it would crumble to pieces without him, when it's the other way around."

"Why not go on your own? The church has tour groups every summer."

"He wouldn't like it." The top of her housedress expanded and deflated as she sighed. "Neither would I, knowing he wasn't looking after himself, or doing anything around the house. There was a time when you girls could have taken over—but he didn't want that."

"Why didn't you tell us? We might have been able to help you talk him into it."

"Ha! Your sister in the kitchen? And you cleaning up after the boys? It didn't seem worth the arguments, Irena, or the havoc I'd have to face when I came back. No." She shook her head. "The world is still out there. One day I may see some of it, when I'm free to."

Her tone was hard to decipher. Resignation; bitterness; but what else? determination? Something new, or at least unexpected. "Aunt Eunice . . . why did you marry him? Were you in love?"

She arched back. "You're asking a lot of questions today."

"I know. Were you?"

Her expression was noncommittal as she swirled the dregs. "I thought so at the time. Handsome. Full of energy; ambitious. I knew he had a temper, but that seemed to come with being Greek, being male—my father, brothers—every man I knew had a temper and felt he was entitled to it." On the verge of sipping, she noticed nothing drinkable was left; perhaps it was losing the prop that made her mouth curve down.

"Was he the first one who ever proposed, or were there others?" Amazing she didn't know that; she truly wanted to.

"He was the first. My best friend had just gotten married and I . . ." Her fingers moved to her lips. "Accepted quickly." It appeared to strike her as a minor revelation, a connection she had just made after all these years. "Funny, I didn't realize . . . Selena, I haven't thought of her in . . ." She couldn't believe her neglect. Judging by the look in her eyes she began making up for it; not just remembering, but sinking into a private world.

Watery gray and glazing over; her aunt seemed accustomed

to this kind of retreating. "I don't think you've ever mentioned her."

"Haven't I?" Her voice was soft, dreamy. "Dear Selena. She was older, brighter, but she chose me to be her friend. We both knew school would be over for us . . . the money was needed for our brothers. Perhaps that was why, what we had in common. Necessity, the future. 'I don't want to marry,' she used to say, 'I want to go out in the world and . . .'" Her hand trembled against her mouth; what she saw distressed her, but she couldn't stop looking.

"Aunt Eunice?" A touch might be too jarring. "Are you okay?"

She nodded and turned away. Irena didn't know what else to do but insert a napkin into her hand clenched on the edge of the table; she clutched it. Brought it around, and dabbed at her hidden eyes. "Isn't this silly?" She sniffled; dabbed. "I don't know what's gotten into me." When she faced forward, a smile was out of control. "You should have heard her! How she described her beaux—she was so beautiful they flocked around her. But she wouldn't give them a thing, not my Selena. The way she went on, making me laugh—having me pretend to be her while she played one of her 'hat-in-hand youths,' she called them, her 'brave but witless fellows.'"

"Was it one of them she married?"

The gaiety disappeared. "Yes," flatly. "It was arranged. Her family was poor; his was not; she had to." Her mouth, a grim line, slackened as she lost focus again. "I stayed away, the night before. She came to our house. She was crying. For hours I held her while she cried. There was nothing I could do for her but that, and yet . . . it seemed enough then."

"What happened to her?"

"They moved to another town," she lilted. "He wanted to give her a finer life." Her parted lips closed; hardened. "She

203

died there. In less than a year, giving birth. Selena had never wanted children. I think . . . she knew." And as it must have then, the thought undid her.

Irena deliberately took her aunt's hand; it squeezed back, held on. The reaction subsided. Her aunt looked down at the hand gripping hers, and realized whose it was. Patting it, she disengaged herself. "So." It was over. She crumpled up the used napkins; stacked their cups. "You are not seeing this boy John Kinsella anymore."

She had to spend a moment readjusting. "That's right."

"I have tried to tell your uncle that your coming home so late has nothing to do with him."

"Oh?"

"He can't understand what else might be keeping you. What does it matter? I tell him. You said she should go out, meet people—she has new friends now. But he is suspicious. So I say, Irena's a big girl; she can take care of herself."

"Thank you. I didn't know you were being subjected to scenes on my account."

"He doesn't notice the change in you. I have to point it out to him. Would you rather she stayed home to stare at you all evening like before? Do you miss being reminded every night by those eyes of hers when you go up to bed? Take advantage, Constantine; relax. You can't put her in a glass case and protect her. And if . . . she should get hurt," her look emphasized the warning, "we won't hear about it, will we. So let it be. She is happier now than I've ever seen her."

My God, she wants to say, searching her eyes for answers. How much do you know?

As much as I want to.

But you understand.

Perhaps more than I wish to.

You even seem to approve.

No, but that doesn't mean I can't envy.

Getting up, Irena went to her side; her aunt tensed, waiting for the next move. Irena made it, wrapping her arms around her shoulders, rubbing a cheek against her thin hair. "I love you, Aunt Eunice. Do you know that?"

She bobbed her head, and began stroking Irena's arm.

Wordless and close; nice, why was she feeling uneasy? She tightened up—she knew what was coming. She couldn't let— she extricated herself from the embrace, Aunt Eunice patting her hand again as it passed without questioning her withdrawal, or the abruptness of her retreat. Safely out of the kitchen, she hurried up the stairs and into her room, just managing to shut the door before it started.

Well, wasn't that touching. God, Alex you almost . . . Almost what? cast a shade on your tender emotions? It was good, can't you see that? Aww, I'll strew a few hearts and flowers—here, have a heart, go on, take a flower. Let up why don't you, please. So you can skip merrily off for applause? listen Little Red Riding Hood, how long do you think I'll keep quiet while you trip around on Cloud Nine? Alex, I'm not skipping, or tripping, I am simply trying to change my ways. Yeah, I've seen how your lesbian lover has changed a whole bunch of your ways. Oh, stop. Why the hell should I? I don't give a damn if you've given up men, but you can't stay away from *him!* I haven't; I'm here. Sure, you're never in the house anymore, and what do you do when you are? you cozy up to Aunt Eunice, as if she mattered one bit in all this. She does to me! Since when, you little hypocrite—you just want to please your lover! You're wrong—that was a meaningful experience. Excuse me I may throw up; look at *my* eyes, you turncoat bitch, you've got an obligation. All right, all right, I'll come back tonight and glare at him for an hour. Don't belittle it, Rena! you've forgotten who you are; you're so busy being *happy*, you don't remember what you did. Alex, I do; you needn't give me a list. Is that what it's come to? something you can write on a slip of paper when it should be engraved inside? I swear, it's indelibly printed. Just wait till your female lover asks you to keep a promise; imagine how *she'll* feel when she sees how you honor your word. Why keep bringing her into it? Because guilty is guilty, Rena; you'll ruin everything you touch, just like you did when I trusted you, after you wouldn't shut up about love. Alex, don't do this, I beg you. You look to me for mercy when I saw how you spared yourself? You have got to stop battering me! a person can only take so much. Then leave—run to your precious lover, but don't expect her to be easy on you, when she learns what a fraud you are.

She couldn't wait to get to the museum, to Maggie. But she had to, thinking up chores, running errands away from the house until it was time for her to be legitimately at her desk. Finally she opened the door to her cubicle, only to see a white memo stuck in her typewriter. She slumped, knowing what it was. Maggie had been debating going to a conference, holding off until she could ascertain which endowment people would be there. Sinking to her desk chair, reading the note Maggie had come in here to type, Irena saw she wouldn't be able to share any of what had happened for the next four days.

The fresh chapter lying on her desk told her. If Maggie were free, she would have been waiting, too. Instead of racing down to greet her, Irena fanned out the pages, making herself settle for what she knew would happen tonight.

There were marginal notes to her on what statistics to insert, how the graphs should be laid out, where to leave space for drawings. It was a difficult job, yet the tale of discovery excited her. Following it was like watching a brilliant detective at work; inspired hunches, mounting evidence meticulously detailed—Maggie was hot on the trail of a mystery, and no one was going to fault her on procedure while she built her case.

"Taa-*daa!*" John, posing in the doorway, held her Styro-

206

foam cup of coffee victoriously aloft.

"Taa-daa and thank you." She was always glad when he stopped by; the only strain between them now came from her having to rebuff his curiosity about Maggie.

"Well? Aren't you going to ask me why I am standing here like the Statue of Liberty in drag?"

"The health clinic test came out negative."

Prancing in, he made a sweeping hook shot with his empty cup into the wastebasket, and thrust her coffee forward. "Guess again, smart face."

She pried off the plastic lid. "The test was positive but you're in love with the guy."

"You," switching to Uncle Sam, "have got a one-track mind."

"And it, gives up. Tell me."

"I," he thumbed his chest, then broke into a huge grin, "am going on a dig! This summer."

"John, that's fantastic! Where?"

"Oh . . ." he looked at his nails from several angles. "Only Orchomenos."

"You lucky! Who's directing?"

"Mark Abrams. Maggie asked me if I'd be interested in getting on his staff. Would I! Whose ass do I—no, I didn't say that—I applied very correctly, and just . . . found out . . . today."

She wasn't proud of the mixture of emotions tumbling through her. "What will you be doing?"

"Field preservation. God, Greece! Minyan ware! Me!" He lifted his arms, twirled around her desk, and landed on her lap, clasping her hands around his middle. "I'd never have gotten it without Maggie's recommendation. Listen," he twisted to speak over his shoulder, "would she rather have yellow roses or red?"

"Yellow, I think."

"Yulloh! Right!" He sprang up. "I'm off to blow a day's

pay! Oh a yellow rose for Maggie . . ." scattering petals, he sang himself out the door.

Irena felt as blank as the paper she was inserting into her typewriter. Maggie hadn't mentioned any of it to her. Not the dig, helping John get a job, anything. Scanning the first paragraph of the new chapter, she blinked rapidly; none of it made sense.

Hours later the muscles in her back ached and her legs hurt. She had been typing steadily, focusing on work to the exclusion of everything else. Successfully, she thought, or she wouldn't have noticed the foul-up in the footnote references. Maggie would have to sort them out before she could continue. Gathering up her official reason, she left her cubicle, fully justified in going to see her.

The flowers hid her from view. They were exquisite, arching proudly out of the vase on her desk. "Hi." She bent to breathe in their fragrance.

"Hello, aren't they beautiful?"

"Gorgeous. John's gamboling through the empyrean thanks to you."

"He's good, Mark's glad—it's one of the nicer things I've been able to accomplish lately."

"Doesn't sound like the conference went too well."

Maggie exhaled disgust.

"No luck?" She fingered a brass paperweight.

"Clement Jackson would've been willing to put his hands on some money, *if* he could've put his hands elsewhere first. I suppose some women might have thought 'Lucky me' and fucked for it." Irena said nothing; her unexpected silence made Maggie quiet. She sat back. "Have we got a problem?" A vigorous denial was coming when Maggie nodded, "Those pages you're holding."

"Oh—yes, the footnote numbering's off."

"Let me see." She took them from her and began skimming for errors. "How's the chapter reading?"

"Okay."

"Just okay? I must be slipping. Damn, when I combined these two I neglected to change the text—they're all off for the rest of the chapter." Inking in the right numbers, "Better do this on the remaining pages or you might get mixed up." She held them out. "Thanks for catching it."

Taking them, she didn't return her smile. "That's what I'm paid for."

Her hand, still out, slowly backed away, and folded under her chin. Irena touched a rose.

"What else?"

"Nothing."

"Really? I rely on your seeing things. What would you have me do to raise this particular chapter beyond 'okay'?"

"It's fine. It's just me today—preperiod."

"So soon? We don't seem destined to get on the same schedule. Would you rather skip tonight?"

"No! I mean, unless you want to."

"Not if I can get some clear time first. The conference wasn't a total disaster, Mark gave me an inside lead and I've got to stop everything to whip up a preliminary proposal. You could help by settling down, with or without a good book."

"Maggie, if you really don't want me to come over, I wish you'd say so."

"And I wish you'd come out with what's bothering you instead of laying the blame on premenstrual tension. Quirky hormones are a handy excuse, but I distinctly remember when your last period ended." A crooked smile softened the accusation. "And so, I hope, do you."

It had been one of their more versatile nights—the mere reference to it made her flush. She fanned herself with the typing paper. "Whew, hot flash. Must be premenopause—my mistake."

"Perhaps you should sit for a minute."

It was only a trace of amusement, but enough; she was torn between talking things out and maintaining some dignity.

"You're busy. I'd better go."

"Irena . . ." From under her chin, her forefinger pointed to the chair.

She sat. Taking advantage of the flowers, making them a little fuller in the vase, she asked, "Who's Mark Abrams?" and hoped it sounded offhand. "The way John mentioned his name, I felt I should know, but I've never heard of him before today."

"Mark's an assistant curator at the Guilford. We were in grad school together, keeping each other's sanity. You might say he was my John equivalent."

"You mean you were involved?"

"For a while, until we realized we were actually meant to help each other through entanglements ranging from inane to intense, of which Mark had dozens." The amusement that had been lingering around her mouth left now. "In his last year Mark stopped playing. He thought he'd met his match for life. Very perversely, it turned out he had. A beautiful, sensitive boy, totally out of his element but pressured to achieve. The day after he flunked his orals for the second time . . . Mark found him. In one week he dumped six years of work. It took him a long time to come back, rebuild. Not many would have—it's a damn shame he never quite caught up with his career again after those missing years."

"Do you see each other often?"

"Occasionally," surveying the landscape of paperwork before her, "when some conference catches us both on the same side of the world. But the bond is there, we don't have to be together to reinforce it. Only now when we help each other," she lifted a folder to peer beneath, "it's by passing on hot tips and good staff." After lifting another, she began riffling through all the work on her desk. "He's pretty well set except for an on-site recorder—do you see my cigarets anywhere in this mess?"

Irena handed her the pack, which had shored up a spilling

hill of paper. "'That's the person who keeps the Daily Register, isn't it? And the Small Finds Index?"

"Mmhm," puffing. "It's a key job." She tossed aside the lighter and opened a drawer. "My God, it's neat in here—I'm certainly not going to recommend that fluffhead who messed me up on my dig. You saw what she did, you're the one who had to make sense of her work." She extended a printed form, "Here," emptying her ashtray into the wastebasket as Irena leaned across to take it, "the applications are fairly standard if you're interested."

"Me! But I've only handled those things at a desk—I haven't had to keep everything straight under field conditions."

"So you'd be under a baking sun instead of fluorescent lights, and instead of reading someone else's entries on level numbers and find descriptions, you'd be coding on the site as the pieces are discovered. You know it's exacting work, but you've never experienced the excitement—nothing compares to being on a dig. I'm envious as hell Mark's able to go ahead with his while mine is stalled."

"Not forever, Maggie. You'll find the money, I know you will. But . . . you're going to be here in the meantime, aren't you? For the summer?"

"I'm surprised Mark hasn't been able to fill this job—I can name half a dozen people who'd give their eyeteeth for it. I honestly don't believe any of them would be better than you. Why not think about it, then if you don't want to try for it, I'll refer someone else."

"You haven't answered my question."

"It shouldn't be a factor in your decision."

"Maggie! how can it not be? What are you saying?"

As if it were self-evident, her hands opened and held the air. They dropped, more beautiful than flowers. "I'm not going to stand between you and an experience like this that will enrich your life. That's not my idea of loving. And if your loving me means you'll deprive yourself of what's exciting and rare and worthwhile, then . . ."

"But that's you—I'm not depriving myself! I don't need anything else—I don't want anything else."

"Irena, *think*. You're comparing what you've known so far. You have no notion of what's waiting out there for you— don't be so willing to wall yourself in with me."

"That's not fair—I'm not doing that, you're loading the image."

"No, I'm telling you I will not be a partner to stifling any-one's life, nor will I simply sit back and watch it happen."

"It *isn't* happening. And it won't—not if both people are in love and they don't want it to."

"That is a charming thought based again on limited ex-perience. I'm sorry, I don't mean to throw mine up to you, but *please* look at what you said. Any two people who want their love to have a long life must keep themselves flourishing first."

"I'm looking. What you're really saying is that *I'm* stifling *you*. And this," she got up brandishing the application, "is a convenient way to get rid of me!"

The wound showed, but the mask quickly covered it. "I'd have to be a masochist to let you get away with that. You'd better leave before I give you a dose of your own cruelty." She bent her head, pulled work over.

"Maggie, I'm sorry—say you forgive me."

"I can't now, close my door on your way out, please."

The finality in her voice sent Irena fleeing from what she had done. Getting to her cubicle, seeing the application still in her hand, she shook it from her as if it were on fire.

She doesn't want you, Rena, you've already served your purpose. No, she's not like that, I know that isn't true. Do you? how can you be so sure? I forgot the trust between us; there was pain because of *me*. You're a fool. Agreed—*agreed*.

Pressing the bell next to M. J. Leland lettered on the mailbox, she tried to rid herself of thoughts. It seemed to take minutes before the buzzer sounded, releasing the door. She knew better than to look up the stairwell expecting to see Maggie lean over the bannister as usual. And she restrained herself from embracing her when the apartment door was opened.

Walking by her, taking in the chamber music and the brightly lit desk, she hung her coat in the closet, laid her book on the armchair, turned on the lamp beside it, went into the kitchen, and got out the makings for herb tea. Maggie hadn't followed, or spoken either. Good. She didn't want to talk, she wanted to be.

When she placed the cup of hot tea on a corner of the desk, Maggie murmured acknowledgment without breaking her concentration. Putting the second cup next to the amber stone on the end table, she kicked off her shoes, and settled.

For the next two hours there was no sound but Mozart and the rustle of paper. Maggie's yawn broke the pattern; stretching, she pushed back her chair. Unwilling to take anything for granted, Irena waited, keeping her eyes on the words in front of her. Maggie's hand, outstretched, appeared above the page.

She was asleep when Irena let herself out, and floated home. Fulfilled, having been touched in a place no hand or tongue could reach. Seeing her face. The puzzled frown she had smoothed away after bringing her, the only thing she needed. The unspoken question in dark tired eyes she had answered with her own. The accepting lips, as a sleep-well kiss finished speaking for her. So real, each physical detail. Yet so much awe surrounded, came from, being with her. It was a strange, empowering combination, being totally immersed in life and at the same time sent to an outer region.

Before she herself could sleep, she would have to come down, brutally. As soon as she entered the house, she would have to wrench herself back to duty. The thought alone started her. She resented having to do it, the pressure seeping into fulfillment, forcing her to come down, hit hardened reality. She had to "see" her uncle, really be there in their confrontations; she knew that, yet it was getting more and more difficult to meet her obligation faithfully. To make nights like tonight no different.

When she went in and reminded him, it was as if layers of gauze stood between them, filtering or subduing her effectiveness. She tried to pierce through, aware of her sister judging. Guilt enfolded her in the midst of failing.

It weighted her limbs as she climbed the familiar stairway, prepared to hear Oh, what a good little girl you've been, the moment she got in her room. She wanted to have it over with. Alex knew it was worse delaying. She grew tenser and tenser, angering herself, undressing irritably. She hated it when Alex toyed with her; made her lie awake in bed, on guard in open territory.

That was real terrific, Rena. One of your better efforts.

She punched her pillow into shape.

You want to dream about your goddess now? The saint you're so obsessed with?

She kicked the sheet free. If the flesh and blood woman were with her here, she'd be warding off her sister.

You should be protecting yourself; you're under her spell too much. You don't understand power, you know; it can't be disguised by adding an s.

That was too absurd to answer. She thrashed and refused to speak.

You can't see, she's pulled the wool over your eyes—eyes that belong to me.

She hurled herself up, "Then for God's sake let me close them and find a little peace!"

You don't deserve it. Not while I'm unable to rest.

Falling backward on the bed, she squeezed her eyes shut. Her hands balled themselves into fists.

What's the matter, Rena? You can't hit out at me; I'm in a place beyond your reach.

She wanted to be in the other one, but she had lost it. Lost it. Alex was doing this to her. Taking—ruining, constantly. She would lose it forever, never be there again—never be free to keep it.

As she covered herself the candle flame swayed, and ceiling shadows undulated in response. Finally she had had the chance to talk about her experience with Aunt Eunice. "Sometimes I think the good isn't real until I've shared it with you."

Maggie plumped up her pillow and fitted it behind her back. "You're not used to affirmation. There was a time when I needed someone to tell me the sky was blue."

"I can't imagine you that way."

"Or yourself any other? Give yourself a chance; let it happen."

"I don't have the faith it will, Maggie."

"I do." She tousled her hair. "I don't lay my bountiful love on just anyone, you know."

She had to angle her head to see her. "I wish you wouldn't make fun of it."

"I'm not, in fact it bothers me. You seem to admire my taste in everything but you—every time you put yourself down, you fault me. I haven't figured out if you think I'm selectively stupid, or indiscriminate, giving myself to someone so unworthy."

"Stop it—you can't be serious." Her face withheld assurance; Irena wasn't going to be let off so easily. "It's hard, existing apart from your reflection. I know that's what I'm supposed to do, and be . . . but it's hard."

"Of course it's hard. No one can give you your core. And you can't trust anyone else's perception of you, until or unless your own vision does some validating. Even then, it's a dangerous process. We all run the risk of distorting, taking in the spurious. It isn't easy to discard that—letting go of the pernicious can still leave us with a sense of loss. But you *are* doing it, Irena."

Dubious, she half turned away. Maggie's hand on her cheek forced her head around. "*You* are." Eyes and fingers gripping; charging her to fuse the vision. The hold on her slackened, and Maggie's gaze roamed across her face. "You don't know your own reflection, or you'd realize. You'll see it one day, your beauty growing right in front of you." She drew back before Irena could clasp her. "You do know, I hope, that a short time ago Alex would have ruined that scene with your aunt."

Just as the mere mention of her caused a separation now. "Sure." She moved away; rested her head against the wall. "No smart remarks or anything while it happened. But she was there at the end. She came. Like she always does, taunting me. Taking it away from me." She looked down, body a blur. "But that's fitting, isn't it."

"Is it? Why?"

"The punishment and the crime. I did it, I deserve it."

"I wonder if there's anyone outside of Alex who agrees with you."

"No one else has to." She rubbed the sheet, ambulance white. "We both know how it went."

"God," intensely whispered frustration. "How I'd like to bump that bitch out of your system."

"Maggie!" jerking forward, shocked it had been *said*. "You don't know what you're saying! You didn't know her—you can't say that." No one could. "Alex was strong. Beautiful! She glowed, she was *passionate*, determined. She was—"

"Brave, loyal, and true. A regular Boy Scout, your sister."

"No! Alex *always* knew what she had to do and did it, and this isn't any different! You don't understand—I robbed her of it—killed everything she had! And she died knowing what I did, it was the last thing she knew, you should have seen her eyes, you should have seen the hatred—she hated me,

216

hated me! And it's too late for forgiveness, it's too late, she's dead, she can't forgive me for what I did, I have to live with that, I have to see it, I have to, I . . ." She was shaking uncontrollably, she clutched herself and bit her lip but couldn't stop the shaking, her face from cracking, she was shaking, cracking, splitting into sobs. "Oh God, Maggie, help me! I can't . . . stand it any longer! Get her out! get her out of me!"

She digs into skin, clawing at flesh. But arms hold on with unceasing strength. And lips press repeatedly, while words flow over without pausing for sense.

Irena's hands fell to the bed. She was dead weight, letting all of herself sag against the woman's body. She felt her head being eased toward a breast. "Take it," crooned. Her lips neared the nipple held for her. "It's all right, it's all right." Timidly she took it in her mouth. "Yes, baby, draw on me, yes, it's all right." Irena did, Maggie rocking, and rhythmically stroking her hair.

VIII

SHE FINGERS the leather-grained binding. The pages are blank in her diary; the name-day gift has never been used, as record, journal, or therapy. Why is she tempted to start it now? Like matter dying and rising transformed, she cannot be documented. Only inferred. And the selection process—the increments of progress and regress—a diary would need an infinite number of witnesses. Or else it would be just slices and bits—samples randomly chosen. No. She is not that little IRENA, embossed in a corner. Smiling, she opens a drawer, and replaces the diary.

The days were getting longer; the evening traffic flowed around them in sharp clear light that edged into dusk. She loved the way Maggie casually controlled a car, it always made her want to kneel under the dashboard and "have" her. "It *is* possible." Not what she was thinking; Maggie was referring to their dinner conversation, the intensity all in her voice as she swung an arm along the back of the seat. "Granted, it takes strength and a fine awareness to separate guilt from grief. And there will be a part of you that mourns forever. But if you're receptive to that part, open to it, it won't do you any damage."

"First I have to separate, then I'm supposed to integrate. Maggie, I'm not an amoeba!" The thought of a lusting amoeba, or an amoeba in love . . . Her hand inched across the seat and slid over Maggie's thigh. "How does a simple person go about doing that?"

"She could start by not romanticizing the dead. And if she doesn't stop sexing up the living, we're going to plough into that embankment." Maggie grinned as the culprit slunk away. "There. Perspective. The dividing lines are *in focus*, you will notice how sedately we are moving between them." It was real, Irena's effect on her; she had been allowed to see it so often and freely, she had come to believe it herself. "Things have started altering for you and I hope you'll keep on letting that happen, keep reviewing her. When you've managed really to look at her, I'd like to know what you see. What you find. However long it takes; wherever you are, let me know. If you can, or care to."

"Maggie." It chilled her.

Her hand dropped down to grasp Irena's and bring it to her lips; the shivers sprang into coils. Lowering their hands together, Maggie kept them clasped in her lap. "I think," her face creasing into a brief smile as she jockeyed around a corner, "defeating one's enemies is a highly glorified impulse. Possibly, just possibly, men have the excuse of Darwinian selection, but women who devote themselves to it? Sorry, they're jumping camps—denying the circle."

"What's bad or wrong about believing in something so much you're willing to die for it?"

Coming to a stoplight, Maggie leaned against the door and looked at her. "You want to be rough on yourself, try believing in something and being willing to live for it—that's harder."

In between bed and the car, Irena's favorite place to "be" with her was the breakfast nook, their talking spot regardless of the hour. "I don't understand how, after all I've told you about her, you can't find anything to admire." She finished peeling the orange and offered half.

Taking off one section, Maggie bit it in two. "Mm . . ." The spurting juice dribbled to the tip of her chin before she could get to it with a napkin. "If I'd met her," she wiped her fingers then her chin again, "I'd probably have responded to her vitality. Her courage. Her rare moments," balling up the moist shreds, she plopped them into an ashtray, "of concern for you."

"She would have liked *you*."

"I doubt it. Wars don't excite me, Irena. No cause strikes me as holy—to destroy in the name of one is the grossest perversion I can think of."

"Then you don't believe people should even *fight* for their principles?"

"Depends on the method and the principle. I don't like power games; once you've made people into pawns, it's too easy to knock them off the board."

"Alex didn't see it as a game, Maggie. I know I accused her of that, but it was serious business."

Her only response was to light a cigaret.

"People can't just sit back and be passive witnesses. My sister was an activist, she believed in putting her body on the line."

"Fine, but bearing witness isn't a passive act. To carry the tale, no matter how horrific, while forging some kind of constructive path—that isn't easy work. And there's no cutoff point where one can say I'm done with that now, I needn't bother any longer; I've won. There is no winning, except in going on. No glory in realizing how minuscule our area of influence is. It's frustrating and dispiriting, and learning to accept takes a long time. To accept, and still make the effort." She frowned; reliving perhaps, seeing whatever it had taken for her to learn. "The most I can do," she said to herself, "is act on a personal level *as if*, and hope other people are doing the same."

"As if what?"

She exhaled slowly, focusing still on some inner place. "As if what I do matters. As if life matters," counting on Irena to follow yet making no attempt to draw her in. " 'To turn a single human being back toward life is to prevent the destruction of the world.' " Resting her thumb against her lips; oblivious to the smoke curling toward her eyes. "Mark was good at throwing the Talmud at me whenever my heat was up." Silence. When a quick smile came, Irena felt more included. "I'd sputter, call him a smug bastard, then go home and think about it." Emerging but not fully with her, Maggie ashed her cigaret. "If the wisdom suits you, take it. Pick and choose, even though it bothers people. Let them attack you for inconsistency—it's better than striding forth under the aegis of generalization."

The image prompted her. "What do you think of Amazons, Maggie?" The only person she saw was in front of her, gazing at the table.

Frowning again. "We shouldn't cut off any womanly part of ourselves in order to win battles. I *know* that. Why was I doing it?" She came out to stare at her intently, as if Irena had answers. "You put a stop to it. When you hit me with my attaché case."

Anxiety alert. "Maggie, please." She didn't like that incident referred to. "I've tried to apologize and apologize."

"I know you have," penetrating now. "Despite my assuring you it's fine. You've never been able to trust me on that one."

Irena looked away; she'd asked for it. Her hand was jostled; enclosed, pulled across the table. "Look at me." Pressure. "Irena." She looked, and saw what Maggie meant her to. "What were you supposed to do with all of that? You said what you needed to say. Maybe it could have been put more gently, but I needed to hear it. Do you imagine I didn't know what lay underneath, what the substance was? Given that, and I mean *given*, who wouldn't have been overwhelmed to the point of immobility?" She let go of her hand. "Now please, hurry up and forgive yourself. And get yourself over here for a hug."

Through with Sunday brunch, they started in on the dishes. "I can't seem to keep it under control, Maggie. Just when I think I've got it down, it comes surging back."

"It will for a while, until you feel significant some other way. You've done something, had an effect; even if it's negative, it's better than nothing. Guilt proves you exist."

Drawing Maggie's arm out of the soapy water, she pulled her nearer and kissed her on the mouth. "I like this kind of proof much better."

Instead of laughing, Maggie returned to her task. "And when you don't have it?" Her voice was remote. "Do you cease to exist when you're not with me?"

She felt slapped. "Of course not." She picked up her towel, would do what she was supposed to.

"You're sure."

"Yes!" Angrily grabbing a dripping plate from the rack, she whipped it dry.

"Are those the times when you need the guilt? Is that when it comes surging back?"

"I do not *need* to feel guilty, dammit!"

The stack clattered as she thrust the plate into the cupboard. Resuming her post at the drainer, she was grasped by the neck, forced to turn; a sudsy finger touched the tip of her nose. "Then don't."

She moved the finger away. "I have an obligation, Maggie. I'll never be rid of it."

Dropping, hands and eyes reverted to the sink. "So long as you choose it. I'm sorry you've had to turn guilt into a moral imperative. Under that kind of cover, it works even more slyly."

"But I haven't done that—responsibility isn't the same thing. By constantly reminding him, I'm bearing witness, aren't I?"

She didn't answer right away. "I don't know."

Stunned. "But you have to see that's what I'm doing—it never occurred to me you wouldn't!"

"Then tell me more about your confrontations. What happens in them?"

"I remind him, with my eyes—no words. I just look at him and he knows he won't be allowed to forget, he's seeing what he's done."

"To whom?"

"Jesus, Maggie! Alex, my brother—both brothers."

"Where's your aunt in all this?"

"Nowhere." The word rebounded from her silence. "That wasn't part of it—Alex's goal was to make him honor my brother." She couldn't duck it but kept trying. "She wanted to show him, turn him around and *make* him have a conscience."

"And in the process, make him honor her? Never mind, you believe in what you're doing. Do you think it's working?"

"I . . . can't tell. Sometimes I think it is. When I do it right."

"Does Alex applaud then?"

"Not like before, but sort of."

"For what? Is your uncle changing?"

"Does a rock? At least I'm making it harder for him to live with himself."

"You're so positive he needs *you* for that." She placed a

fistful of silverware in the drainer. "What about you and your aunt living with him? Is that harder or easier now?"

Lifting the wet silver, she slowly set it down, her hand slackening. "Ever since we talked . . . it's been easier." Merging, the other kitchen, her aunt, Maggie's voice coming and leaving.

". . . applause though, appeasing ghosts is a tricky business . . . angry when you act on your own behalf instead of . . ."

A surprising bite on her shoulder. She was back in the shared domesticity she loved. The silverware gleamed.

"The early Greeks knew what to do about the *biaiothanotoi*. Most so-called primitive groups had words and rituals for the living dead." She swirled the water in search of submerged items, then let it out and reached for the cleanser. "Especially those who died before their time, by their own hand—they were the most vengeful and dangerous. They were seductive, and no tribe could let itself be lured into devaluing survival. But we're such a *civilized* people, we're out of touch. Our welfare's threatened by the same forces, but we don't have access to the ancient rites of appeasement. It's lost knowledge again." Through with scouring the sink, she began wiping her hands on the tag end of Irena's towel. "There's too damn much of it. And not enough time, money, or sensibility diverted from the uncritical quest for anything new."

The lines in her face had deepened; they did when she was tired or intense. Touching the severity around her mouth, Irena failed to alter it. "That's my Maggie," sometimes her voice could ease her, "asking for the moon goddess."

Fake exasperation, then she was playing along, cocking her hands on her hips. "Not asking. Going for. If for no other reason, then because she's there." That lithe stride to the kitchen table, her cigarets. "You'd think—no, you wouldn't.

I've given up expecting them to understand, or accept, or support, even though I've tried to present the challenge according to their mystique."

"You'll *get* the money, Maggie. I've said it over and over. Talk about faith, I've always had it in that—doesn't it count when it comes to you?"

Motionless within a haze of smoke, she scrutinized her from where she stood. "It counts." When she drew the cigaret out of her mouth, her expression matched the quiet seriousness Irena had heard. "A great deal." Her head bent in profile and she slid an ashtray closer. "You don't lay your bountiful love on just anyone, do you."

Irena hooked the tea caddy onto the rim of the pot. "I'm still surprised you don't see anything wrong with going over there. Tacitly you're giving consent to dictatorship."

"Which will be, for a time, whether I consent or not. There's no point in my squandering what moral fervor I'm capable of. The Greeks are survivors, they've lived through worse regimes. But, if you can tell me how I'm supposed to look at the repressions here, and then adopt a superior attitude about what's happening there, I'll be glad to rethink my position."

She had become an expert at judging the exact amount of boiling water. The lid clinked into place, nicely worn from years of accommodating the chain. "It just doesn't seem right, to ignore it all, and go digging for Bronze Age plates."

"It won't be, if that's your perspective."

"I didn't mean to make it sound so frivolous, Maggie."

As she arrived with the pot Maggie scooted the trivet to the middle of the table. "Only because you haven't had enough frivolity in your life to be comfortable with it yet."

"Oh, really? *Who* made a graceful leap onto the curb last night and pirouetted herself right into a fire hydrant?" She sat down to laughter, broken when Maggie tossed a smacking kiss across to her. "I happen to be black and blue from frivolity, but I do not regard Orchomenos as a Tupperware hunt."

"Why not? People in the next millennium will be digging for it."

"Come on." She checked the tea and poured. "Minyan ware's exquisite—I've seen pictures. Name me a museum that wouldn't hunger after one piece, Bronze Age or not."

"It isn't your everyday experience, scraping away and discovering that kind of find—when you unearth the beautiful, by any age's standard, it's a blessed event. But you know there's no junk in archaeology, thousand-year-old trash heaps are treasure troves to us."

"Well, I'm glad I'll be spared the sight of a plastic plate under glass, with futuristic crowds thronging through oohing and ahhing."

"They won't, the crowds. If we're lucky, a few will." Her face, like her voice, was subdued. "We'll be alive then."

She couldn't read it; sometimes Maggie assumed a level of understanding in her she didn't think she had. Finishing her cup, she withheld the failure to comprehend. "More?"

"Please."

She concentrated on pouring, that and china clinking the only sounds.

"You've gone quiet—what's happened?"

"Nothing!" Lightly said, but it wouldn't mask her feelings of inadequacy, not with Maggie looking on.

"I'd like to think that someday someone sifting through a ton of rubble will unearth the shards of that teapot. It's certainly no work of art. Just an object of the times, a future relic from a life. The fragments will be taken somewhere, and out of a lot more than curiosity or aesthetics, that article —these times, this life—will be reconstructed. They'll never know two women who loved each other spent their midnight hours talking over it, but they will touch what we've touched. We'll be linked then, continuous. And as they're piecing

226

together not us exactly, but people like us, they'll begin to know."

She could never predict when Maggie would be rough on her or gentle, like now, sharing a vision. She traced the teapot's contours. "You make me want to leave a note inside, just in case."

"A find *is* a message, a sign to those who follow. Perhaps that's why I feel I'm participating in one of the ancient mysteries when I'm on a dig. I go underground, and I'm initiated, restored by revelations." She stared at her hands, enclosing the cup as if for warmth. "I lose some of it here. Always. I get frazzled, too far away from the source."

"What's it like, Maggie? Being there and feeling that?"

When pain shadowed her, Irena knew she was seeing beauty. "I can't describe it because I'm within it, so completely myself that I'm part of the experience. My capacities, my reason and intuition and ability to accomplish, are at their peak there. I accept it. And I've seen it in others—there's a wholeness, a vitality—you can't go into their orbit without coming away enriched somehow."

"Did you feel that way the very first time you went there?"

She laughed. "No. I wasn't prepared. I hadn't done enough work yet—on me. I could have tripped over the winged victory at that point and not seen it."

"Maggie, that's not credible."

"Only to you. Believe me, I take full credit for discovering her, but I am very humble about the timing. I'll always be grateful for the summer I had the year before, in someone else's orbit."

Irena picked at a spot on the table. "Lucky someone." Neither of them spoke again; when she glanced up, Maggie was looking at her.

"I know you won't take this the right way. You can't yet. But one day, someone else will feel lucky for having done enough work to be ready for you."

Disbelief and denial ice inside her body. Only a part of her, small and indistinct, is free of it, wrapped within a future.

Not wanting or knowing how to respond, she shook the teapot, and got up to heat more water. In a moment Maggie was behind her, holding her, murmuring, "If you can stay, I'd rather taste something else now."

"I want to hear everything—everything!" But she was squeezing Irena speechless. "Come *on,*" pulling her hand, leading her to the sofa. "Sit—speak!" Backing into a cushioned corner, Maggie tucked her denimed legs under and leaned forward with her elbows on her knees.

Now she couldn't talk because she was marveling at a face that could have been twenty-five years old.

"Ireenah, *what happened? How* did they take it?"

"What happened," she repeated, trying to call herself out of the daze, away from fascination. "Oh . . ." She forced her eyes up from the enlivening lines of her mouth and brow, the increasing amusement. "Well . . ." This was dumb, she had been looking forward all day to telling her. "He ranted of course," she shook back her hair, her head started clearing. "And naturally she cried."

"Thanks—I could have told myself that part."

Able to enter into it finally, she put her hands on her hips. "Listen, whose story is this?"

Maggie grew calmer. "Yours, darling," grasping Irena's knee. "All yours." Hand withdrawn, she settled against the cushions.

"All right, then," squaring her shoulders as if she had won a realistic point. "I will not recount every item in his objecting routine because it went on and on, from the tedious to the bizarre with quite a bit of perversity thrown in. I'm not sure . . ." she faked thinking about it, forefinger at her temple, "it might have been his fantasies of barbaric assaults on my maidenhood that got her going. Anyway, the more his imagination whipped him up, the louder she sniffled. So—picture—I had him in front of me screaming about Turks and her in back of me yanking out Kleenex, when suddenly . . . Are you ready for this?"

"Ready. I think."

"Suddenly she came up beside me, put her arm timidly around my waist, and said, 'Constantine, she's going.'"

"She didn't!"

"She did. Just like that. He couldn't believe it, he was openmouthed, struck mute in mid-invective."

"Good for her."

"Well, her voice was quavering. You know."

"Even so."

"But it got stronger."

"You're making this up."

"I'm not! 'She is going and you have no right to stand in her way. She has an opportunity, she must take it. You want to give yourself a blood pressure attack, that is your business, but Irena and I do not have to watch it.' I swear to you, Maggie, she piloted me right out of there. 'He'll carry on for days,' we were in the kitchen then, 'but don't worry. It's settled, and if he won't help you with the plane fare, I will.' And then—"

"*Then?* You mean there's more?"

"Yes, *more.*"

"Irena, you're sure you didn't dream this."

"Positive. That was a bone-crushing hug we gave each other, I know it happened because I'm a little sore right here," touching her rib cage which didn't hurt at all. "And I can see her face after it was over—we were about a foot apart and she was trying to speak, but, Maggie, it was so hard for her. I didn't know what else to do except wait."

"Right," there with her at every step.

"It wasn't easy for me either, seeing her, struggling . . ." Without warning she wasn't recounting but reliving and her eyes were tearing, mirroring the image of her aunt's. "She said," lifting them to Maggie's to complete it, " 'I want you to tell your friend . . . I said thank you.' "

Maggie's face lost all expression. It wasn't a mask.

Leaning across, she kissed a numb cheek. "My aunt thanks you, Maggie." There was no response. She neared her mouth. "I . . ." closing in unsteadily, "thank you." Her kiss was passively received. She drew back. Her voice wouldn't cope with her feelings any longer; forcing it, she managed a final, whispered "Thank you."

With eyes that would fix on Irena forever, Maggie riveted an answer. Emotions overran her face and she let them find their own expressions. Not moving, she simply let Irena see them. Giving her everything. Exposing. Trusting until, fully aged and suffering, she reached out and clasped Irena to her.

The black-lit hours are hardest. Lying awake and alone; the day's brave fronts dismantled. She knows there is no luster to Maggie's honest rejoicing. Loss and foreshadowed yearning reappear, like tarnish, during the night. She knows. Just as Maggie knows what Irena is fighting. How fear looms before her and she cannot make it fade. Shrouded at the foot of her bed; watching, while resolution weakens.

It's a cliche that decisions, once made, put one's mind at rest. It's a lie—she is shaking with mental tremors, no one mentions the aftereffect. Yes, the act has been decided upon, but the deed—it is the deed that will be torture. Yet she has to undergo it. The timing is right, it is the right thing to do—she remembers the prediction. Small comfort. Parting can only mean diminishment.

If they surrender to it. Distance is the enemy—when two are in one, their forces must overcome it. She knows. They are together in this. Each, in her private darkness, can arm against separation, by summoning dreams and replenishing her inner store of the other.

Maggie stretched to peek behind the curtain. "That's a beautiful Saturday afternoon out there—let's get in the car and find a good craggy beach."

Irena rolled over. "Can I go like this?"

"If you've got the guts to." She was already up, energetically pulling out clothes.

"You mean you don't mind if the entire world sees my fabulous naked body?"

For answer, Maggie tossed Irena's sweatshirt and jeans at her.

"*Well.*" She held up the garments that had landed on her midriff. "Signs of jealousy, I do believe."

"Nonsense. I was only thinking of the poor passing sailors who'd have to lash themselves to their masts."

"You lie, Maggie Leland."

She turned on her way to the shower. "No lie. Simple projection."

In half an hour she had made every green light and was laughingly declining an offer to drag from two teenagers who barreled alongside. She let them gun ahead. "You're in a fine mood today." To her, their route was a speeding backdrop for Maggie's profile.

"It's grant time." Every feature was playing. "That old goat Marcotte better not have packed his bags."

Her own suitcase was lying open on her bedroom floor; a hinged and gaping mouth waiting to be filled. "Wouldn't it be neat . . . if he'd already taken the shots and was having a horrible reaction to every one of them?"

"What a nasty thought. I love it!" Her smile—Irena couldn't watch. She groped for Maggie's hand. Fingers slid between hers; firm, assuring. A spasm shot through, Maggie was gripping her violently. In seconds she'd gone. "*Surf.* There has to be surf *and* rocks *and* a good stretch of beach. I insist on it." As they swung onto the coast highway Irena slid closer; she squeezed the back of Maggie's neck, making her stiffen, and for a moment, close her eyes. "Just keep it up, *run* us off the road."

"I love you." It came out huskily, no match.

The look she gave her then was fully weighted. "I know." Solemn eyes, back on the road. Suddenly she was pointing, "There!" all eager again. Barely slowing for the approach, she swerved into a small gravel area gouged out of a hill.

"I hope nobody else comes."

"They wouldn't dare."

"Then I won't bother to lock."

"Don't!" Maggie grinned over the roof of the car and ran.

Going after her, cresting the sandy incline, she came upon Maggie and the world, etched against vivid blue sky. Glistening to the horizon in gentle swells, the ocean sighed from below. The air smelled of it, and the wind held a fine mist to their faces. "Ah," Maggie exhaled a deep breath. "Perfection," Irena finished, despite the scattered dots of people.

With the tide out, the coves beneath were connected by a strip of sand, curving around the cliffs for miles. A steep, spiraling path led down; they had to slide part of the way on their hands and heels. From the beach they saw what had been hidden to them above; caves, battered by eons of ocean slamming, wave against rock, the rock losing.

"We'd better be careful the tide doesn't turn on us."

"It's in our favor now—let's make the most of it."

Beyond each rocky bend; at every tide pool. On huge bleached trees that had washed ashore. When the gulls flew away from them, myriad claw prints stayed in the sand. Sandpipers scurried daintily along the surf line. In rock crevices crabs scuttled for cover, then peered back thinking they were invisible. A small hermit one gave itself away when a mounded black shell rose and walked into the water, settling between two sea anemones; rubbery, retracting at a touch.

The sand was cool by the time they were sprawled on it, watching the waves suck and take from the shore. "All that force coming on and on." She listened to the pebbles rushing backward. "Do you find it frightening?"

"I should. If I knew the sea intimately—had my home by it or needed to make my living from it—I'm sure I would. But I'm free to let it soothe me." Almost as proof, a cigaret lay unlit between her fingers. "It has gone on and on, and will. Time means nothing. Civilizations rise and fall, continents disappear. Yet there it still is, in its own motion. A ceaseless witness. Connecting us." Head propped on her hand, she turned from the sea to her. "Always."

Irena veered to the hills behind. She wouldn't be able to sustain this. She wanted to accept, but her vision was marred by the plane high over water, carrying her, taking her away.

Maggie sprang up. "Let's climb to that jut of rock before we go." Starting to jog down the nearly empty beach, she threw back, "The waves are crashing past the top!"

By cutting to the hard-packed sand, Irena managed to narrow the distance between them. Ahead of her, Maggie was turning boulders into steppingstones, then leaping to a path that hid half her body while she climbed, up and across the side of the rock. Just as Irena gained the last boulder, her figure appeared, lit by the late rays of the sun, against the wind and waiting for the sea to come.

Transfixed, she saw the wave, booming upward, Maggie, lifting her arms high, the spray rising beyond her, spuming and falling, flicking itself onto her upturned face. She couldn't breathe. Again a wave boomed and the figure, wind-whipped and sun-bronzed, joyously opened her arms to it.

The victory, "Maggie!" Scrambling to reach her. "Maggie!" She had to be with her, had to be, she couldn't leave, she had to . . . "I can't!" Heaving arms around her. "I can't leave you!" Holding and clinging, crying into her shoulder.

"Please, don't do this." Lips on her neck, her hair. "Don't. You promised."

"I can't!"

"You have to, you have to."

"No!" Impossible to clutch her tighter.

"Please. Help me let you go—help me."

"No I love you, I want to be with you!"

"You will be. You are." Fingers, her back. "I'll think of you, I'll dream of you." Steadily pressing. "I'll be there for you, inside, as you are for me." Imprinting their feel. "You must help me stay behind. You must, it's harder here. I'll be reminded of you everywhere," moving, loosening her grasp, "but you'll be in new places, exposed to so many new sensations you won't have time to miss me."

"That isn't true!" Holding on through the space between them. "All I'll do is miss you, I'll be going away just to spend all my time missing you! It's stupid!"

"It won't . . . *happen* that way," strong hands underscoring.

"What if you find someone else while I'm gone?"

"What if *you* do?"

"That's not possible, I won't want anyone else, ever."

"Irena, we must act . . . as if . . . the sky won't fall. Please."

The hands dropped away. More air came between their bodies. The earth at her feet dissolved. She shut her eyes, trying to find what was being asked for. Squeezing until there were points of light. Searching for what was expected. Summoning up, calling on it, so she could be. And keep the promise.

Her efforts were being seen; she could see herself, as Maggie must be seeing. Eyelids resting—when had it become easier? The sun must have set, she was shivering. Opening her eyes, she met the dark ones opposite. Reflecting what hers were. Coming to her.

"You know."

"Yes."

Joined, treading over stones and dirt, they walked to the path. At the narrow opening, Maggie stepped aside. Irena went ahead, slipping and righting herself with occasional help from behind.

*